"You came for me," I whispered in a voice I barely recognized as my own.

There was a rumble in Gabriel's chest. One that quickly changed to a sexually charged roar as he pulled me to him. He was hard, and I could feel the wave of lust that enveloped me as he answered in the best way he knew how. The only way he knew how. He kissed me.

I grabbed a handful of thick, white hair as his mouth covered mine. I had never been kissed like this before. Not by Gabriel, not by anyone. It was a kiss that had me drowning in a sea of possession. It said he was claiming me as his own, branding me as belonging to him, and he didn't give a damn who knew it. It was pure alpha male, and I had no doubt that if he could have found a way to tattoo his name on my tongue with his, he would have done so.

Also by Carla Susan Smith

A Vampire's Promise

A Vampire's Soul

A Vampire's Honor

Carla Susan Smith

LYRICAL PRESS
Kensington Publishing Corp.
www.kensingtonbooks.com

LYRICAL PRESS BOOKS are published by

Kensington Publishing Corp.
119 West 40th Street
New York, NY 10018

All Kensington titles, imprints, and distributed lines are available at special quantity discounts for bulk purchases for sales promotion, premiums, fund-raising, educational, or institutional use.

Special book excerpts or customized printings can also be created to fit specific needs. For details, write or phone the office of the Kensington Sales Manager: Kensington Publishing Corp., 119 West 40th Street, New York, NY 10018. Attn. Sales Department. Phone: 1-800-221-2647.

Lyrical Press and Lyrical Press logo Reg. U.S. Pat. & TM Off.

First Electronic Edition: September 2016
eISBN-13: 978-1-60183-958-9
eISBN-10: 1-60183-958-8

First Print Edition: September 2016
ISBN-13: 978-1-60183-959-6
ISBN-10: 1-60183-959-6

Printed in the United States of America

Acknowledgments

No book is ever truly the result of a single effort. While the original concept may have been mine, getting the story to the finish line would not have been possible without the help from some very special people:

To my husband Jack whose belief in me has never wavered.

To Joe and Cayden for just being who you are.

To Ruth Guillot who is my first reader, and who came up with the title *A Vampire's Honor*—much better than my *Book Number Three*.

To Lynne Harter for having the patience to correct all my mistakes and share the most amazing nuggets of information along the way (loved learning about blended and single malt scotch!).

To Liz O'Connor, my friend and fellow author, for allowing me to vent when necessary and for offering encouragement when needed. Only another author truly understands.

And last but not least, to Alicia Condon and all the wonderful people at Kensington who continue to keep me on this crazy rollercoaster ride.

Thank you. Thank you. Thank you.

Chapter 1

The real estate woman was flirting with Gabriel . . . and really starting to piss me off. Even though I knew women were going to come on to him, it wasn't always easy to accept. Or watch. I've often wondered if they'd be just as enthusiastic if they knew he was a vampire. Honestly? I don't think it would make the slightest difference. I've seen little old ladies throw out the most amazing innuendoes when he's helped them to a seat, and little girls play peek-a-boo from behind their mother's skirts because he smiled at them. I have no problem with old ladies and little girls. It's the ages in between.

I realize that much sex appeal is going to arouse any healthy libido, so I do my best to ignore the suggestive glances, fluttering lashes, and breathy voices. Especially as I know the interest is never going to be reciprocated. I can even turn a blind eye to the occasional *oops-I-didn't-really-mean-to-press-my-boobs-against-you* contact, because when that happens—and it has—Gabriel uses the moment to demonstrate that he's with me. Usually with his tongue in my mouth. But every now and then there's a woman who views his affection for me as some sort of unspoken challenge. And Claudia Benton—Exclusive Properties was such a woman.

I stood at one of the apartment's large picture windows, pretending to be mesmerized by the view of nighttime Greenley Heights. The city's neon splendor sparkled like a Christmas tree, but I was too busy surreptitiously observing my would-be antagonist to give it more than passing notice. Busy pointing out the features of the kitchen's built-in wine cooler, Claudia Benton was hanging on Gabriel's every word. He said something I didn't quite catch, but it made Ms. Benton laugh, and I watched as she put her hand on his muscular forearm, keeping it there far longer than a real estate agent should. Even if she did want to make her commission.

"Oh please, you must call me Claudia," she said, looking up at him. "I feel like we're such good friends already."

She pronounced her name *Cloud-ia*, which struck me as somewhat pretentious, but she could call herself Ophelia, Queen of the Outhouse, for all I cared. I knew the first-name invitation didn't include me.

Narrowing my eyes, I took her in from head to toe. If I had to guess, I'd put her in her early thirties. Her dark suit was tailored and looked expensive, as did her high heels. The blond hair may or may not have come from a bottle. Unless I could see roots, I couldn't tell for sure. And she wore no wedding ring.

Having exhausted the finer points of the wine cooler, *Cloud-ia* was extolling the virtues of the kitchen's other appliances when she suddenly stumbled, managing to save herself from kissing the hardwood floor only by grabbing the arm she'd just been caressing. Apparently flustered by her clumsiness, she apologized and thanked Gabriel for his gallantry.

I was fully prepared to give her the benefit of the doubt. Sometimes a stumble is just that, and she did seem embarrassed by her clumsiness. But then she glanced over at me, and the smile on her face told a different story. It was a sly, malicious smile. One that said if she tried a little harder, she could make Gabriel look her way, and once she had him looking, who knows what else he might want to do?

It was absolute crap, of course. She stood no chance of persuading him to sample what she was offering, but she didn't know that. Vampires, once they make a commitment, don't cheat. At least not while the object of their affection is still able to draw breath. And as one of the most possessive creatures ever, a vampire's focus becomes a problem only if those feelings aren't reciprocated. Gabriel and I had no worries in that regard. The proof of our devotion to each other had sent a tremor through the Dark Realm that blew the lid off the Richter scale.

But even if all of this was known to my wannabe rival, I suspect it would have simply made her more determined. Some women think they're irresistible. My inner bitch, who hadn't had much to harangue me about recently, now tapped my mental shoulder. *You gonna let her get away with that?*

No fucking way.

"Ms. Benton." I'd stab myself in the eye with a pencil before I called her by her first name, no matter how she pronounced it. "Would you mind showing me the bathroom?" I asked.

"But you've already seen it, dear," she replied in a condescending tone.

"Yes, I know, but if it's not too much trouble, I'd like to see it again. There's something I need to check out."

"Oh?" The lift of her brow was as condescending as her smile. "And what might that be?"

"Counter height." If my smile was any sweeter, I'd give myself a cavity, but as I passed Gabriel, I made sure my fingers brushed the back of his hand, causing a spark to flash in his neon-blue eyes.

There was a pleasing warmth about the bathroom, even if the décor reflected the taste of a strong male presence. Tile that looked like bricks covered the walls and floor in a color palette ranging from beach sand to a dark, coppery red. An old-fashioned claw-foot tub with curved sides took up a good amount of space, but there was enough left over for a spacious, modern shower with a glass door. The toilet was hidden behind a discreet half wall, and a double-sink vanity completed the necessary appointments. I stared at the space between the two sinks. It certainly looked like it would be adequate.

"I never thought of the shower as being small . . . until now," Ms. Benton murmured, her eyes glazing over as she gave Gabriel's wide shoulders a lingering look. I could just imagine what was going on inside her head and decided I'd had enough. Standing next to the open bathroom door, I put one hand on my hip and gripped the doorknob with the other. "Ms. Benton, would you give us a moment, please?" I really wish I could have seen her expression when she heard the lock engage.

I turned and reached for Gabriel, my fingers slipping inside the waistband of his jeans as I pulled him to me. I saw a glimpse of white as his mouth covered mine. He'd dropped his fangs, and a tremor of anticipated pleasure ran down my spine as my tongue slid between them.

When Gabriel makes love to me, that's exactly what he does. He takes my body on a long, sexy thrill ride, stopping at every erogenous zone to ignite a fire that burns white hot inside me. Radiating a sensuality that threatens to steal the breath from my body, he electrifies every nerve ending I possess until my need to feel him moving inside me eclipses everything else. It is without a doubt the most glorious carnal experience I could ever hope to have.

But then there are other times when a girl just wants to be fucked . . . and this was one of those times.

I quickly unbuckled his belt, slipping free the button on his jeans, and had the metal tab of the zipper between my finger and thumb when his hand grasped my wrist lightly.

"Careful," he murmured, his lips next to my ear.

He was fully erect, and I could feel the hard length of him pushing back against my hand through the heavy denim, but his warning was not without merit. It would be too awful if, in my eagerness, metal teeth caught something they shouldn't. Especially as there was nothing between skin and zipper.

I opened his fly, and his cock practically leaped into my hand. My fingers wrapped around him, my palm sliding up and down his thick shaft, pausing only so my thumb could graze across the dimple in the head. Gabriel shuddered, his muscular thighs responding to my touch. To be able to produce this reaction in him was an aphrodisiac all by itself.

As I continued to stroke him, I yanked his shirt free of his jeans, and slid my hand up his back, my nails scraping across his skin. The growl that emanated from deep in his chest vibrated off the tiled walls. He tilted my head back and ran his tongue across my collar bone and up my neck. Reaching my mouth, he kissed me. It was a long, lingering kiss that guaranteed I would leave the bathroom looking like I'd been schooled by someone who definitely knew how to use his tongue to do more than talk.

Gabriel tugged at my skirt, sliding it up past my hips. His hand went between my legs, and the growl in his throat became deeper as his fingers stroked the inside of my thigh. I trembled and let go of his cock, my hand clutching his upper arms and pulling him closer. He looked down at me and smiled knowingly, and I felt his clever fingers push aside the silky fabric of my panties and slip inside me.

I was ready for him, and the pressure of his fingers made my muscles clench. I was at a loss to describe the sound that escaped me as I arched my back and ground myself against the heel of his hand, but the smile on Gabriel's face was one of pure satisfaction. Withdrawing his fingers, he pulled down my panties. I kicked off my shoes so

I wouldn't catch my heel on the flimsy fabric. A scrap of scarlet silk lay on the floor as Gabriel gently muscled me back to the section of countertop separating the two sinks. His hands on my waist, he boosted me up and set me down on the marble. It felt deliciously cool against my bare ass.

I gasped and clutched the front of Gabriel's shirt as he pushed himself inside me. No matter how prepared I think I am, my body always seems shocked to feel him filling me. Now he cupped a foot in each hand, drawing my knees up, and began to move his hips slowly back. I dropped my gaze and watched as he slowly withdrew. His cock was engorged and glistening, the thick length coated with my silk. He stopped when he was almost completely out, and I raised my eyes back to his. Watching my reaction is always a big turn-on for him. I licked my lips and scraped my teeth over my lower lip and saw the pulse at the base of his throat quicken. I could feel the accelerated beat of his heart beneath the hand I held against his chest. He drew in a ragged breath and dropped his fangs. Heat raced through me as the neon blue of his eyes began to bleed into the surrounding sclera.

I let go of the countertop and moved my hand to the back of Gabriel's neck, curling my fingers and pricking him with my nails. He smiled and thrust himself back inside me. With each rhythmic drive I clenched my muscles, taking him in deeper, pushing him closer to his orgasm until a jolting spasm at the base of his spine told me to let go and blur my climax with his. He emptied himself inside me with a violent tremor that shook both of us.

"That," Gabriel said, his voice a husky whisper as he tried to catch his breath, "was . . . very . . . intense." He smiled down at me and smoothed a wayward curl from my cheek. "You should get jealous a little more often."

"You think I was jealous?" I asked, pretending indifference.

"I know you were. I could feel it." He brushed his lips against mine. "And I want you to know how much I approve of your method of dealing with it."

Reaching above my head, he took a washcloth from the towel rack and quickly cleaned both of us before gently pulling my skirt back down and setting me on my feet.

"Um, where are my panties?" I asked, checking out the floor.

Gabriel opened his hand, revealing red silk. I reached for it, but he quickly pushed the fabric in the front pocket of his jeans. "I think

I'll keep them for the time being," he said, his mouth curling into a sly grin. "Just in case you decide not to get jealous again."

"Is that really how I look to you?" Being bare-assed inside my skirt was making me feel deliciously shameless.

"No," Gabriel admitted. "You look like a woman who just got exactly what she wanted."

Chapter 2

By the time I walked out of the bathroom, Gabriel was gently ushering a mildly protesting Claudia Benton through the front door. I caught a glimpse of her face, and the expression she wore was not going to get her nominated for Realtor of the Year. It occurred to me that perhaps she was worried about losing her commission. Oh well, the bitch should've thought about that before trying to put the moves on my man.

"She had another appointment," Gabriel told me, seeing the questioning look on my face. "I told her we'd lock up." Another appointment this close to midnight? Yeah, right, of course she did. Still, I knew better than to say anything. "I think I saw a decent bottle of wine in the cooler," Gabriel said. "Would you like some?"

"That would be nice," I said with a smile. "I seem to have worked up quite a thirst."

I know next to nothing about wine, and Gabriel's efforts to educate me on the subject have not been a stellar success. He took me to a nighttime tasting event at some posh winery, only by the time I realized the operative word was *tasting* and not swallowing, it was too late. A half-dozen glasses, all on an empty stomach, and I was the life of the party. Who knew fermented grape juice could be so intoxicating? Or so sneaky. I was in the middle of a perfectly wonderful conversation with a very nice gray-haired man who was a professor of something at a college somewhere, when the next mouthful of Cabernet du Plonk had me slurring my words and sliding off the bar stool. According to the general consensus, I was the most delightful drunk they'd had at this particular winery in years. Something my lover made certain he shared with me once my head stopped spinning. But now I knew better. Accepting the glass of wine, I kicked off my shoes and sat down on the oversized couch, tucking one leg under me.

"So what do you think?" Gabriel asked, taking up his own sizable amount of space at the other end of the couch.

"About what?"

"The apartment." He made an expansive sweep with the hand that wasn't holding his wineglass. "Do you like it?"

To be honest, I hadn't really paid that much attention to it. I'd been too busy letting myself get annoyed by Ms. I-really-wanna-get-in-your-pants realtor, but as she was no longer an issue, I viewed my surroundings with a new perspective. Something about the way Gabriel was looking at me set a red flag waving in my head.

The building was close to the Greenley Heights financial district, and if the décor was anything to go by, the target buyers were young up-and-comers in banking or a similar profession. Clean lines, lots of white, with expensive neutral rugs covering the hardwood floor. All the appliances were top of the line, but I doubt the wall oven would ever get used and the range top only minimally. However, I could see the fridge and microwave getting quite a workout.

Whoever bought this apartment would be still hungry to make their mark. I imagined them to be single with no children, working long hours, and spending very little actual time inside these walls. Which was a shame, because the apartment had a lot of potential. Personally I loved the sections of open brickwork that made otherwise plain walls interesting, and the huge picture windows were a wonderful feature. As was the view, which I could now fully appreciate. But the feature that was the apartment's crown jewel was the floor-to-ceiling, built-in bookcase covering one entire wall.

"Yes," I said, nodding and taking a satisfied sip of my wine. "It's very nice."

"Would you like it?" Gabriel asked in a low voice.

"Would I like what?"

"This apartment. Would you like to have it?"

Normally when Gabriel makes my stomach roll, it's a good thing—an indication that I can expect some heavy-duty skin-on-skin contact taking place—but what my stomach was doing now was nowhere near that pleasant. A sudden jolt of anxiety made it curdle, causing a tremor that, if it reached my hand, would guarantee the light-colored couch would be wearing an abstract splash of the not-too-shabby merlot Gabriel had poured me.

You're being ridiculous! my inner bitch scolded. *What was that in the bathroom just now? A pity fuck?*

No, at least that's not how it seemed to me, and Gabriel would never be that cruel. So why did he want to give me an apartment?

Living with Gabriel had its own unique challenges, and while I had very little difficulty getting my head around most of the ones that related directly to his being a vampire, it was the human ones I found harder to deal with. Like the fact that he was beyond stinking rich.

"I need you to close your bank account," he'd told me a few days after I'd moved in with him.

"Why?" I was in the kitchen, trying to figure out how the coffee-maker worked. The damn thing had more lights and switches than a flight-control desk at NASA.

"It will make dealing with your finances easier," Gabriel said, coming up behind me and pushing the button that made the brew cycle kick into life. "Besides, isn't that what married people do?"

"Not necessarily," I murmured, frustrated that I'd missed which button he'd pressed. "And, anyway, we're not married."

The open cupboard door did a wonderful job of distorting his comment, which was probably just as well. I had no doubt he was making some pithy remark about my inability to set a wedding date.

"I still need you to close your bank account," he said, handing me a mug.

"Um, you do realize I don't actually have any finances, right?"

Being with Gabriel meant I now lived a nocturnal life, which pretty much wrote my pink slip for me. With no job, and having more or less given my house to my BFF Laycee and her boyfriend Jake to live in, I had less than a thousand dollars to my name. I'm ashamed to say my sudden lack of income hadn't crossed my mind . . . until now.

"That's what we need to talk about," Gabriel told me. "Are you going to have a problem with me providing for you?" It was an old-fashioned phrase that sounded as if it belonged in the Victorian era, but it was also something I would expect Gabriel to say.

He wants to provide for you? I could almost see my inner bitch rolling her eyes. *What does that mean . . . exactly?*

I filled my coffee cup with premium roast, added a splash of half-and-half, and sat down at the breakfast bar while Gabriel stood, waiting for my response. What he was really asking was whether or not I was going to have a problem taking his money. Truthfully, I didn't know. I'd never had a man offer to provide for me before, and from the way Gabriel was looking at me, I was pretty sure it wasn't something he made a habit of. "You're not going to leave a wad of bills on the bedside table, are you?"

He tried hiding his grin behind his mug, but the dimple in his cheek gave him away. "Only if that's what you prefer."

I tucked a stray curl behind my ear. "No, I'm more of a cookie jar type of girl."

A puzzled frown replaced the grin. "I know what a cookie jar is, but what's a cookie jar girl?"

I explained. "Every payday we both put an agreed-upon amount of cash into an empty cookie jar, so either of us can take what we need, as we need it." He seemed surprised by the concept, and I could almost hear the cogs turning inside his head as he weighed the practicality of such an arrangement. "Of course, it's not going to be exactly fair in this situation, because only one of us is going to be putting anything *into* the jar."

"Hmmm, well, I was thinking of something more along these lines," he said, fishing something out of his back pocket.

He placed a credit card on the marble countertop and pushed it toward me with his forefinger. It was copper-colored and had what appeared to be a smart chip embedded in it and my name etched on the front. I recognized the familiar Visa logo, but the moniker in the top right-hand corner was something I'd only seen in my schoolbooks. I picked it up and stared at Gabriel. "J. P. Morgan? Is this like the banking guy?"

"*The banking guy,*" Gabriel repeated, chuckling softly. "I think John Pierpont would have liked you very much."

My heel slipped off the lower rail of the breakfast bar stool I'd perched my butt on. "Did you . . . did you . . . are you saying you actually *knew* him?"

"We met a couple of times," Gabriel said, shrugging his wide shoulders nonchalantly, "when he wanted some advice."

"About what?"

"Mergers, acquisitions, financial investments."

"What did you do?" I was fascinated as my brain went on a trip through high school history lessons. "Tell him to create U.S. Steel?"

"No, that I can't take the credit for, but I did mention that I thought electricity was definitely a sound investment."

I was stunned. "You're responsible for General Electric?"

Gabriel laughed out loud. "Of course not! I just offered an opinion when it was asked for."

"And that's why you have an account at his bank?"

"I have accounts with many banks."

If there was some other meaning in his statement, I had no idea what it was. Instead, I looked down at the credit card in my hand. "What's the limit on this thing?"

"There isn't one."

Oh goody!

I might not be that savvy about finances, and certainly no banker is ever going to ask for my advice about anything, but I do know that credit cards with no pre-set spending limit are issued only to accounts with a lot of numbers coming before the decimal point. As if it might suddenly sprout teeth and bite me, I put the card back on the countertop and pushed it in Gabriel's direction. "I don't think so," I told him.

He folded his arms and stared at me for a full minute before asking, "Why not?"

"It's too much, Gabriel. Too big. I don't think I can handle it."

It wasn't just the card we were talking about, and we both knew it. It was accepting the lifestyle his wealth was going to give me. Of course, I knew he had money. He didn't just live in the penthouse of the swankiest apartment complex in town, he owned the building itself. His shirts were made in England, and he wore watches with names like Rolex and Patek Philippe. And then there were his cars. I'd been stunned to learn there was a second sub-level garage for his vehicles only.

I read an article once about people who won multi-state lotteries. Seventy percent of the winners either lost or spent their entire fortune within five years. I remember thinking I would never squander such an opportunity; only now I could truly appreciate how terrifying a sudden fortune could be. Gabriel wanting to give me a J. P. Morgan Palladium credit card was like winning the lottery, and like that seventy percent of overnight winners, I wasn't equipped to deal with the reality of such an abundant cash flow.

"You sure we can't do the cookie jar thing?" I muttered wistfully.

Gabriel said nothing as he took back the plastic bearing John Pierpont's name, but the next evening a colorful jar was sitting on the breakfast bar. Next to it was a note written in his beautiful copperplate script.

Better? And please, don't make a fuss. Your limit is 100K.

Inside the jar was an assortment of tens and twenties, with a few fifties thrown in for good measure. And a credit card. A black American Express with my name stamped on the front. Smiling, I took a couple of the twenties and slipped them with my new credit card into my wallet.

And now he wanted to buy me . . . an apartment?

"What do I need an apartment for?" I asked, trying to sound conversational while at the same time doing my best to ignore the seasick feeling washing through me. I looked up and found myself gazing into a pair of neon blue eyes, and I turned my head away. Gabriel's ability to move quickly—and silently—was still unnerving.

"What is it, Rowan?" he asked, placing a finger under my chin and turning my head back so I was looking at him once more.

"N-nothing."

My response was met with a raised brow. "You're not being truthful with me." He began stroking the side of my jaw with his thumb. "If you don't like this apartment, we can always look for another."

Oh yeah, like that was going to make a difference. It wasn't the apartment that was a problem, it was the reason for it. Apparently the novelty of living with me had lost its charm. Oh, I didn't doubt that Gabriel loved me and would want to keep seeing me. I was his Promise, after all, but being around me twenty-four-seven was an entirely different prospect from being able to pick and choose as the mood—or hunger—struck him.

I leaned back, pulling my face out of his grasp, and shook my head. "The apartment's fine," I said, although I already knew the bathroom was going to have to be gutted and redecorated. It already had the wrong sort of memories.

"If it's not the apartment," Gabriel said, "then what are you upset about?"

I downed the contents of my glass in one go and, emboldened by the sudden rush of fermented grapes, blurted out, "Why don't you just say you want me to leave?"

He looked startled. "What? Who said anything about you leaving?"

"Well, isn't that what this is all about?" I wasn't sure how much boldness I was going to find in one glass of wine, but I was determined to make the most of it. "It's okay, Gabriel, you can be honest with me."

"Aw, shit, Rowan—no! You've got this all wrong."

He jumped up from the couch and proceeded to pace. I watched him do an entire circumference of the open living space before coming to a stop in front of me. He dropped his gaze to the floor, and I watched his chest move as he took in a deep breath. My thighs twitched in appreciation of his muscle control.

"I should have known," he said, running his fingers through his hair, "that this was going to blow up in my face."

"What was?"

Picking up the bottle of merlot, he refilled my glass. "I thought you might like a place of your own."

"Whatever for?"

"For your . . . stuff."

"My what?"

"I don't like the idea of all your possessions being boxed up and sitting on a ten-by-twenty slab of concrete surrounded by corrugated metal walls. You don't seem to want to bring anything to the penthouse, so I thought if you had an apartment of your own, you could get everything out of storage." He paused.

"What?"

He sighed. "And I thought perhaps Laycee might be more comfortable visiting you in a place that felt like it was more you and less . . . me."

He had a point. Had I become involved with a regular non-vampire guy and moved into his penthouse apartment, my BFF would have already found a way to get invited for an extended stay, just so she could see how the other half lived. I loved Laycee dearly and always would, but if I thought my introduction to the presence of vampires had been shocking, her experience had been brutal.

Katja was the only female vampire I'd met so far. Gorgeous enough to be on the cover of any high-end fashion magazine, she was also obsessed with Gabriel. When her attempt to get me to dump him failed, she took it upon herself to reveal the truth about my boyfriend. It wasn't the ideal way to learn I'd been sleeping with a vampire, but it didn't have the outcome Katja had been hoping for. Being Gabriel's Promise meant more than just a casual fling. The beautiful vampire wasn't about to give up, however, and decided to use my best friend as coercion. But after hearing that her psychotic abductor was a vampire, Laycee's knee-jerk reaction had been to laugh. Which was not appreciated by Katja. In retaliation, she broke Laycee's wrist with a squeeze of her fingers, something hard to believe from a girl who looked as if she'd have difficulty opening the packaging inside a cereal box. But a flash of Katja's dental work had sealed the deal, and when the realization hit Laycee that I'd been sleeping with a vampire . . . well, it was asking a lot for anyone to accept. Even if they had known you since second grade.

When Laycee and I finally discussed the events of that particular night, we both knew there was no going back. Laycee wanted a normal life. One that involved marriage, children, and PTA meetings. What she didn't want were supernatural creatures that might tag along with me. So the only way she knew to protect herself, and her new family, was by letting me go. It might have been the right thing to do, but that didn't mean it didn't hurt. On both sides. You don't just walk away from someone you've known since you were six years old. A fact Gabriel recognized.

"Having a baby changes everything," Gabriel said in a voice that told me he'd given the matter some thought. "I can't imagine Laycee not wanting to share this with you. I understand her concerns, especially about me, but I don't think it's going to be possible for her to shut you out of her life completely. No matter what either of you think. Perhaps having your own place will make it easier for both of you." I hoped he was right because I really missed my best friend. "I'm sorry. I should have discussed this with you first. I thought it would be a nice surprise."

It was a wonderful gesture and another example of how well Gabriel knew me—sometimes better than I knew myself. "I don't know if she'll . . ." I let the rest of my sentence stay unspoken. We both knew if Laycee and I were to resume anything close to a friendship, she had to be the one to make the first move. The decision to put some distance between us had been hers; the olive branch had to come from her also.

"She just needs some time," Gabriel said as he sat down next to me. "But if it makes you feel better, do this for me. I really don't want your possessions kept in storage, and there's a spare bedroom that you could use for your father's things."

He had a point about my belongings. Apart from my clothes, the only other items I'd brought to his penthouse were a few books and one or two photographs. All of which I kept in the master bedroom, because somehow pictures of my dad didn't look right perched on a shelf next to a vase that was probably from the Ming dynasty.

"I realize what you've given up for me, Rowan. It's going to take time getting used to being with each other—"

"You mean it's going to take me some time," I amended quietly.

He sighed. "I don't ever want you to regret the decision you made." Raising my hands, he turned them over and kissed the inside of each wrist. It was a gesture filled with tenderness and warmth.

"Can I ask you a favor?" There was a lump in my throat, and it took a couple of swallows to dislodge it.

Gabriel's long, slender fingers tightened around my hand, and his face took on an earnest, yet guarded, expression. "Of course, anything you want."

"As we've already christened the bathroom . . . do you think we could do the rest of the apartment now?"

It really was too bad that a few days later my wonderful, thoughtful vampire lover proved he could be just as stupid as anyone else on the planet with two legs and a cock.

Chapter 3

I stared down at the colorful array of silky material that filled the drawer before me and didn't recognize a single item. "What the . . ." I muttered as my hand rifled through the contents. Hitching my towel a little higher, I closed the drawer and opened the one below, and then the next. All of them were filled with the most exquisite items of lingerie, and none of them were mine. Trust me, a woman recognizes her own underwear.

When I moved in with Gabriel, I didn't have to ask him to empty a dresser drawer or give up wardrobe space for me. One side of the massive walk-in closet in the master bedroom had deliberately been left empty. Gabriel had never doubted that it would hold my clothes. I had stared, open-mouthed, at what looked like a half mile of empty padded hangers on the rail above my head. I was equally astounded by the custom-built cabinetry below it—empty drawers interspersed with sections of open shelving that I was expected to fill with my shoes, purses, and other fashionable accessories. Hah! My idea of accessorizing was to actually carry a purse. It never occurred to me to see if it matched my shoes or anything else I was wearing. *Fashionable* was not in my vocabulary.

As I began making my way toward the open doorway, my progress was halted by a set of drawers that were partially open. Lined with a pretty floral silk, the vibrant colors caught my eye. I pulled open the drawer a little further, and the light scent of freesias filled the air. "And what am I supposed to put in here?" I asked, looking over my shoulder at Gabriel.

"Your lingerie," he replied, giving me a smile that was very wolfish and completely alpha male.

But now, as I opened the familiar silk-lined drawers, I was horrified to find there was nothing within that was even remotely familiar. "Oh no, please tell me he didn't," I said in a voice that clearly illustrated my displeasure to anyone listening.

I pulled out a coffee-colored satin bra. Exquisitely decorated with small bows and tiny seed pearls, it could have qualified as a work of art. I let it fall from my fingers onto the plush carpet at my feet as I reached for another beautiful item. This one was a daring magenta trimmed with black lace. It joined its mate on the floor. My frenzied hands removed one gorgeous item after the other. There were satin bras, wispy camisoles, and lace panties, along with a few other items that looked as if an engineering degree might be required in order to put them on.

I stared down at the froth of aquamarine lace I held in my hand. Any prior admiration for the skill and dexterity required to produce such an item, even if it was done by machine, was suddenly wiped away by another feeling altogether. This scrap of fabric was actually supposed to cover my ass? I snorted in disgust at the garment's complete lack of practical usefulness. There was only one reason a woman would wear something like this. Resentment, as thick and viscous as anything from the La Brea Tar Pits, began to bubble inside me. What the hell had Gabriel been thinking?

Um . . . I think that's pretty obvious, don't you?

My inner bitch sometimes had problems differentiating between rhetorical questions and real ones.

None of this was me. I was a Fruit of the Loom and Bali bra type of girl. Making a purchase from Victoria's Secret was about as exotic as I got. I didn't frequent shops that sold . . . I began checking labels: La Perla—Fleur of England—Agent Provocateur. Agent Provocateur? You gotta be kidding me—what idiot came up with that one?

Probably some guy who hadn't been laid in a while? my inner bitch offered helpfully.

Yeah, I could believe that.

"Rowan . . . what's wrong?"

I wasn't surprised to hear his voice or note the deliberate mildness of his tone. Always able to sense my mood, Gabriel was only too keenly aware of my simmering anger. I turned around and glared at him.

"Where's my underwear?" I demanded.

"It would appear that you are standing in it," he answered reasonably.

I didn't want reasonable. I wanted to stomp my foot, but it isn't quite the same when you're standing on plush carpet. "No, where's *my* underwear?" I demanded.

"Rowan, sweetheart, that *is* your underwear. Who else's would it be?" he added in an even voice.

"This isn't mine," I insisted stubbornly. "It's yours."

He chuckled and flexed his biceps, which in turn made my thigh muscle twitch. "I don't think I'd look half as good in any of it as you would."

Oh fuck me sideways, my inner bitch groaned, *he thinks you're trying to be funny.*

It was disappointing to know that male vampire DNA could be just as idiotic as its human counterpart.

I took a deep breath in through my nose and exhaled slowly before I spoke. "This isn't my underwear, Gabriel, this is all *yours.* Everything here is something *you* want to see me wear."

"Of course it is." If he was any more agreeable, he'd leave me no choice but to slap him. "But these are all items you would have bought for yourself . . . eventually."

I stared at him, appalled by his chauvinistic attitude. What was wrong with my underwear? It had been good enough before I moved in with him, so what had changed? Did he really think that living with him meant he was entitled to make decisions for me? Indignation made me bristle and my temper climb a notch higher. I picked up a hanger and waved the item at him. At first glance, the lingerie appeared to be a black bra and matching pair of panties, joined together in some bizarre fashion with a number of buckled straps. It seemed to me that a contortionist might experience some difficulty putting it on. "You think I would actually buy something like this? For myself?"

Of course not, my inner bitch chimed in, *but you gotta admit, it does look very interesting . . . and sexy.*

"Ah, that . . ." Unfolding his arms, Gabriel ran his fingers through his hair and had the grace to look a little shamefaced. "The saleslady assured me Lady Gaga has something just like it."

I stared at him, aghast. "And that's supposed to make me feel better?"

"It doesn't?" he asked, mildly surprised by my apparent lack of enthusiasm.

"Knowing Lady Gaga has something like this doesn't make me feel better, Gabriel. It scares the shit out of me."

He shook his head, moving the white waterfall of hair across his shoulders. It was obvious he wasn't grasping why I was upset that *my* underwear, my perfectly good one-hundred-percent-cotton bikini panties and underwire bras, had all disappeared. Replaced, apparently, with ridiculously expensive designer lingerie.

He folded his arms again, and I forced my thighs to behave. "Okay, I'll admit it might have been a little presumptuous of me to get that for you." He tilted his chin at the Lady Gaga outfit still in my hands.

You think?

"But aren't I allowed to give you a gift?"

For someone who was normally so in tune with me emotionally, Gabriel was now being maddeningly obtuse.

"A gift would be a negligee for Christmas or my birthday or Valentine's Day, and it would be a single item. It wouldn't be replacing everything I own with stuff *I didn't choose.*" I forced myself to take a deep breath and push aside my anger. How could I get him to see that replacing all my underwear with lingerie he'd selected made me feel like I was being objectified. "You can't do this, Gabriel," I said, struggling to keep my temper on an even keel. The fact that I had to actually explain how I felt was starting to piss me off. "Replacing all my underwear is just . . . wrong."

"Why?"

"Because it's too . . . it's too . . . *Fifty Shades,*" I blurted out.

His eyes narrowed as he considered the frame of reference I'd used. "You think," he said slowly, "buying you lingerie means I want to control you?"

Thank God there's at least one guy on the planet who understands that book ain't a primer for a healthy, loving relationship!

"Not deliberately," I said, mentally shushing my inner bitch, "but that's how it makes me feel."

I watched his brows pull together even further as he considered my words. If Gabriel thought this was covered under "providing" for me, then he and I had very different ideas of what that concept meant. Besides, this had nothing to do with gift buying. It was all about respect. For me. As a person. Any minute now, I told myself, the floodgates would open and comprehension would wash through him, along with a healthy dose of shame for taking so long to grasp what I was getting at. I waited for him to apologize.

He didn't.

Instead his sudden sympathetic expression, coupled with an ever so slightly condescending smile, made me nervous. Whatever he was thinking, I was pretty sure he was way off base. "Are you PMS-ing?" he asked.

Awww—fuck! Tell me he did not just say that.

"W-w-what?" I stuttered.

A ball of fire exploded in my solar plexus, and I suddenly felt . . . all wrong. I didn't feel ill exactly, but I definitely felt off-kilter. As if I was out of sync with everything around me. Especially Gabriel. I was hot, and not in a sexual fantasy way, even with all the lingerie on the floor. I was hot because my core temperature was rising, and what was worse, I was dangerously close to bawling my eyes out. What the fuck was wrong with me? Why did I feel so bad?

Because you're disappointed, you idiot! Your hunky vampire just fucked up, and if you don't want to make it any worse—by saying something you'll regret—then you'd better get the hell out of Dodge and go find someone who can tell you how to deal with him.

Sometimes my inner bitch really does make sense.

I turned around, heading for the door that would take me back into the bedroom, but a gust of wind across my cheek was a rude reminder of vampire speed. Barring the opening with his arm, Gabriel blocked my exit. I guess the look on my face told him he'd just opened mouth and inserted foot. Big-time.

"Let me out," I said through gritted teeth.

"Not until we've sorted this out."

Ordinarily I would have applauded his willingness to discuss a problem between us. Most guys would be only too happy to let their woman pout, sulk, or go shopping just so they could avoid the possibility of talking about their *feelings*. But now wasn't the time.

"If you don't let me by, I'm going to rip off your fucking arm and beat you to death with it!" I snarled. My threat couldn't have been more ludicrous, and how Gabriel managed to keep a straight face was beyond me.

"Rowan, please—"

My legs began to shake. I really needed to start moving while I still had the ability. "Gabriel, listen carefully because I'm only going to say this once. I don't want to sort out anything with you, at least not right now." Hot tears pricked the back of my eyelids. "Let me by—*now!*"

"At least tell me where you're going," he said as he let me push by him.

He was a vampire, and it was his nature to be possessive, something I still hadn't quite come to terms with. What Gabriel would grudgingly admit to as being slightly overprotective, I saw as irrational, borderline obsessive behavior. But, as upset as I was, I didn't want to provoke him into doing something we'd both regret.

I took a deep breath and forced myself to speak calmly. "I'm going to talk to someone who will understand without my having to explain."

"Anasztaizia?" He sounded relieved.

"Yes, Anasztaizia."

I could feel his eyes boring holes into my back as I dropped the towel I was wearing and pulled on a pair of jeans and a loose fitting T-shirt.

And no underwear.

Chapter 4

"Oh, dahlink!" Anasztaizia declared, taking one look at my teary-eyed expression and overall pathetic state. "This is going to take more than coffee, I am thinking."

She pointed to a bar stool by one of the kitchen's prep areas and instructed me to sit. When I had called the lovely Magyar, she had simply told me to come to the restaurant she and her family owned. "I am taking inventory. No one is here, so we can talk in private." Which I took to mean that her vampire boyfriend Aleksei was down for the day at her apartment and she already had a good idea why I needed to see her.

After slamming the penthouse door behind me, I'd half-expected Gabriel to wrench it off its hinges and drag me back inside, or to find him waiting for me in the garage when the elevator doors opened. But he didn't, and he wasn't. Stepping into the garage's concrete coolness, I let loose the breath I'd been holding. As an Original Vampire, Gabriel could tolerate the daylight in measured doses, and I wasn't completely certain that he might not decide to continue our discussion by coming after me. It appeared he'd seen reason and thought better of it. Good. If he was really smart, he'd go lie in his sarcophagus and look for the answer while in a state of unconsciousness.

Wouldn't that be kind of difficult, what with him being unconscious and all?

It seemed my inner bitch had enjoyed this difference of opinion between Gabriel and myself a little too much.

Now I watched as Anasztaizia emerged from one of the restaurant's large walk-in coolers, a decadent-looking confection in her hands. It was some sort of cake, and the fondant glaze on the top had been decorated in a spider-web pattern.

"Esterházy torte," Anasztaizia told me. "Guaranteed to cure everything but the stupidity of the male sex!"

She cut me a slice and set it before me, along with a fork, a napkin, and a large mug of the special-blend Russian coffee that I loved. As I ate my cake, giving my taste buds an orgasm, she told me about Prince Paul III Anton Esterházy de Galántha, whom the cake was named after. It wasn't until she was refilling my coffee mug that she asked me softly what Gabriel had done. So I told her.

Being able to talk to another female who was also involved with a vampire was a godsend. Anasztaizia had made herself available to me from the moment I'd accepted that vampires were very real and that I'd been sleeping with one. At first I'd been hesitant to burden her with my endless questions and anxieties, especially as vampires are, by necessity, secretive. I wasn't sure how Gabriel would react if he thought I was blabbing bedroom secrets to Aleksei's girlfriend.

"It's all right," he'd assured me, making his dimple wink sexily. "I understand there are some things you would feel more comfortable discussing with another female, and I think it might be good for Anasztaizia also."

His instinct had been correct.

"You have no idea, dahlink, how long I have wanted another woman to talk to," Anasztaizia told me, making me realize that keeping her boyfriend's secret had been harder on her than I'd thought. "But I have no wish to come between you and your friend, Laycee." Her smooth brow puckered with an uncharacteristic frown. "You have been friends for a long time, but I am thinking perhaps there are things you cannot say to her, yes?"

It was true. Even if Laycee had wanted to embrace wholeheartedly having vampires in her life, there were still things I wouldn't be able to share with her because she would always be on the periphery. And this particular episode with Gabriel? Laycee would have shrugged it off as nothing more than one of the perks of having a rich boyfriend. She certainly wouldn't have felt objectified or disrespected and might not have understood why I did. And why was that?

Because no matter how much you care for Laycee, you aren't cut from the same bolt of cloth, my inner bitch whispered in a voice that seemed surprised I hadn't figured this out for myself. The truth could be very disheartening at times.

So no, Anasztaizia wasn't going to come between us.

"He replaced *everything?*" she said, the incredulity in her voice telling me I hadn't been overreacting. Anasztaizia understood completely why I was upset about Gabriel wanting to dress me up like an X-rated Barbie doll.

"Has Aleksei ever done anything like this?" I asked hesitantly.

She laughed. "Of course, dahlink—he's male."

"Yeah, but has he ever done anything to make you feel . . ." I trailed off, unable to verbalize what I was feeling.

"Like he had absolutely no idea who I was?" Anasztaizia asked gently. I nodded, and she sighed. "Oh yes, he's guilty of that, but I think it is something every male on the planet has done, and it makes no difference if they're human or vampire." She reached out and patted me on the back of the hand. "Only Aleksei would never buy me lingerie."

"What—not ever?"

Anasztaizia shook her head. "He would be far too embarrassed to actually walk into a store and buy something so intimate."

"He should ask Gabriel to go with him. I'm sure he could give him some tips."

"Could you imagine the two of them together in a lingerie store?"

A sudden image of the big Russian vampire filled my head. I pictured him dressed in his beloved army greatcoat, military garb, and combat boots, checking out a thong on a hanger. It was too ridiculous for words, and I snorted in a very unladylike way.

Anasztaizia shook her head. "Well, thankfully he doesn't have to, dahlink. I know what he likes."

"Yeah, I thought I did too, but I guess I was wrong. Apparently Gabriel wants to see me wear something called La Perla."

Her brows rose in admiration. "He bought you La Perla?"

"Yeah and Flora England and some Agent or the other."

"Fleur of England and Agent Provocateur." The names rolled off her tongue with ease. "Well, you certainly can't accuse him of having bad taste. Were they pretty?"

"Exquisite," I sighed, recalling the lovely satin bra with ribbons and pearls. An unexpected wave of shame swept through me at the way I'd manhandled them. "I guess they were pretty expensive, huh?"

"The cost makes no difference, dahlink. Gabriel was wrong to do what he did, and if you don't want it happening again, then it is up to you to let him know, although . . ."

I stared at her as her voice trailed off. "Although what?"

"Well, you did let him buy you an apartment and a new car," she pointed out.

"But at least I had some say in both of those things."

The apartment was one thing, but the car was a different matter altogether. I'd been upset when Gabriel had insisted I give up the POS. Iffy brakes, which had been on my needing-to-get-checked-out list, made the vehicle, according to him, unsafe to drive. I might have been able to swing the odds in my favor if new brakes were all that were required, but the POS had other problems. The kind that required a mechanic who would relish the challenge of working without the help of computer-aided diagnostics.

"So it's the scrap yard then?" I'd asked, feeling an unexpected prick behind my eyes.

"Absolutely not," Gabriel assured me. "This car is a link to your father, and you can keep her for as long as you want. I'd just feel better if you didn't drive her." He'd held me close, surprising me that he understood how strong a pull a couple of tons of steel had on me. "Let's see if we can get her fixed up, and maybe restore the original paint job?"

"What's wrong with the color she is now?" After all these years I'd grown quite fond of the unique Pimping-It-Purple shade a previous owner had chosen.

"Absolutely nothing," Gabriel said, his attempt at nonchalance not quite disguising his shudder. "In the meantime you can take your pick of anything here."

I was far too intimidated to drive anything in his garage, and as most of his vehicles had stick shifts, it was the perfect excuse to decline his generous offer. Which left me with no choice but to allow him to buy me a new car. And that, I suspected, was his intention all along. The Dodge Charger met with his approval, the Plum Crazy color not so much. Still, he was smart enough not to make any disparaging comments, and for that I thanked him.

So how could a man who was so wonderfully sensitive about my beat-up car, and who recognized my need for a place of my own, be so brainless as to replace all my underwear? "This is different," I continued, "it's more personal. I can't believe it never crossed his mind to talk to me about this first. What if La Perla reminded me of an old boyfriend or something?"

"Does it?" she asked curiously.

"No, of course not." I shook my head. "But he doesn't know that."

Hmmm, I wouldn't be so sure . . .

"Ah dahlink, sometimes I forget how it was in the beginning with Aleksei."

I hesitated a moment before asking, "How did you and Aleksei meet?" She gave me an odd look, one that said she'd been waiting for me to ask, and blew out a sigh. I couldn't tell if this was because she really didn't want to answer, or because she was concerned what my reaction would be. I apologized, "If it's too personal—"

"No, it's not that. I was a different person back then." A slight frown crinkled her brow, and she gave me a hesitant smile. "My mother and father, the ones who run this restaurant with me"—she waved a hand in the air—"are not my real parents. They are good, kind people who took me in and saved me from what could have been a very different kind of life."

"They adopted you?"

She shook her head. "Not formally, but as far as I am concerned, they are my parents. I never knew my real father; he died when I was very young, and so my mother remarried. I was thirteen the first time my stepfather got into my bed. When I was fifteen, I told my mother what he'd been doing. She called me a liar. Somehow it was easier for her to believe I had seduced him. So she threw me out."

"Oh my God—how could she do such a thing?" Although I knew it happened, I still found it hard to believe a parent would turn against a child in this way. "What did you do?" I asked.

"Took money from her purse and ran away. Like a lot of girls, I went to Budapest. I thought I would become a model." She snorted in disgust at her own naïveté. I thought she was being too hard on herself. "Anyway," she continued, "I met a girl who had a boyfriend, and pretty soon I was doing drugs and selling myself for the next high." She leaned back and folded her arms across her chest. "You understand what I am telling you, Rowan, about what I was doing?"

I nodded. Yeah, I understood, but it was in the past, and I wasn't going to condemn her for it. Realizing that, Anasztaizia relaxed her arms. "Is that how you met Aleksei?" I asked. "When you were on the streets?"

She nodded. "It was in an alley behind a nightclub. The man I was with decided he wanted his money back. Of course I refused, so he hit me a couple of times, and then suddenly Aleksei was there. I remember the man started to cry and pissed his pants, he was so scared. Aleksei took me to a café, got me something to eat, and asked if I wanted to be a prostitute all my life. I was only sixteen, but I'd already seen too much. Not many girls made it to nineteen. I didn't want to be one of them. So Aleksei took care of me. When I was clean, he sent me to live with my new parents, made me promise to go back to school . . . and became my boyfriend."

"He was your boyfriend? At sixteen?"

"It's not like you're thinking." She smiled at me. "It was all very proper. Aleksei is very old-fashioned. He wouldn't even kiss me until I was twenty-one."

Seeing how lovely Anasztaizia was now, it wasn't hard to imagine how she must have looked at sixteen. I had to admire the big guy's restraint. "Is that when you found out he was a vampire?"

"That was when he told me, but I think I always knew what he was. You must remember, Rowan, I grew up hearing stories about vampires."

"And it didn't scare you?"

She smiled and toyed with the diamond ring on her finger. "A little, but by then it was too late. I was already in love with him."

"And the heart wants what the heart wants," I said softly. Her eyes shone brightly as she looked at me. Oh yeah, I could absolutely understand what it was like to fall, and fall hard. "So what do I do about Gabriel?"

"Easy!" Her smile was dazzling, and filled with relief at knowing her past made absolutely no difference to me. "You set boundaries, Rowan. You tell Gabriel what is acceptable and what is not. And wanting to dress you like a high-priced hooker is definitely not acceptable—unless, of course, it's something you want to do. But that decision has to be yours, not his."

Her reference to the hooker was because I'd told her about the Lady Gaga outfit. "The only thing missing was the spike heels," I muttered glumly.

"Oh, I'm pretty sure they were there, you just didn't find them.

He's a vampire," Anasztaizia reminded me softly, "one of the most possessive creatures ever created."

"I know, I know," I muttered, trying my best not to sound irritated, "but if you're saying that to make me feel better, then I gotta tell you it isn't working."

"I don't know about making you feel better, dahlink, but perhaps when I say possessive you are thinking one thing when I am meaning another, hmmm?"

She tilted her head and, resting her elbow on the prep surface, cupped her chin in her hand. The huge diamond Aleksei had given her twinkled in the overhead light. Perhaps she was right; maybe my definition of everything was completely different when applied to a vampire, although how many different definitions of possessiveness could there be?

"Anasztaizia, I'm not some teenager straight out of high school having her first love affair. I know Gabriel has had other women, and for all I know, they welcomed this type of possessiveness, expected it even. Maybe they were happy at not having to make decisions for themselves. But I'm not one of those women, and I don't want Gabriel thinking he can just make decisions for me. Please don't misunderstand me," I said, quickly seeing the alarmed look on her face. "I love his attentiveness, but it's easy to blur the line between consideration and obsession."

"Perhaps the problem is not just his," Anasztaizia said, looking thoughtful. "Perhaps the problem is with you also."

"What do you mean?"

"You're not just another woman to him, Rowan." I opened my mouth to protest, but she held up her hand. "Please let me explain. Vampires are not by design solitary creatures. They live a solitary existence for the most part because it is in their own best interest to do so, but there is always a part of them that craves connection with another human being. And yes, being able to feed freely is a big part of it, but that isn't all a vampire wants from a human. If they are able to form a bond, then it is as if a huge weight has been lifted, and they have the freedom to be exactly who, and what, they are with that one person." She paused, and this time her smile looked sad.

"Can you imagine how it must feel to spend every waking moment always in fear of discovery?" she continued. "Making sure every move, every word, every gesture does not betray you? For a vampire to know the need for blood will not be refused is nothing compared to being able to talk openly and frankly about his life. How the world has changed, lovers that have died, discoveries they have witnessed." She gave a little laugh. "And of course being able to drop their fangs without making anyone scream is quite wonderful—or so I am told!"

Now I knew why Aleksei had been so pleased when I didn't keel over the first time he showed me his fangs—and why he continued to do so every time he saw me.

"But in the back of their mind is the knowledge that this will not last forever. A human life span is so short, and that fact alone is responsible for how their possessive instinct manifests itself. I can't tell you that all vampires fall in love with their human companions, but a very real affection does exist. They do what they think is necessary to protect their human companion, and also to show their appreciation for what is being given, even if it is sometimes a little overwhelming." Putting her hand on my arm, Anasztaizia squeezed gently. "I understand completely why you feel the way you do, but I don't believe it was Gabriel's intention to deliberately belittle or objectify you in any way. He just wants to give you . . . everything."

"But I've never asked him for anything—"

"It doesn't matter. To him this is no less than you deserve."

"Well, I'm not sure how high heels and kinky underwear fit into that category."

She shrugged. "He's male—what can I say?"

I sighed and carried my dirty mug and plate to the large sink. "This is going to happen again, isn't it? Oh, I don't mean replacing my underwear," I quickly clarified. "I mean Gabriel doing stupid things."

"Probably," Anasztaizia agreed, "but it's up to you to make him listen whenever he does something you don't like. This may not be your first love affair, Rowan, but in many ways it is Gabriel's." It was every bit as much my first love affair too, but I didn't tell her that. "If it makes you feel any better," she continued, "Aleksei's stupid moment was to fill my closet with fur coats."

"What?"

The lovely Magyar nodded. "Yes. More than twenty full-length coats. Mink, fox, rabbit, chinchilla, wolf. I burst into tears when I saw the leopard skin."

"What did you do?" I asked, shuddering at the number of lives lost to make so many coats.

"I threw him out, which was a little embarrassing because he was naked at the time, and we were staying at the Hotel Imperial in Vienna." That I would have liked to have seen—or maybe not. "He thought I might want to thank him for his generosity by making love on them."

"Oh Jeez," I muttered under my breath.

"Exactly. It took him two days to realize I wasn't going to speak to him again until he got rid of them all."

"I'm surprised it took him that long," I blurted out.

"So was I, but thankfully he did. And then he explained that this was how he had pampered the last woman he had been with—"

"The last one?" Despite what she'd just told me, I'd assumed Anasztaizia was the only woman in the big guy's life. The only one with any meaning at least.

"Aleksei is over three hundred years old," she said softly, patiently. "He had other women before me. This particular one was a dancer at the Moulin Rouge. I think she might have been painted by Lautrec, or maybe he wanted to paint her. In any case, Aleksei became jealous, and they almost broke up."

"And you're okay with this?"

"Rowan, dahlink, she was a can-can dancer who's been dead for over a century. What can she do to hurt me?"

I sat back down and looked at her. She was lovely and wonderful and had fully accepted that however much time she was going to have with Aleksei, she would make the most of it.

"If it's important to you, Rowan, then it's important to Gabriel." She reached over and patted my hand. "But remember, he's a vampire, not a mind reader, and while he may be incredibly intuitive, even he needs to have things spelled out for him every now and then."

She was right, and I knew it. Anasztaizia made me see my problem with Gabriel from a different perspective. One that was going to let me put down some ground rules without being confrontational. "You really are the best!" I said, giving her a hug.

"I'm happy to help," she replied, handing me the rest of the Esterházy torte, which she'd boxed up.

I had parked the Charger close to the brick wall at the far end of the alley behind the restaurant, only now I was blocked in. A black delivery van was parked behind me, and so close I had zero maneuvering room. Freaking moron! Clutching my car keys, I opened the restaurant's back door and called Anasztaizia's name. "You know whose van this is?" I asked as she came down the hallway, her pointy-toed Manolo Blahnik pumps clicking on the tiled floor.

She frowned as she looked at the van and then shook her head. "Sorry, dahlink, I've never seen it before."

"You think someone's getting a delivery?"

"On a Sunday?" Her face told me that was a big no. "It's probably someone having lunch."

"But why park here? It's kind of out of the way."

"Perhaps that's reason enough. Why don't you take my car?"

"Oh, I can't do that," I said, turning down her generosity.

"Why not? I'm going to be here for at least another two hours. By that time the van will probably be gone and I can drive your car home. If not, I can get a ride with one of my guys." One of her guys meant any of the kitchen staff who would be working in a few hours.

"You sure you don't mind?"

She grinned. "Didn't you already tell me I was the best? Let me get you the keys."

Chapter 5

Anasztaizia drove a red Mazda MX-5 Miata with a retractable hard top that I would have loved to have put down, but an unfamiliar car always makes me nervous. Especially when it's someone else's pride and joy. I thought perhaps I might indulge myself when I returned the car to her later, but right now I needed to familiarize myself with the dashboard. Leaving the hard top up was probably the reason my injuries weren't more extensive, because I never saw the truck that hit me.

The green light said I had the right-of-way, which meant the truck that crossed the intersection at the same time I did obviously ran a red light. Who does that at 2:00 p.m. on a Sunday afternoon? One minute I'd been having a lively dialogue with my inner bitch about the art of compromise—*tell him the thongs have got to go, but you'll keep the bras and the Lady Gaga number*—and the next my world was a cacophony of screaming metal, screeching tires, and crunching glass.

I ricocheted forward and hit my head on the steering wheel, realizing, in a moment of absolute clarity, that the Miata's air bag had failed to deploy. Thankfully the seat belt kept its part of the deal, and stopped me from taking a header out the windshield. The strap, cutting across my chest, was agonizing, but it was, all in all, a fair exchange.

Anasztaizia's sexy little sports car came to a stop in the middle of the intersection, and, from what I could tell in a dazed glance out the driver's window, it was now facing the wrong way. The force of the impact had popped the hood open, obscuring my view through the windshield, telling me I owed the seat belt more than I realized. The smell of gasoline and burnt rubber filled the car along with the faint aroma of something citrus that had to be the air freshener plugged into the air vent.

The passenger side of the Miata had taken the brunt of the collision, which resulted in the door buckling to create a noticeable gap. I figured the only way it was going to open was with some help from the jaws of life or some similar device. A soft plopping sound startled me as a big dollop of cake fell from the ceiling to the floor. Apparently Esterházy torte didn't survive a violent impact too well.

I needed to get out of the car. The smell of gasoline was getting stronger, and I didn't want to wait around to see if anything was going to blow. The driver's-side door appeared to be intact, a detail that was confirmed a moment later when it was wrenched open. A hand reached toward me, and I gave an involuntary shriek as the blade of a very large knife was waved in front of my face.

What? Couldn't kill us with your truck so you've come to finish off the job by getting up close and personal?

The idea that the accident was anything but what it seemed was preposterous, and I can only blame the absurdity of my thought process on the blow to my head. At least I was spared the embarrassment of voicing my accusation, but only because my tongue seemed to be bigger than normal. In that same second I tasted blood and realized I'd bitten it. The knife danced in the air before slicing through my seat belt in a single, easy swipe. And then it magically changed into a syringe. I turned my head and forced myself to focus on the figure squatting next to the open door. Dressed in jeans, boots, and a wifebeater, he didn't strike me as being qualified to give me a shot of anything. At least nothing that was legal.

"Call . . . nine . . . one . . . one . . ." I mumbled awkwardly through lips that were swollen and a tongue that was getting decidedly thicker.

Ignoring me, the man grabbed my arm and pulled it toward him. There came a sharp pinch, and then I was being lifted out of the driver's seat as the rest of the world turned black.

I came to with a violent, full-body spasm that banged my head and hands against something with a hard edge. Disoriented, I sucked in a breath and almost choked. There was some sort of covering over my head. A bag or hood that, judging from the scratchy feel against my skin, was made of a type of rough sacking. It smelled foul. A mix of stale sweat, dried vomit, and old blood. The smell of fear.

My mouth was dry. I was so thirsty I could easily drain one of those water cooler bottles and ask for a refill. It had to be a side effect of whatever shit I'd been injected with. My tongue had been replaced with 200-grit sandpaper. Panic began to rise, and I had to stomp it down before it could escalate and run wild. If that happened, I had no chance of getting out of whatever hell I was in.

Yeah, well, you've gotten out of this kind of shit before.

Call me crazy, but I was pretty sure my departure from the Dark Realm was more a result of being thrown out by a demon than anything I'd done on my own. Still, it was kind of nice to know my inner bitch was still with me, even if her advice wasn't exactly helpful.

I decided to check for injuries from the car crash, but this was difficult because not only was I hooded, I was also handcuffed. And who knew handcuffs were so heavy?

Anyone who's ever flirted with the idea of kinky sex, I imagine.

Yeah, well, that isn't me.

I know.

Gabriel had definitely expanded my knowledge of sex with some experimentation that could qualify as borderline kinky, but we hadn't gotten around to using restraints. And it wasn't like anything we did required a pre-agreed "safe" word. Besides, my idea of kinky was probably everyone else's normal, but I made the decision right then that no matter how many orgasms Gabriel promised me, I was never going to wear handcuffs for him. Not even fur-lined ones.

From what I could discern, I was shackled to metal bars. Was I in some sort of cage? I stretched my fingers, and the distance between each bar seemed to confirm this. As did the fact my arms couldn't slide down past my shoulders. And the bars weren't round, but square-cut, which explained why it had hurt so much when I'd smacked my head against them.

Cautiously I moved my lower extremities. If the numbness in my butt was any indication, I was sitting on a concrete floor. Okay, that confirmed it. Concrete floor and bars spelled cage in my world. A careful flexing of joints and muscles told me nothing was broken, and other than feeling sore and bruised in places I expected to feel sore and bruised, I seemed to be okay.

We're alive, and that's a plus.

My inner bitch . . . always looking for the silver lining.

The worst pain was in my chest, and had to be from the seat belt. I couldn't take a deep breath without it hurting, so I made myself take shallow ones. Kind of like one of those dogs with the squashed-in noses. I was more than a little miffed at the air bag's failure to deploy, and someone was going to get a really nasty letter from me about that, but I've also seen pictures of people punched black-and-blue from kissing one. It's not like being whacked in the face with your bed pillow.

Once I got past my catalog of aches, I was surprised to realize how clear-headed I was. This was unexpected, because I figured that whatever had been in the syringe hadn't been a round of antibiotics. If my chronic thirst was the only side effect, it was something I could deal with. The bastard who'd injected me had no idea my boyfriend could rip his head off—literally—and I wanted to be the one to tell him he'd just made the last mistake of his miserable life. All I had to do was stay calm and wait. Gabriel would come for me. He had told me the bond between us was a strong one, so I was confident he'd already plugged into my emotional grid.

Assuming he's awake.

Yeah, well, there was that. I had no idea what time it was, or how long I'd been unconscious. After my abrupt departure this morning, Gabriel had probably taken advantage of my absence to catch a few zzzs of his own. As an Original Vampire, he could go quite a while without sleep, but even he needed to recharge every now and then. And it had been almost a week since he'd last done that.

I could only imagine how angry he was with my storming out this morning, and I know if I were he, I'd go crash and give myself time to cool off. He wouldn't sense anything until he awoke, so yeah . . . that might be a problem.

Hope for the best . . . but prepare for the worst?

I guess so.

The sound of approaching footsteps made me hold my breath as I tried to make out how many sets there were. Definitely more than one person, but the footfalls were muffled, and it was difficult to know if they belonged to more than two people. I figured the confusion might have something to do with the bag over my head. Then came a voice, an unintelligible garble that made no sense. Maybe I wasn't as clearheaded as I thought.

The covering over my head was suddenly pulled off, and I gasped in a mouthful of air that was a lot cleaner than what I'd been breathing through the foul sack. I opened my eyes and then snapped them shut almost immediately. The single fluorescent bulb in the ceiling was strong enough to trigger a sudden unrelenting pounding in the back of my head—one that ice-picked its way down my neck, across my shoulders, and halfway down my back. Chronic thirst wasn't enough. Now I was a candidate for a possible seizure. Although I was grateful to no longer be forced to inhale the odors left in the burlap sacking, I was of two minds about having the hood removed. I've watched enough cop shows on TV to know the inability to identify an abductor goes a long way toward ensuring the release of a kidnap victim. I had three kidnappers, and they either didn't watch much TV or had already decided identification wasn't going to be a problem. I was hoping for the former.

I peered into the gloomy shadows beyond the metal bars, and determined I was underground. Possibly a parking garage or some similar structure. And yes, I was in a cage. Shaped like an octagon, it made me think of an MMA fighting ring. The only way in or out was through a door cut into one of the sections of bars, and that was secured by a heavy link chain and a big, shiny padlock. Considering the fact I was handcuffed to the cage bars, it seemed like overkill to me.

The man standing next to the cage door was the same asshole who'd injected me while I sat, dazed and disoriented, in Anasztaizia's crumpled car. I thought it seemed more than likely he was also responsible for the accident in the first place. His partner in crime stood next to him, watching me with beady little eyes. Half the size of his buddy, he had dirty, unkempt hair that fell over a thin face with a sharp nose and pointed chin. He bounced from foot to foot, his hands darting in and out of his jacket pockets, his upper torso rocking from side to side. If he was a rodent, he'd be scurrying all over the place, so of course I christened him Rat Boy.

But it was the last member of this happy little threesome that I needed to pay close attention to. Dressed in a suit that looked expensive, as did the pale shirt and dark silk tie he wore, he was obviously the one in charge. His dark hair was slicked back from a face with chiseled cheekbones, a long nose, and a thin-lipped mouth. He also had a moustache, but truthfully I've seen women with more hair on their upper lip than he had.

He was also a vampire.

There was nothing blatantly overt about his behavior. Nothing that said *regular infusion of blood required* or *deadly allergic reaction to sunlight,* but I knew he was a vampire nevertheless. I think it was his skin that gave him away. The tone was too uniform, and there was something about the way he moved. It was as if he had calculated how every gesture would look when observed through human eyes. It was freaky weird, but I was learning not to question my own intuition.

He gave me a long look, took a few steps forward, and then narrowed his eyes as he continued to stare at me. I got the oddest feeling that I had disappointed him, that I wasn't what he'd been expecting. Yeah? Well, disappointment was a two-way street, because I found him seriously lacking as a vampire. Maybe being around Gabriel and Aleksei had skewed my ideas on how a vampire should look. Still, there was no doubt in my mind that this guy had his own set of fangs. Only neither of his two companions knew that.

"Is this some sort of a joke?" he asked them in a voice that was a little nasal and held enough of an accent to tell me English was not his native tongue. Rat Boy and the big guy looked at each other and then at the vampire. From the expressions they wore, it was plain to see his question flummoxed them. The vampire waited for one of them to answer, and I got the feeling he didn't have much in the way of a funny bone. "Who is this?" he snapped irritably, pointing a finger at me.

Two sets of eyes looked at him, then at me, and then at each other. It was quite a pantomime, and under different circumstances I would have laughed my ass off. Both of them looked horribly, almost comically, dismayed. Someone had fucked up. Royally.

"That's her—the woman you told us to grab," the big guy said, sounding puzzled. He hesitated a beat before adding, "Isn't it?"

"Which one of you did I give my instructions to?" A slight movement of Rat Boy's head indicated he was the lucky winner. "And were they not explicit enough?"

I didn't think *explicit* was in Rat Boy's vocabulary.

"I guess," he mumbled with what had to be the slowest shoulder shrug in the history of mankind.

The vampire suddenly yanked him across the floor, pushing him to his knees before me, and bringing him close enough I could tell it had been a while since Rat Boy had acquainted himself with a bar of soap.

"Does her hair look blond to you?" he snarled menacingly. Blond? Had they actually meant to grab Anasztaizia? "Did I not say the woman you were to acquire had blond hair?"

Not waiting for a reply, the vampire jerked Rat Boy to his feet and backhanded him across the face. It's got to be humiliating for a guy to be bitch-slapped by another guy in front of his pal. I couldn't tell if the big guy had participated in the screwup, but he absolved himself of blame by giving Rat Boy a hard look and saying, "You didn't tell me she was blond."

"Sorry, Gus, must've slipped my mind," Rat Boy mumbled as he rubbed the vivid scarlet imprint on his cheek. "She was in the car, and I didn't think anyone else would be driving, know what I mean?"

"Well . . . fuck it!"

"Succinctly put," the vampire commented on Gus's assessment of their predicament.

In whatever world Gus and Rat Boy inhabited, a car being driven by someone other than the owner just didn't happen. But, unable to change a mistake already made, Gus accepted there was no point in dwelling on it. "How can I make this right, Mr. Petrov?"

Another name to add to my vampire address book. At least this one had a *mister* in front of his name.

"I'm not sure that you can." The vampire tapped a finger against his mouth as he considered his options. I was pretty sure letting me go unharmed wasn't one of them. He stopped and looked at me, narrowing his eyes. "But perhaps she can be of use, after all."

"You don't want to use the blond woman now?" Gus sounded disappointed by the possibility, making me suspect he might have a thing for blondes.

"I would love to," Petrov told him. "Especially as she remains an integral part of my plan." If Rat Boy didn't know *explicit,* then I was willing to bet Gus hadn't heard of *integral.* "But due to your incompetence, I am forced to rethink my strategy." He gave both of them a scathing look. "Still, I might be able to salvage something from the situation."

There was a heavy silence as three heads turned almost in unison, and I felt the grim weight of unknown possibilities being put on my shoulders.

Chapter 6

Petrov came toward me and dropped to his haunches. Taking hold of my chin in his fingers, he turned my head one way and then the other, his fingers brushing down either side of my neck. I knew what he was looking for—bite marks, and forty-eight hours ago he would have found some. But I'd long since healed. I doubt even a shadow of a bruise existed, especially not with the care Gabriel took when feeding from me.

A dozen questions bounced around inside my head, looking for a way out. If he was searching for evidence of bite marks, then he must also know that Anasztaizia fed Aleksei, and that Aleksei was a vampire like him. Should I tell him I was a Promise, and hope he knew what that was? Anasztaizia had surprised me by revealing not every vampire did, just as some vampires couldn't name a single Original Vampire. She had even heard rumors that the existence of the Originals was being questioned.

But if he knows Anasztaizia feeds a vampire, what does he want with her? To feed him?

I thought that was highly unlikely.

Opening his jacket, Petrov took something out from his inside pocket. It was a slim black case that looked a little like a jewelry box, the kind that usually contains something bright and sparkly and very expensive. This one held two syringes.

"No thanks, I'll pass," I said, watching as he removed one from the molded insert. "Your boy there already inoculated me."

"Mmmm, I know," Petrov said, "but that was something different, and as you weren't the intended recipient, it was completely wasted."

"Why? What did you expect it to do to Anasztaizia?"

He pulled his brows together and gave me a puzzled look. "Who? Oh, so that's her name. I didn't know."

Really? What kind of shithead arranges an abduction but doesn't know who he's kidnapping? And what the hell could Anasztaizia possibly be involved in—a conspiracy to corner the world market in paprika?

Ignoring my question, Petrov removed the needle cap and tapped the cylindrical tube with a nail. Holding it upright, he depressed the plunger slightly. A small fountain of liquid sprayed in the air. Narcotic rain. He turned his head. "Gus, come unlock the young lady's handcuffs, if you please."

The big man hesitated. "Do you think that's a good idea, Mr. Petrov?"

"I only need one arm free, Gus. That shouldn't be a problem."

Although unhappy with the request, Gus was smart enough to keep his mouth shut and did as the vampire asked. I wondered what was making him nervous. How much of a threat could I be with one arm free and one still handcuffed? I gritted my teeth as my left arm fell to my side like a lead weight. Stinging pins-and-needles pain shot from my fingers to my shoulder as blood began to flow.

Petrov turned my arm over and pulled what looked like a length of thin rubber tubing from his pocket. Using it as a tourniquet, he deftly knotted it around my upper arm before stretching it out and tapping the inside of my elbow with two fingers. I have good veins, or so the people at the Red Cross have told me whenever I've donated blood. Gabriel has also said the same thing. My abductor grunted in satisfaction as my vein popped up, begging to be poked with something sharp.

"Will you at least tell me what it is you're giving me?" I said, trying not to sound panicked.

This close up, I could sense there was something *off* about him. Not *off* because he was a vampire; it was something else entirely. Something I couldn't put my finger on but knew intuitively was horribly bad. Homicidal maniac-slash-serial killer bad. The best way I could describe it was to say if I was walking down a dark alley late at night, and Petrov was coming the other way, I'd turn around and run like hell before he got the chance to pass me.

As he rubbed the ball of his thumb over my vein, I wondered how long it had been since he last fed. Had to have been recently because he was controlling himself well. "It's just something I've been playing with," he said, answering my question about the contents of the syringe.

He obviously wasn't going to share the recipe for his creation with me. Either that or he figured I was too dumb to understand the chemistry. He might have been right, but even I knew lysergic acid diethylamide was LSD. Ah shit! Was that what he was doing? Making me OD on an acid trip? Fuck! I hoped to God he was giving me the good stuff.

But you can't die . . . can you?

Oh shit! Yeah, that's right . . . well, I don't think so.

Being told you have an extended life span is one thing, but *knowing* you have an extended life span is something else. Because how could you really be sure, unless it was put to the ultimate test?

I had made a bargain with a demon, a master of deceit, trickery, and lies. I had no way to know if he would honor the terms of our agreement, but I had no reason to think he wouldn't either. If he could be convinced the love Gabriel and I shared was true, then my vampire lover would be released from the rule of the Dark Realm, and I would keep my soul. So I had bargained, and my life span had been extended as part of the deal, or so I'd been told. What I hadn't anticipated was my demonic pact being sealed with a kiss. A kiss that allowed a piece of my soul to be stolen.

You didn't ask?

Sorry, I was kind of distracted at the time.

Yeah, I guess having a demon's tongue halfway down your throat could be considered a distraction.

You really need to go there?

My demon had told me that my life would be extended to match Gabriel's, and he'd also said I would not fall prey to disease or infirmity or perish at another's hand. I wasn't completely sure whether the definitions of disease and infirmity were the same in the Dark Realm as in my world, but I was pretty confident that *perish at another's hand* was self-explanatory. If that was true, then whatever was in Petrov's syringe couldn't kill me.

Yeah, but we're talking about a demon . . .

A trickster, a deceiver, a liar.

Believing the potion might not kill me didn't mean it couldn't fuck me up so badly I might wish I was dead. What if it totally screwed with my brain and I didn't even know I was still alive? The devil, as they say, is in the details.

Or maybe the demon is in the lack of them?

Just couldn't resist that one, could you?

How are you feeling?

Are you kidding me?

No, I'm being serious. You've already been given something, right? So . . . how do you feel?

Pretty damn good actually, apart from still wanting to drain Lake Michigan. I still ached and was sore in places, but that was more from the physical toll of the car crash. My head wasn't anywhere near as messed up as I might have expected, especially after being injected with an unknown substance.

Think you can get him to tell you what it was you were given?

Maybe . . . "Is this more of the same shit Dickless Wonder gave me earlier?"

Petrov shook his head. "No, I already told you that was different and completely ineffectual."

"How do you know?" I challenged. "How do you know it's not working on me right now?"

He snickered as he considered my question. "The formula was designed to interact and react with a certain type of blood chemistry. Chemistry you don't have," he added smugly.

"How do you know that? Did you do a test while I was unconscious?" The idea that he might have was more than a little scary.

Petrov shook his head. "No testing needed. I just *know*."

Oh, but you don't, you asshole!

He'd just confirmed he didn't know I was a Promise, and I was glad I hadn't told him. "Well, why don't you tell me what it was supposed to do," I said. "I mean what can it hurt if it's not working on me?"

I could almost see the cogs whirling in his head as he weighed the pros and cons of full disclosure before he sighed and decided what the heck. "Not every drug produces a physical response or is designed to get you high in the way you're thinking." He sounded like some college professor giving a lecture. "This particular formulary is designed to be an inhibitor, to prevent a specific reaction from occurring."

I shook my head and frowned. What reaction? "I don't understand," I told him.

"Of course you don't." He was so condescending it took me by surprise when he continued. Maybe he liked having a truly captive audience. "How much do you know about, what was her name, Anasztaizia?" I nodded. "Mmmm, yes, well, what do you know about her boyfriend?"

"Only that she has one," I answered cautiously. "She doesn't talk much about him."

"I would imagine not," he murmured, more to himself than to me. "Well, if she did talk about him to you, she might tell you they share a unique connection."

"What kind of connection?"

"You wouldn't understand even if I were to tell you. Suffice it to say, the drug's objective is to block this connection."

My heart skipped a beat as the impact of his words washed over me. He knew Aleksei was a vampire. He might just as well have shouted it from the rooftops. Aleksei and Anasztaizia had been together long enough that tuning in to her emotional state was second nature to the Russian vampire. If she was hurt or frightened or on any kind of emotional roller-coaster ride—kidnapped by a couple of psychos, for example—Aleksei would be able to sense it. And he could use their *unique connection* to find her.

But supposing the link between them could be disrupted in some way? It would leave Aleksei stumbling around in the dark, while giving Gus and Rat Boy the time to finish whatever it was Petrov wanted them to do to Anasztaizia. And it didn't take a genius to figure out what that might be. Or what kind of effect it would have on Aleksei when he did find her.

Shit! Shit! Shit!

This was all about Aleksei.

Unfortunately, I had to assume the inhibitor intended for Anasztaizia could very well be working on me. My stomach suddenly churned at the thought, and the sting of bile coated the back of my throat. But I refused to give in to the feeling of defeat that threatened to wrap itself around me. There was no way to know if Petrov's chemical compound was effective, but the vampire didn't know about the ace up my sleeve.

I was a Promise, bound to an Original Vampire, and willing to bet the connection existing between Gabriel and myself was far stronger than the one Aleksei and Anasztaizia shared. It was certainly older, and that had to count for something. Would Petrov have taken such a factor into account while swishing his magic potion in his lab beaker? There was no way to know for sure, but I doubted it. If he hadn't been able to recognize I was a Promise, then I felt confident his formula was effective only on bonds that were less than a hundred years old.

All you have to do is wait until your honey wakes up . . . he'll find you. Mark my words, he will find you.

Providing of course that physical distance wasn't a problem, because I had no idea where I was. Professor Aleksei's Vampire 101 class hadn't covered limitations that might compromise the strength of the bond between vampire and human. That was an unknown I could do nothing about. It seemed that Petrov wasn't going to tell me anything more about the first drug. Why would he when he assumed it was a dud? But if he intended to inject me with anything else, then I needed to find out what it was. Knowledge is a powerful tool, and any information I could give Gabriel would help him find the right way to flush this crap from my body.

"So is this going to make me think Rat Boy is irresistible?" I asked Petrov.

"Rat . . . who?" The vampire raised a brow as I jerked my head toward the space over his shoulder. "Oh, I see." He smirked. "No, I'm not sure there's anything that can do that."

He held my elbow, and I made myself relax my arm. It would be easier if he thought I'd already accepted the inevitable. Just as he was about to slide the point of the needle into my skin, I jerked my arm back. A drop of blood, brilliant as a ruby, glistened in the crook of my arm.

Petrov sucked in a breath between clenched teeth, making a hissing sound. His nostrils flared, and his eyes looked strangely glazed. "Bitch!" he snarled, waving the still full syringe in the air. "You've been keeping secrets!"

"Not really, you just made the wrong assumptions about me." His reaction told me he knew I was *something*, but he wasn't sure exactly what that might be. "It didn't cross your mind that if Anasztaizia had a vampire for a boyfriend, I might have one as well?"

From the look on his face it was apparent this had never occurred to him. What an idiot! For a few moments he seemed lost in thought, probably wondering how he was going to get his sorry ass out of this mess. And then I watched as hubris got the better of him.

"Perhaps I should thank you," he said.

"What for?" I asked uneasily.

"The opportunity to prove my inhibitor formula works."

I snorted. "What makes you think it's working?"

A frown creased his brow. "You're right. I don't, not really. I don't even know if you feed a vampire, but let's assume for the sake of argument you do. And let's also assume a similar bond exists between you and said vampire." He leaned forward and gave me a sick smile.

"That's an awful lot of assumptions you're making."

"Ah, but I don't think they're assumptions at all." He looked at the blood stain on my arm. "I think you do feed a vampire, only you haven't been doing it for long, which means the bond between you hasn't had time to mature and strengthen. I want to know whether my serum will work, so we're going to amplify your emotions, just to make certain your vampire lover is given every opportunity to come to your rescue." He placed the still-full syringe on the ground before getting to his feet. "I need one of you to hold her and the other to stretch out her arm, palm flat on the ground," he said, pointing to both Gus and Rat Boy.

I tried struggling, but I was no match for Gus. He unlocked the other manacle and had me face down on the concrete floor with such a minimum amount of effort, I knew I wasn't the first woman he'd immobilized this way. With his knee on my back, he turned my head, pressing it to the ground, but making sure I could see Rat Boy as he yanked on my arm. Both of them laughed as Petrov broke my fingers one at a time.

I shrieked and screamed and made sounds I'd only ever heard from wild animals on TV nature programs. And when he was done, and Gus had rolled off me and Rat Boy had let go of my arm, I curled myself into a ball, barely able to hold my injured hand to my chest, and sobbed because it hurt so much.

"So . . . where is your vampire lover?" Petrov asked, his voice next to my ear. The pain in my hand was now coursing through my body and was so intense I couldn't have uttered a single syllable even if I'd wanted to. I was certain having a single finger broken was bad enough, but Petrov had relished breaking all four, leaving my hand a swollen, misshapen mess. "It would seem that no one is coming for you," he told me, feigning disappointment.

I couldn't stop him as he pulled my swollen hand from my chest, but I snarled through my tears. He picked up the discarded syringe and injected the full dose into my arm, and when he was done, he followed it up by giving me the second one. A double dose. There was no way to know what I'd been injected with. It could be the Ebola virus or bubonic plague or mad cow disease. But I was very aware that I couldn't allow Gabriel to feed from me as long as my blood was tainted.

Perhaps that was his plan . . .

"Did you make that for Anasztaizia too?" I sobbed as he put the empty syringes back in the case.

"Yes, but it can be used on any human."

Are you still human? I mean, technically?

I gave my inner bitch the mental equivalent of a *who knows?* shoulder shrug.

"What do you want to do with her?" Gus asked. He seemed a little hesitant, but I think that was due more to Petrov's unexpected reaction to me than to any real threat I might pose.

"I really don't care. She's of no use to me," Petrov told him. "Do whatever you want."

"Really?" Rat Boy, snickering like a perverted schoolboy with his first porno magazine, gave me a speculative look.

"Just make it quick, although I don't think that will be a problem for you." He gave Rat Boy a disdainful look before turning and addressing Gus. "She should last for about thirty minutes, but if I were you, I'd be gone long before that."

"Why?"

"Just in case someone does come looking for her."

"What's gonna happen in thirty minutes?" Rat Boy piped up.

I don't know if it was the second injection suddenly kicking in and giving me a rush, or maybe my brain releasing endorphins. Either way, my body recognized that if I was to survive whatever was coming, I needed help. The pain in my hand began to subside, changing from an agonizing shriek to a manageable pulsating throb. The change allowed me to focus on what was going on around me.

"What's gonna happen in thirty minutes?" Rat Boy repeated, and I could hear the curiosity mingle with his excitement.

"She'll be dead," Petrov told him, "but if your sexual proclivities run to necrophilia . . ." He let the rest of his sentence hang.

Rat Boy looked confused.

"Fucking a corpse," Gus told him.

I hurt too much to be impressed that he knew what Petrov was talking about. But at least I now knew what a double dose of his just-something-I've-been-playing-with formula was supposed to do.

Yeah, but that still doesn't mean you're going to die.

Well, I guessed we'd find out in about thirty minutes.

Chapter 7

Petrov vanished. One minute he was there, and the next he was gone. I didn't know how it was that he could be awake during the day anyway, but for all I knew the stars could already be twinkling in a midnight sky.

If they were, Gabriel would already be here.

Okay, not nighttime then, but maybe close to sunset, and being in a pretty dark place—in more ways than one—was probably okay for the vampire.

I'd been telling myself that I could survive anything because Gabriel was coming for me. That was as certain as celebrating Independence Day on July 4, but the throbbing in my hand was making it difficult to hold onto that belief. Was Petrov's inhibitor drug actually working as he intended? If so, then Gabriel wouldn't be showing up anytime soon, and until he did I was on my own with homicidal Tweedledum and Tweedledee.

As for whether or not I was going to die, the validity of my demonic deal was about to get its first real test.

I dropped my swollen hand to my side, gritting my teeth as the tips of my fingers brushed against my leg. The pain had definitely lessened, but I think that was due to a combination of released endorphins and compressed nerves numbing my fingers. I gripped the bars with my good hand and pulled myself to my feet. No way in hell was I going to let these bastards touch me while I was on my knees.

"You have no idea what he is, do you?" I said, panting from exertion and looking at the morons watching me.

"What do you mean?" Rat Boy asked suspiciously. The constant movement of his hands was starting to give me a headache. Fiddling with his collar, tugging at his jacket, hitching up his jeans.

"Petrov. You're completely clueless about what he really is."

"He's the guy who's gonna give me a lot of cash to mess you up," Gus said in a cold, calm voice that sent a shiver of fear down my spine.

I shook my head and realized trying to enlighten them was futile. They would never believe me.

"So what d'you think, Gus? You think she's still got some fight in her?" Rat Boy had watched me struggle to my feet with something that could pass for reluctant admiration.

"Hard to say," Gus replied. "Any bitch that's cornered is unpredictable."

"Yeah, but she's only got one good hand, Gus. I don't think she'll fight. Maybe she would've before, but not now."

The bigger man shrugged his shoulders. "Doesn't make much difference either way. I just need to hear her scream."

"Well, you've always been good at making them do that." Rat Boy clearly idolized his bosom companion. "So, you wanna get started?"

I didn't have to ask what Gus was going to get started on. The look on his face said it all.

Rape has its own particular violence, its own savagery, and the man who succumbs to its cruel lure, using it to crush the body and conquer the will of its victim, cannot help but be forever tainted by its evil. Make no mistake . . . rape is a weapon. Which explains why it was—and still is—such an effective way for conquering armies to subjugate and terrorize entire populations.

Knowing that you're going to be raped is its own torture. Deciding how to react to the violence that will be committed is a choice I believe most women make without any hesitation. God knows, I've watched enough TV to know the most important thing a victim can do is survive. But when survival has already been taken off the table, it becomes a completely different ball game.

But was I going to survive? Until I had proof of the effect of my demonic bargain, I was taking nothing for granted. Besides, why would I think a demon would tell me the truth?

Because you kissed him?

Wow, you just can't let that go, can you?

You would have known if he was lying.

When my inner bitch sounds this smug, it's because what she's about to tell me is something I either already know or should know.

You would have tasted it on his breath.

See what I mean?

Unfortunately, her words didn't exactly fill me with confidence as I watched Gus pull his T-shirt over his head, revealing a tattoo of a coiled snake on his left pectoral. Dropping his hand to the waist of his jeans, he slowly unbuckled the belt at his waist before popping open the button on his fly. His zipper seemed unnaturally loud as he pulled it down, but to be honest, my own anxiety acted as an amplifier. I watched in disgust as he slipped a hand inside his pants and began stroking himself. With his gaze firmly fixed on my face, he watched for my reaction. I curled my lip and, with moisture I didn't know I had in me, spat in his direction.

Unfazed, Gus continued to stroke himself. There was absolutely nothing sexual or erotic about what he was doing. No pump or grind accompanying the masturbation, and judging by the expression on his face, he didn't seem to be getting any pleasure from it, which I found even more disturbing. But then again I've only ever watched one other man masturbate, and he definitely enjoyed it. Not as much as having me do it, but seeing Gabriel pleasure himself is something I find extremely erotic. And highly arousing.

It took me a moment or two to understand Gus's intent. His indifference to the physical response his hand was eliciting made me realize this obscene perversion was an act of pure intimidation. Along with his well-muscled torso, the proof of his superior physical strength, the sight of his fully erect cock cresting from the opening of his jeans was an unspoken vile threat. And his composure was telling me he was in complete control.

"Just out of curiosity," I said in a voice that was as indifferent as I could make it, "what makes you think someone isn't already looking for me?"

"Why would they be?" Rat Boy sounded genuinely puzzled.

"I was in an accident, asshole."

"Really?" His snickering was getting on my nerves and made me want to smack the ever-living snot out of him. "Where? When?" he taunted.

"The car—"

"—has gone. Mr. Petrov is very good at what he does." Rat Boy sounded more than a little awed.

"That won't stop my boyfriend," I told him defiantly. "He'll be looking for me—"

"He'd better get a move on then, 'cause your clock's winding down."

I looked at Gus. The coiled-snake tattoo seemed to sway slightly as he breathed.

Do you think if he gets real excited he can make it dance? You know, like those Indian snake charmers . . .

Gus peeled back the top of his jeans. His cock waved gently from side to side, and I forced a smile to stretch my lips. He answered with one of his own, so I made my smile expand to a grin, and then backed that up with a giggle, which in turn became a throaty laugh. His smile disappeared and was replaced by a look of confusion that quickly morphed into simmering anger. Rat Boy just looked bewildered.

"Do you actually know what to do with that," I asked, pointing a finger on my good hand at his crotch, "or is that all it does?" I waved my finger back and forth, goading him. Probably not the smartest thing to do—okay, definitely not the smartest thing to do—but I figured if I was going to be raped, I sure as shit wasn't going down without a fight.

My kidnappers looked at each other. I'm not sure, but I think Rat Boy offered his opinion with a gesture that said I-think-she's-off-her-rocker. I snapped my fingers in the air, making both of them look back at me. Taking a step forward, I stared Gus in the eye. The longer it took, the worse it was going to be, and I could only hide my fear with bravado for so long. It was time to dance.

"Okay, big boy," I said scornfully, "you want to hear me scream? Let's see if you can make me." And crooking my forefinger, I beckoned him to me.

He narrowed his eyes and stared at me like I was deranged, which, at that precise moment, I probably was. There's nothing more unpredictable than someone who truly believes they have nothing left to lose. It didn't matter that the chemical cocktail I'd been given wasn't meant for me in the first place. Petrov's plan had been to make sure Aleksei couldn't find Anasztaizia before these assholes had finished with her. Breaking my fingers had not brought Gabriel to my rescue, so I had to assume either I was too far away geographically or the drug was affecting his ability to find me. Either way, Gus and I were going to get to know each other.

And just in case my demon was wrong, I wanted Gabriel to know I'd not made it easy for my attacker.

I watched as Gus licked his lips. The physical disparity between us definitely was to his advantage, and my injured hand tipped the odds even more in his favor, but I could see he was rethinking how to approach me. I could read it in his eyes, in his expression, in the way the muscle below his right eye suddenly began to twitch. I didn't need a college degree to know that I wasn't being as submissive as his usual victims. There was no weeping or screaming or emotional breakdown. No begging him not to hurt me. All of which were probably triggers that got him off. Instead he was facing someone who gave the outward appearance of being calm and collected, and made him have doubts about who was really in charge.

I saw the moment he made his mind up to come for me. He took one swaggering step forward, and stopped. A grunt of surprise escaped him, making his expression change from brutal confidence to a look of shocked disbelief.

The sudden, high-pitched shriek Rat Boy emitted made me swivel my head in his direction, noting that a high C wasn't the only thing he'd let loose. The dark stain at his crotch became a line that ran down the inside of his leg before ending in a puddle on the floor. The smell of ammonia was strong as he fell to his knees with a whimper.

Another grunt, this one wet-sounding, had me turning my attention back to Gus. A dark red blotch had mysteriously appeared on his chest and was growing bigger. I could tell something was moving behind him, but I was so mesmerized by the stain on his smooth chest, I paid it no attention. And then Gus's sternum split open as something inside his chest cavity exploded outward, sending blood and pieces of shattered bone flying in my direction. I don't know if it was flesh or muscle or blood, but something splattered on my cheek. I barely registered it because my eyes were fixed on the fist that was poking out the middle of Gus's chest.

Long familiar fingers uncurled themselves. Like petals of an alien flower, they opened to show me the secret they held. Gus's heart. I watched as the organ contracted, muscle memory making it obey the final directive of a brain it was no longer connected to. And then it stopped. The hand, shimmering with blood and tissue matter, released its prize, and there came a sickening, indescribable sound as the dead heart dropped on the floor. The only thing keeping Gus's two-hundred-plus-pound body in an upright position now withdrew itself from his torso, and without Gabriel's arm to support it, the lifeless body collapsed.

I stared at the vampire who had come for me.

I could feel Gabriel's eyes on me, waiting for me to acknowledge his presence. I continued to stare, seeing, for the first time, what the lesser beasts had seen when they'd approached the Dark Realm, needing a champion of their own. A predator that was different from anything that already walked the earth. One that would make mankind fear the night. I wondered if the lesser beasts ever knew how successful they had been in their quest.

Gabriel's expression was a mask of tightly controlled violence. His eyes had turned completely black, and his razor-sharp fangs, glistening with saliva, were extended longer than I had ever seen them. One arm was bloody from fingertip to elbow, and I noticed a sliver of white protruding from between his knuckles. A piece of bone embedded in his skin.

His lungs were bellows that moved his chest with each inhale of breath. A sheen of sweat turned his skin an iridescent gold beneath the pale light, and I could see the pulse thrumming at the base of his throat, see the blood pumping through his veins. He had never looked more beautiful or more deadly, and I felt my legs tremble as a wave of lust almost brought me to my knees. A dead man lay on the floor before me, his partner on the verge of insanity, and I was aroused. For the first time in my life I understood how closely entwined are sex and death.

Gabriel's eyes narrowed, and I saw the corner of his mouth move. It was almost imperceptible, but it told me he'd caught the scent of my lust and was just as stimulated. I have often wondered who decided the Grim Reaper should be a faceless, hooded robe with skeletal hands wrapped around a scythe. I mean . . . really? This is the best you could come up with to depict the specter of death? The scythe and its symbolism I got, but if anyone could see what I was looking at now, they would have no problem giving death a face.

Perhaps, my inner bitch murmured, *they have seen him, and that's why the Grim Reaper has no face . . .*

I conceded the possibility.

A palpable tension thickened the air. I didn't need Gabriel to tell me this was a side of him he had not intended me to see. At least not yet, and I could sense his frustration. Just as the decision to reveal his true vampire nature had been taken out of his hands by Katja's interference, this too was a premature disclosure forced by events outside his control. The timing, however, made no difference. It would always be wrong for any number of reasons. How I chose to handle it was the only thing that mattered.

I stepped forward, skirting the pool of blood slowly spreading from beneath Gus's inert form. Reaching for Gabriel's hand with my good one, I felt his fingers curl around mine. He radiated a power and strength that I suspected had barely been tapped.

Do you know who I am . . . truly?

I had no way of knowing what he saw as he looked at me. Was it the girl who wept at seeing him crucified, or the one who grasped his hand and pulled him from the Void? Perhaps he saw the woman-child who gave herself to him as she promised to safeguard his soul. The lover who had been his from the very first. Did he see all of that as he now looked at me? Did he see *any* of that as he looked at me? His eyes, normally so expressive, were like pieces of jet glass, reflecting back my own image and telling me nothing about what he was feeling.

And yes, even though I loved him more than my own life, this version of Gabriel truly scared me.

For all I knew, I might be reduced to nothing more than a combination of scents and sounds and impulses. Familiar enough to alert his senses, strong enough to trigger a response. Except I refused to believe that. Even with Gabriel's transformation into a glorious killing machine, I knew on some level he recognized exactly who I was. It wasn't dumb luck or a twist of fate that had brought him here to me. He had come looking for me.

Carefully I raised his hand and placed his palm against my chest so he could feel the pounding beat of my heart. His fingers curled, cupping my breast, and I blushed suddenly as I remembered why I wasn't wearing a bra. Grasping the shard of bone with my thumb and forefinger, I pulled it from his flesh. I was suddenly envious of those girls who always seemed to have a tissue or wet wipe in their pocket, thinking it might be nice to clean Gabriel's arm. I guess I could have improvised and used my T-shirt, but I wasn't sure if I could get it off using only one hand, and besides, it was probably better if only one of us was bare-chested.

I looked up at him as my fingers moved slowly over the back of his hand, caressing the skin, brushing lightly over his knuckles. He remained impassive, saying nothing, and yet I could tell he still needed something from me.

My approval?

My understanding?

My support?

Now it was my turn to place my palm against his chest, my hand rising and falling with each tortured intake of breath. His heart beat strong and true beneath my fingers. He was my avenging angel, and no matter what, he would always be there for me. God have mercy on those responsible for summoning forth this side of his nature, because Gabriel, I knew, would have none.

A tremor ran through him, and I felt his body quiver with rage as he carefully took my damaged hand in his. He looked at my grotesquely swollen fingers, and I barely felt him lock his thumb and forefinger around my wrist, immobilizing my hand. I had no idea if it was fear or relief that started my own body trembling, but I reached up and cradled his face in my good palm.

His eyes were beginning to lighten. His irises were still inky black, but the surrounding sclera had now turned a lighter gray. A few more minutes and it would become white once more. I stared up at him, losing myself in unfathomable depths.

"You came for me," I whispered in a voice I barely recognized as my own. The fear that I might be hallucinating, that the pollutant in my blood was having a final laugh at my expense, was very real.

There was a rumble in Gabriel's chest. One that quickly changed to a sexually charged roar as he pulled me to him. He was hard, and I could feel the wave of lust that enveloped me as he answered in the best way he knew how. The only way he knew how. He kissed me.

I grabbed a handful of thick, white hair as his mouth covered mine. I had never been kissed like this before. Not by Gabriel, not by anyone. It was a kiss that had me drowning in a sea of possession. It said he was claiming me as his own, branding me as belonging to him, and he didn't give a damn who knew it. It was pure alpha male, and I had no doubt that if he could have found a way to tattoo his name on my tongue with his, he would have done so.

And I gave myself to him. Reconfirming all I'd felt when I'd first pulled him from the Void. I relished the feel of his tongue pushing its way inside my mouth, searing me with a heat that promised desires I'd not yet realized, and when he withdrew, I followed. Sliding between his lips I felt the razor-sharp edges of his fangs scrape against my tongue, and I felt him shudder with his need for me.

Gently fisting a handful of curls, he pulled back my head and looked down at me. The pulse in his throat was throbbing wildly, and a thin circle of gold now rimmed the dark blue of his eyes. Another appetite had awakened.

"I was going to fight," I told him. It was important that he knew, no matter how desperate my situation, I was never going to let anyone think they could just take what I freely gave to him.

"I know . . . I heard . . . I saw. You were magnificent."

An unexpected jolt of pleasure ran through me at hearing the pride in his voice. He had expected no less from me. His lips brushed my ear as he began to murmur in a voice that was melting honey. It liquefied my spine and ramped up my lust, making me wet. Gabriel pulled back, his nostrils flaring as he ran his tongue up the side of my neck.

"You've been drugged!" he hissed, able to taste the change in my blood through the pores of my skin.

"Yes—you mustn't feed from me!"

Urgency gripped me. There were things I had to tell him. Important details that I needed both Aleksei and Anasztaizia to know, but a flicker of movement distracted me. I'd totally forgotten about Rat Boy. His face was a mask of absolute terror as he stared at Gabriel. He was convinced he would never leave this place alive, and his immediate concern was how much pain he was going to suffer before his death. He flicked his eyes in my direction, his mouth an open, silent plea for mercy.

"Quick or slow?" Gabriel murmured in my ear.

Rat Boy had never intended to rape me. I don't know if that was because he was impotent, or didn't like girls, or just got off on watching his buddy, but it was the truth. Even holding my hand so Petrov could break my fingers was done because he was more scared of Petrov than he let on. And he had a right to be scared. Rat Boy and Gus might not have known they were taking orders from a vampire, but they were smart enough to recognize a predator that stood several rungs higher on the food chain.

Rat Boy was on his knees, having pissed his pants, and begging for mercy. His eyes flickered between Gabriel and myself, and the color drained from his face when Gabriel dropped his fangs.

"Now you know," I told him.

"Know? Know what?" he squeaked in a terrified voice.

"That vampires are real."

He stared at his partner's lifeless form on the floor. He'd been wasting his last few minutes of life convincing himself that he was trapped in some macabre joke, spinning Gus's death into something his brain could handle without going insane. And now I'd just blown that all to shit.

"Let him go," I said, turning my head away. Gabriel snarled in frustration. The ruthless, aggressive side of his nature was unhappy at my request. I put my hand on his arm and waited for him to look at me, waited until all sides of him were focused only on me. "I don't think he's going to be a problem, do you?"

"He wanted to hurt you, Rowan. I can't—"

"But he didn't," I interrupted. "Do you really think he's going to come after me? After what he's just seen? Every time he closes his eyes he's going to see what you did to his pal. I doubt he's going to sleep much anymore." Gabriel stared down at me, and I could see him battling his aggression. "Do it for me, Gabriel," I said in a low voice. "I can only take having so much blood on my hands."

He kissed me, hard and fast, and then picked Rat Boy up by the neck. If it wasn't so serious I would have laughed at the comical way his feet dangled in the air.

"Don't you ever forget you owe her your life. If it were up to me, I'd snap your neck like a twig without a second thought. But if you ever come near her again, I will hunt you down and kill you. I will make what happened to him"—he pointed to Gus's body—"seem like a kindness. Do you understand me?"

It took a couple of false starts before Rat Boy was able to nod his head, dropping to the ground when Gabriel let him go.

How long would it take for the police to arrive? I supposed that would depend on how long it took Rat Boy to pull himself together and make a 9-1-1 call. Would forensics be able to tell what had made the hole in Gus's chest? Would they think some sort of satanic ritual was involved as the heart had been removed? Was I losing my humanity because I felt absolutely no remorse about his death?

My head began to swim, and I suddenly had difficulty keeping my balance. I felt as if someone had given me an overdose of Alka-Seltzer, but instead of doing its plop-plop-fizz-fizz routine in my stomach, it had taken a wrong turn somewhere and was now in my bloodstream. I could actually feel my veins popping, my blood effervescing as it moved through me. Was this Petrov's drug doing its job? Had my demon lied to me, and was I now actually dying? I put out my good hand, feeling Gabriel catch it in his own before sweeping me up into his arms and carrying me out of the cage.

Chapter 8

I don't remember much about the drive home, except being grateful that Gabriel had come in a vehicle big enough for me to remain sitting in his lap while he kept one hand on the steering wheel. Neither one of us was about to let go of the other. I had a vague recollection a new mirror had been installed in the private elevator that took us directly from the garage to the penthouse. Some crazy abstract spiderweb design that reflected my face back in multiple images. It was odd, but I kind of liked it.

I'd never appreciated the level of privacy I was afforded by this simple mechanical box until now. Explaining my appearance would have been bad enough, but Gabriel still had body goop smeared on his arm. Of course it was a safe bet that none of the building's other tenants, had they seen us, would have been so tactless as to have commented on our appearance. At least not to our faces. Gabriel was the wealthy recluse who lived in the penthouse. I was an unknown factor, but being with Gabriel made me acceptable.

And then my lover was barking orders at Tomas as he carried me through the penthouse door. Now that adrenalin was no longer surging through my body, I was a road map of aches and pains. Some I could attribute to the Mazda being used as a bumper car, and some I figured could be blamed on Petrov's concoctions—both of them. It was foolish to assume that just because I couldn't die—and to be honest I was still sitting on the fence about that—there wouldn't be any physical effects from the unknown chemicals in my system.

I took it for granted Gabriel was going to put me to bed, but he bypassed the massive king-sized-and-then-some in our bedroom and continued to the walk-in closet. It wasn't until I saw him punch the numbered keypad on the back wall that I understood what he was doing. Taking a step back, and refusing to put me on the ground, he waited for the section of wall to slide silently open and reveal the hidden room.

Built originally as a panic room, it was the perfect place for his sarcophagus.

Living with a vampire had some unique challenges, one of which was learning to adapt to a nocturnal lifestyle. It wasn't easy. For twenty-five years my body had followed the rhythm of the sun. Behavior that's more instinctive than learned. But now I was asking it to do a complete one-eighty and adopt a nocturnal lifestyle. And trying to synchronize my sleep pattern with Gabriel's was still a work in progress. There were nights when I couldn't keep my eyes open past four a.m., and days when they wouldn't stay closed past four p.m. And although Gabriel always made certain I fell asleep in his arms, I didn't always wake up in them. Two or three times a month he would slip out of the huge bed we shared and bring himself here, to the hidden room and his sarcophagus.

Of course I'd been excited to see it the first time. Images of the boy king Tutankhamun swirled in my head, so you can understand my disappointment when the sarcophagus didn't look the way I imagined it ought to. It was bad enough that there was no pharaoh wearing more eyeliner than your average heavy-metal rocker, and it wasn't even shaped like the coffin of an Egyptian ruler.

A sarcophagus is actually the name for a stone or marble coffin, shape unspecified, my inner bitch pointed out.

Yep, that was this, all right. A block of solid marble, it reflected every possible shade of blue in the spectrum. Some of the colors were *fluid,* changeable, and while I was pretty sure I was looking at the color blue, I wouldn't have bet my life on it. If these hues were in our color spectrum, then they were at a place human eyesight didn't register. But all of them, even the funky, way-out-there colors, made me think of Gabriel's eyes.

The block itself was approximately ten feet in length and six feet wide, and it was the only item inside the reinforced room. Carved into the top were symbols that held a certain familiarity. I just couldn't place where I might have seen them . . . or when.

"They are runes," Gabriel had told me, standing behind me with his hands resting on my shoulders.

"What do they do?" I didn't think they were to make the top look pretty.

"They protect me."

"How?" I turned and looked at him, all curiosity.

Closing his eyes, he tilted his head back until his long white hair fell free of his shoulders, turning into a heavy curtain that covered the scars there. His nostrils flared slightly, as if he was searching for a specific scent in the air. I sniffed too, trying to be discreet, but unable to dismiss the suspicion that I probably looked more like a cocaine addict. I couldn't smell anything save for a faint woodsy scent. Kind of like one of those plug-in air fresheners that needed replacing.

"What time is it?" Gabriel asked as he straightened up.

I checked the Altiplano on my wrist. Part of Piaget's Skeleton Collection. I refused to think about the sixty-thousand-dollar price tag because if I did, then I'd talk myself into giving the damn watch back. And I didn't want to. Being able to see the inner workings of the timepiece fascinated me. "Six seventeen," I said, answering his question.

"Sunrise," he murmured. Un-tucking his T-shirt from the waistband of his jeans, he pulled it up over his head.

"Um . . . what are you doing?"

While Gabriel and I had had sex on every conceivable surface in his apartment, I was more than a little hesitant about this hunk of marble. The distinct possibility that my ass might slide off the glasslike surface was reason enough, but I also had the strangest feeling that fornicating anywhere near it would be akin to an act of blasphemy. Like having sex in a church. Any church. Any part of any church. There were just some things you simply didn't do. At least I didn't.

Gabriel's fingers, now busy with the buckle at his waist, stayed their movement. "I thought it was time you knew where I am when you wake up alone." He looked slightly puzzled by my question.

"And you have to take your clothes off to do that?"

He nodded. "Yes. I always sleep naked, Rowan, whether I am with you or not."

"Oh, so you're going to sleep then?" It was my turn to be puzzled.

He took both my hands in his, turning them over so he could kiss the inside of each wrist. The gesture always struck me as being seductively intimate. "Yes, and so should you," he said, giving me a knowing look.

Of course, six a.m., sunrise—well, duh!

Like I said . . . a work in progress. That was the first and only time since moving in with Gabriel that I did not fall asleep in his arms.

Completely nude, he lay down on the top of the marble slab, arms by his sides, hands relaxed. It was difficult not to notice he also had a raging hard-on. I could have run a flag up the damn thing, except I had enough on my mind dealing with the unexpected flame that had ignited somewhere in my pelvis. After licking its way up between my breasts, it now scorched my face.

"Yes, I do," Gabriel's voice murmured to me.

"Yes, you do what?"

"Go to sleep with an erection. You are the last thing I picture in my mind, so it's a natural reaction." Keeping his eyes closed, he pulled his mouth into a grin at hearing me gasp. "I know that's what you were wondering."

I muttered something under my breath that I was certain he heard but was too sensible to comment on. And then I gasped for an entirely different reason.

A soft blue glow began to pulse from the marble, washing over Gabriel's body and filling every part of the otherwise empty room. It took me a few moments to realize the light was keeping time with the beat of his heart, and it was slowing down. A moment later I covered my mouth to stifle a shriek as Gabriel's body sank into the marble block and disappeared from view. I stood completely transfixed before a rush of adrenaline carried my legs to his coffin.

The top had changed from an opaque, impenetrable covering to one that was now transparent, allowing the inside of the crystallized rock to be viewed. Gabriel lay cradled in a depression that was shaped to fit his muscular frame perfectly. I stared down at him. His eyes remained closed, his features relaxed, and I knew that his mind and body had entered a quiescent state, completely closed off from his surroundings. The lack of stimuli would permit him to disconnect from the physical world and reconnect to the inner essence that made him . . . well . . . Gabriel.

It was something every Original Vampire had to do in order to stay sane through the passing of the centuries. And why, on a less-intense level, all vampires found it necessary to sleep during the daylight hours.

Movement dragged my eyes away from his face. The mystical runes carved in the top of the sarcophagus now began to move. Whether by their own inclination or responding to the presence inside the sarcophagus I had no way of knowing, but each throbbed with a soft glow. One after the other, they lit up and then darkened, reminding me of flashing Christmas lights. I covered my mouth with a hand to stifle a giggle, although I didn't think Gabriel could hear me.

I took a moment to catch my breath, finding the entire spectacle mystifying, awe-inspiring, and breathtakingly beautiful. As my eyes moved from the runes to Gabriel's still form, which I could see clearly through the top of the sarcophagus, I pressed my lips against the cool surface directly above his mouth. Almost immediately the room was filled with the most glorious scent of pine trees, crisp, fresh snow, and something that I recognized but still couldn't name. It was an aroma I was all too familiar with. It was the scent of Gabriel's blood.

And now my lover was crossing the threshold of the panic room, and I had a pretty good idea why. He intended to put me inside his own sensory deprivation chamber.

Carefully he set me down, placing my bare feet on the cool marble ledge that sat at the base of his coffin. The extra height didn't put me on the same level as Gabriel, but I didn't have to tilt my head back quite as much in order to look up at him.

His eyes were now almost all the way back to the neon blue I was used to seeing. I smiled, much preferring this color to the stormy sea shade they became when his temper was riled. The tips of his fingers brushed against the side of my breast, causing heat to arrow through me and making me realize I was naked. My clothes, the T-shirt and jeans I'd put on in a snit after our earlier disagreement, lay in a pile on the floor. When had he undressed me?

"What the—"

"You can't wear anything to sleep with me," Gabriel said in a low voice.

"Sleep . . . with . . ." Panic made me step back, or try to. The feel of cold stone against my ass propelled me forward, back into his arms. I looked over my shoulder at the sarcophagus, then at Gabriel, then at the sarcophagus again. "You mean in there?" I whispered.

"Uh-huh."

"With you?"

"Yes, with me." A frown appeared, marring his smooth brow. "You haven't become claustrophobic over the years, have you?" I shook my head. I didn't think so, but then I hadn't put myself in a sensory-deprivation chamber recently. "Well, we'll find out soon enough," Gabriel said confidently.

"Yes, I suppose we—no, wait! I-I can't get in there, not with you."

He put both hands on my shoulders, and strangely enough I wasn't bothered that one was caked in dried blood and other . . . stuff. Instead I was mildly disturbed to notice he wasn't wearing any pants. Gabriel was now as naked as I was, only I didn't recall at what point he'd stopped to undress not only me but himself as well. Had I passed out?

His hand moved from my shoulder and lifted my chin. He gazed at me. "Rowan, sweetheart, you have to get in there, and the only way you can be in there is with me."

I shook my head and winced. The icepick throb at the base of my skull didn't want me to forget it was there. I took hold of Gabriel's hands, clutching them tightly, and forced myself to focus. "But why do I have to get in there?"

"Because I don't know what that fucking bastard injected you with, but I do know what it's doing to you isn't good. This is the only way to purge it from your blood."

I wasn't so out of it I couldn't tell that Gabriel was having a hard time holding on to his temper. If I pushed him any further, he might snap. "Oh," I said in a small voice. There really wasn't anything else to say, so I slipped my hand in his. "Then let's do it."

Gabriel lay on his back and positioned me on top of him. He tucked my head beneath his chin, and I put my hands around his neck while his arms encircled me. We lay together on the surface of the marble coffin, and then suddenly we were inside it. I sucked in a breath and raised my head, wanting to tell Gabriel his cock was poking me in the hip, but he just chuckled and moved his hand between my shoulder blades. I could feel the stone expanding and contracting to accommodate my body, and then came a series of light, almost ticklish pricks as the protective runes moved over my skin. I felt them on the soles of my feet, the back of my thighs, and my buttocks, back, and shoulders. They clung to me, intent on completing their appointed task.

I pressed my head against Gabriel's chest, breathing in his scent and hearing the steady beat of his heart and the hypnotic inhale-exhale of his breathing. Listening as each breath stretched out longer and longer, as each beat of his heart grew fainter, until I couldn't hear either anymore.

And then I was all alone.

Awash in a sea of pitch black, I didn't even realize Gabriel was no longer holding me until I stretched out my hand and connected with . . . nothing. How had I lost hold of him? One moment his arms were around me, and I could taste the sweat of his skin on my lips, and then he was gone. As far as I could tell, there was no violence to our separation. He wasn't yanked from my arms, nor I from his. It was as if we had simply drifted away from each other. Loosened our hold and slipped away. Only I hadn't noticed.

I couldn't tell if my eyes were open or shut, because there was nothing to mark the difference. Open or closed was all the same. The darkness surrounding me was absolute. Every grain of light had been snuffed out of existence. The energy used to produce such a phenomenon had simply been eliminated.

This is how it must have been before God brought forth the light.

If I was supposed to be afraid, I wasn't. I didn't really feel much of anything, truth be told. No fear, no anxiety pulling at me. Nothing sending my nervous system on a roller-coaster ride or making my heart skip a beat or two. Assuming, of course, that it actually was still beating.

And then I heard a whisper in the darkness. No, not a whisper, more of a . . . sigh. A sigh that sang my name.

Rooooowaaaaaan . . .

A sound that was capable of physical touch. It stroked my skin, brushed over my nipples, fluttered between my legs. It aroused me, making me feel warm and safe. Making me feel that I was exactly where I was supposed to be.

Making me feel like I had come home.

Chapter 9

I woke to find Gabriel on his side, propped up on one arm, watching me. My mouth stretched into a smile as his other hand made a lazy, circular sweep across my back. He smiled back, and I blinked sleepily at him through the tangle of curls that fell across my face. "You came for me," I said in a voice that was still in awe of the vision I'd beheld.

He regarded me with a puzzled frown, halting his hand at the tattoo in the small of my back. The group of symbols that was his name in a language I'd never known existed. "You doubted that I would?"

"I didn't know," I confessed, pushing the hair from my face. "One of the drugs I was given . . . he said it was an inhibitor, that you wouldn't be able to sense me. Actually it was meant for Anasztaizia so Aleksei wouldn't be able to find her."

"Ah, so that was the reason." His fingers brushed lightly over my inking before resuming their course along my spine.

"The reason for what?"

"The reason you felt like quicksilver in my mind."

Quicksilver, I knew from one of my high school science classes, was another name for mercury. The stuff they used to put in thermometers, and it's also the reason for the phrase *mad as a hatter*. If memory serves, back in the day, mercury was used as part of the hat-making process, but prolonged exposure to its vapors resulted in madness. Having seen pictures of what passed as fashionable headgear during that time, I think the insanity was pretty self-evident.

"One minute I could reach you," Gabriel continued, "and the next you were slipping away from me."

"But it didn't stop you from finding me."

Well . . . duh.

"No, it just took me longer." Frustration and anger flashed quickly across his face.

"Gabriel, it wasn't your fault. You couldn't have known."

He stroked a finger across my cheek. "Nothing will ever stop me from coming for you, Rowan, and I will always find you. *Always*."

My stomach muscles clenched at hearing his words, and I found it incredible that this gorgeous man, this gorgeous vampire, was in love with me. "You're so beautiful," I murmured. Gabriel looked startled, enough so that I apologized. "Ah jeez, I'm sorry. I didn't mean to embarrass you."

"I'm not embarrassed," he reassured me. "I'm just a little surprised."

I sat up and looked down at him. "You don't think I ever noticed how incredibly good-looking you are?"

"Oh, I figured you'd noticed," he said, clearly distracted by the sight of my naked breasts. "I just thought it would take you longer to say it out loud." His dimple winked at me.

Despite his teasing tone, Gabriel had a valid point. I didn't verbalize nearly enough all the things I felt about him. And shrieking while on the verge of an orgasm didn't count. We'd declared our love to each other, in word and deed. Any doubt about the latter could be confirmed by a certain demon still trying to make sense of it, but I think this was the first time I'd actually commented on his looks. Normally I was so overwhelmed by the sheer perfection of Gabriel's features, I became tongue-tied. Which was quite shameful because he was always telling me how beautiful I was to him.

He reached up and smoothed a curl between his fingers, watching as it coiled in his hand. "How are you feeling?" he asked.

"Good. Did you . . . were you able to get it all out of me?"

"Not all of it," he told me, looking a little troubled, "but what remains cannot hurt you." I was about to ask him how he could be so certain some residue was still in me when I suddenly became aware of where it was located. If I concentrated, I could feel it moving in a lethargic roll in the cold place deep inside me. The place left empty by the missing piece of my soul. I wasn't worried. Nothing could survive in there.

I was grateful to be alive, in one piece and relatively undamaged. It was too horrible to contemplate what Gus and Rat Boy might have done to me if Gabriel hadn't stopped them. Saying thank you seemed so inadequate, but I didn't know how else to convey what I was feeling. Fortunately, my brain decided to save me from blurting out something inane or wildly inappropriate or possibly both. It told my heart to take a road trip and lodge itself in my throat. Unable to speak, I began to tremble, and my tears went into overdrive.

Gabriel held me close, and I snaked an arm around his neck while at the same time pushing my leg between his thighs. There was nothing sexual about this; it was a gesture of comfort. Then, with my face in the hollow of his neck, I wept.

His voice was a soothing murmur as he spoke to me in a language I'd never heard before. It made no difference. The words were secondary. In Gabriel's arms I was safe. What had happened to me, what had *nearly* happened to me, had been a mistake. A true case of being in the wrong place at the wrong time, because it wasn't me that Gus and Rat Boy were supposed to abduct, but—*Anasztaizia!*

I yanked myself rudely out of Gabriel's embrace, saying, "I have to talk to Aleksei!"

His hands caught hold of my upper arms, preventing me from rolling off him. "Of course, and you can, but later—"

"No, you don't understand—I have to talk to him *now.*"

"Rowan, you can talk to Aleksei all you want, but not right—"

"But you don't understand—it's important!" Surely the urgency in my voice, the way I was struggling to get out of his hold told him that?

"More important than Anasztaizia?" Gabriel asked, giving me a shake.

"Anasztaizia?" My voice became fearful. Oh, dear God, no! Don't tell me Petrov had managed to get to her after all.

"Yes, she saw you on the news and became hysterical." In a quick move, Gabriel reversed our positions, so I was now looking up at him.

"I was on the news?"

"Well, not you exactly, but there was a report about a traffic accident downtown. It seems a big pickup plowed into a little red sports car."

"And they reported that?" I was incredulous. Vehicle accidents happened all the time. I couldn't imagine anything less than a multi-car pileup being newsworthy.

"It arouses curiosity when there are no victims at the scene," Gabriel said quietly. "For now it's being passed off as kids joyriding or some such nonsense." So much for Rat Boy's proclamation about Petrov's vehicular cleanup skills.

"And Anasztaizia recognized her car on TV," I said. I don't know why I was surprised. I would have recognized mine. Well, the POS anyway.

"Thankfully it was right before the police showed up at her apartment," Gabriel said.

"The police?" Of course, they would have gotten her information from the registration. "W-what did she tell them?"

Gabriel raised a brow. "She told them she hadn't realized her car had been stolen."

Now it was my turn to be puzzled. "Why would she tell the police that?"

"Because, sweetheart, it was obvious you were missing."

It made sense. Anasztaizia's experience would tell her which events were best left in the hands of human law enforcement, and which were better suited to vampire retribution. And anything concerning me would automatically be turned over to Gabriel.

"But she gave me the key," I told him, pointing out what I thought was an obvious flaw in the lovely Magyar's explanation. "If her car was stolen, wouldn't it have been hot-wired or something?"

"If the police ask, she'll confess she might have forgotten to lock the car, might even have left the key in the ignition."

I didn't ask if he thought the police, or more likely the insurance company, would believe her. This was Anasztaizia we were talking about, always so calm, cool, collected—"You said she got hysterical?"

"Yes." His mouth became a grim line. "She came here as soon as the police had left. Tomas said she was crying, making no sense and demanding to see me. When he told her I was already searching for you she became quite hysterical. He gave her something to calm her down, put her in one of the guest bedrooms, and called Aleksei." A little smile curled the corners of his mouth. "Trust me, there is no way that woman is leaving until she's seen with her own eyes that you're in one piece."

"Oh."

The relief of knowing Anasztaizia and Aleksei were both safe and only a few rooms away drained the tension right out of me. I tried to sit up, but the leg I had put between Gabriel's thighs was still there.

Somehow he'd managed to keep it locked in place when he'd rolled me. He squeezed gently before releasing me. The subtle pressure felt good.

I stretched. One of those full-body, throw your arms above your head and push out from the tips of your fingers to the end of your toes kind of stretches. Every muscle expanded, every ligament lengthened, and my body elongated so it was firm and taut. I held my breath when it became almost too much, before collapsing back into the pillows.

Gabriel brushed his thumb over my lower lip before asking, "How are you feeling . . . really?"

"I've never felt more grateful to be alive . . . really."

And it was true. I'd never felt this good in my entire life. The throb in my skull was gone; the ache across my shoulders and chest had vanished. I looked down at myself, fully expecting to see bruises or some evidence that I'd been involved in a vehicular mishap, but my skin was perfectly clear. Not a contusion in sight, not even where my forehead had hit the steering wheel. I raised my hand and looked at my fingers. There was no swelling or discoloration; my joints looked perfectly normal. My hand was in perfect working order. Tentatively I wiggled my fingers, and then moved them faster, playing air chopsticks. I stopped as I recalled the look on Gabriel's face when he'd told me the reason I had to get in the sarcophagus with him.

"Would I have died?" I asked quietly. "You said you didn't know what I'd been given, but you knew what it was doing to me. Would it have killed me?"

"I don't know."

"But what about my deal—"

"Sorry, sweetheart, but that's a chance I'm never going to be willing to take. I can tell you that if you weren't a Promise, I believe what was in your body was toxic enough to kill you."

Meaning it would most certainly have killed Anasztaizia.

"Would you have put me in your sarcophagus if I wasn't your Promise?"

"Rowan, the only reason I could even consider it is because you *are*."

Oh, I hadn't realized that. "And you have no idea what I was given?"

He shook his head. "No, but I'm pretty sure it started out as heroin."

"Started out?"

He nodded. "Yes, it had been enhanced with some unknown additives."

"How long was I out for?" I asked.

"I don't know." Seeing my frown, he went on to explain, "The runes will only keep you for as long as is necessary."

"Didn't you know what was happening to me?"

"Only vaguely," he admitted. "Once you were healed, you could no longer remain with me."

I tapped him on the shoulder, and he rolled over so I could move. Settling on my side, I propped myself up on one arm, mirroring his position. "So how did I get here?" I sure as hell didn't remember walking out of the panic room under my own steam.

"Tomas," Gabriel said quietly.

My face exploded like a fireball. If I'd been naked going into the sarcophagus, it stood to reason I had also been naked coming out of it. Something I was certain Tomas could not have failed to notice. And Gabriel's apparent nonchalance at his sentinel carrying me, in all my bare-assed glory, from the panic room to the bedroom, seemed completely at odds with what I knew of a vampire's possessive nature. "Tomas?"

"Uh-huh." He nodded.

"And you're okay with this?" I asked, watching his face carefully.

He sighed. "Had it been anyone else, they would already be dead," he confessed, "but I trust Tomas with your safety." His expression turned solemn. "However, if this is going to make you feel uncomfortable, then I will send him away."

I might not fully understand the role Tomas played in Gabriel's life, but I knew he was bound to Gabriel just as surely as I was. The burden of breaking such a bond was not a weight I was prepared to carry, but I had no idea how I was going to face the sentinel again, knowing he'd not only seen me in my birthday suit, he'd also got a pretty good feel for it.

Maybe he put you over his shoulder instead, with his hand on your ass.

I growled mentally at my inner bitch.

Sorry . . . just trying to be helpful.

If that's your idea of helpful—it isn't.

Now that I knew Tomas had played a role in my recovery, there was going to be one extremely awkward conversation taking place in my not-so-distant future.

"No," I said, shaking my head. "I don't want you to send Tomas away."

"Thank you." Gabriel looked relieved, and then another look crossed his face. It was more than just desire, it was a hunger—a need—that could be satisfied only one way. A circle of gold banded the rapidly darkening iris in his eyes. My stomach made a delicious roll, and my heart skipped a beat. "Rowan . . ." My name was a husky groan on his lips, and I watched his bicep flex as he gripped himself beneath the sheet.

My breasts were achy, my nipples hard, and I wanted Gabriel as much as he wanted me. Maybe more. But I needed to make sure that every physical trace of what I'd been through no longer existed. And real or symbolic, there was only one way to do that. Slowly crawling backward off the bed, I crooked my finger, beckoning him to follow me.

Chapter 10

The feel of hot water sluicing down my back and between my shoulder blades was therapeutic. Being in the sarcophagus had cleansed the drugs from my body, healed my broken bones and bruises, and taken care of my physical well-being. But standing beneath the hot shower spray was cathartic in a way the runes on Gabriel's coffin could never be. This was what I needed. To purify myself. To wash away the stench of Gus and Rat Boy and Petrov—especially Petrov—even if the odor of their combined foulness existed only in my mind.

The opening of the shower door, a lovely piece of glass sandblasted with images of long-legged wading birds, displaced some of the hot, steamy air. I felt a slight change in the water pressure as Gabriel activated the other showerhead set in the wall behind me. I started to turn around, but he took my hands and placed them firmly on the marble tiled wall in front of me. Obediently I kept my back to him, bending my head as the spray cascaded down my shoulders.

The fragrant scent of jasmine and ginger filled my nose as Gabriel, using his hands as a sponge, washed me. His strong fingers kneaded my shoulders before working their way down my back, paying individual attention to each vertebra in my spine. A trail of soapy suds ran down the back of my thighs.

Replenishing the soap in his hand, Gabriel turned me around and continued washing me. Cupping the fullness of each breast in a palm, his fingers slicked across my skin as he continued to lather me. I sucked in a breath as he gently pinched my nipple, gasping at the sensation that made a sudden heat explode between my legs.

Slippery hands glided down my rib cage, my waist, and across my lower belly. A finger dipped playfully into my belly button, making me giggle. He turned me back around and placed my hands flat against the tiled wall. Then he pushed his thigh between my legs, encouraging me to widen my stance. Long fingers soaped the inside of each thigh, and the feel of his nails lightly drawing over the sensitive skin made my muscles jump in anticipation.

I looked down to see him rinse his hands clean of the perfumed soap, and I heard his breath as it quickened next to my ear. His cock was long and hard, and it pressed up against me. His fingers found their way between my legs, slipping inside the folds of my flesh and pushing inside my body. I groaned and bucked at the feel of him.

"Do you want me to stop?" he murmured in a husky voice.

"I want you to make me come," I gasped.

He obeyed, moving his fingers in and out, creating a friction that made me clench my pelvic muscles and taking me to the edge of my climax. And just when I was certain my pleasure couldn't possibly be any more intense, Gabriel rubbed his thumb over my clitoris and sent me tumbling into an abyss of sensual gratification I had no idea existed.

I was swimming in a sea of orgasmic bliss and would have fallen to my knees if not for his arm around my waist. Waves of carnal ecstasy crashed over me, electrifying every nerve ending in my body . . . and then he pushed himself inside me.

The arm around my waist tightened, and he braced himself against the shower wall with his other hand. I wrapped my fingers around his muscular forearm and felt the muscles in his body clench as he drew back and then thrust forward, hips slamming into me. His own release was imminent. His thighs began to tremble as he prolonged the moment, and I felt the scrape of fully extended fangs down the side of my neck.

I pulled my wet hair to one side and offered myself to him. Gabriel struck at the exact moment I felt him move inside me, giving and taking at the same time. I have never felt anything so perfectly blissful.

All the lingerie I had thrown on the closet floor during my temper tantrum had been folded and put back in the silk-lined drawers. Somewhere between making me come either the third or fourth time, Gabriel and I had both apologized to each other over the matter. He promised not to do anything so outrageous again, while I, on the verge of sexual implosion, agreed to keep most of the lingerie. Even the Lady Gaga outfit.

Sex in the shower is a great way to reach a compromise.

Now, as I quickly plaited my wet hair in a single braid, I stared at my reflection in the full-length mirror. Not too shabby for a gal who was on the verge of death what, ten, twelve hours ago?

More like sixteen.

Whoa. I'd been out that long? Five minutes later I was dressed, my ultra-expensive underwear hidden beneath sweat pants and an NFL T-shirt. I didn't know who this gal Fleur was, or even if she really was from England, but she sure knew how to make a girl feel special in one of her bras.

Opening the bedroom door, I was immediately enveloped in a bear hug that had my feet dangling a good six inches off the ground and left me squeaking for breath. When over six feet of Russian vampire decides to hug you, it's best to just go with it and pray his enthusiasm doesn't accidentally crack a rib. My name came out with a deep growl, followed by a whole lot of Russian I didn't understand. Putting me back on solid footing, Aleksei released me, but took my hand and swallowed it up inside both of his.

I stared at him, feeling ridiculously happy to see he looked the same as ever. Tucked into military-style camouflage pants was a Marine Corps T-shirt bearing the slogan "First In, Last Out." I was convinced at some point in his life, perhaps more than once, Aleksei had been one of Uncle Sam's Misguided Children. "What happened to your boots?" I asked, looking down at his black-socked feet.

"Tomas said not on hardwood floors." He made a clucking sound with his tongue.

"Yeah, he tells me the same thing about my high heels. I've learned to take them off at the front door." I took my left hand and placed it atop the two that held my right prisoner. "Sorry if I gave you guys a scare, but I'm glad you're here, because there's something—"

"ROWAAAAAAAN!"

The rest of my sentence was drowned out by Anasztaizia's voice screaming my name, followed by an emotional flow that I assumed was Hungarian. Like her boyfriend, she reverted to her native tongue in times of stress. Thankfully, Aleksei let go of my hand at the moment she flung herself at me. We hugged, saw each other's eyes well up with tears, and hugged some more. The girlfriend-slash-sister bond that we shared now felt stronger and more meaningful.

I opened my mouth to say something, but Aleksei decided the estrogen flowing in the hallway was thick enough. Placing a hand on each shoulder, he turned Anasztaizia and me toward the kitchen.

"Eat first, talk later," he boomed.

The smell of bacon made my mouth water and my stomach grumble. Aleksei went to stand by the stove, while Anasztaizia set about getting plates and silverware on the table. Gabriel, watching me with a look that said he was ready to take another shower, fixed me a mug of hot coffee.

"Where's Tomas?" I asked, taking the mug from Gabriel's outstretched hand.

"Getting the mirror in the elevator replaced." Ah, so the spiderweb design hadn't been some form of artistic expression. I thought it looked suspiciously as if someone's fist had punched the glass, and I was willing to bet the person responsible wasn't standing more than a foot or so away from me. "You're going to talk to him? Now?"

"No time like the present." Putting off the face-to-face was pointless. The sooner Tomas and I got over any embarrassment we felt with each other, the better. Besides, there was no way I was going to be able to keep down—*was that blueberry waffles Aleksei was making?*—anything I ate until we'd cleared the air. Or I had. Gabriel made a move to go with me, but that was the last thing I wanted. "No, you stay." It sounded like I was giving orders to a golden retriever. "This shouldn't take more than a minute." I leaned forward and kissed him quickly on the mouth. "In the meantime, could you make sure the big guy doesn't eat all the bacon? Oh, and I want one of those waffles—and some scrambled eggs."

The door to the penthouse was standing wide open, as were the doors to the elevator that faced it. Tomas was giving instructions to the building's maintenance man on the best way to remove the damaged mirror without mutilating the surrounding paneling in the process. Henry, or so the name on the man's shirt said, was listening carefully.

Although I felt certain it wasn't the first broken mirror Henry had ever replaced, this time was different. He would be able to share with the rest of the building staff that *someone* had used their fist to vent their frustration. Seeing me standing in the open doorway, Tomas left Henry to start without him.

When I'd first learned Gabriel had a sentinel, someone to protect him as he lay in his sarcophagus in a state of inertia, I imagined a beefy ex–Special Forces guy. A muscle-bound assassin trained to kill with his bare hands or a paperclip. What I got was Mr. Rogers, complete with a cardigan that had leather patches on the elbows. I soon learned, however, that protection came in many forms, with physical strength being only one of them. As a runecaster, Tomas was uniquely suited to protect Gabriel. Or me.

When I asked what part of Scotland Tomas was from, Gabriel had chuckled and informed me his sentinel wasn't Scottish. I protested, citing Tomas's accent and use of idioms.

"Tomas," Gabriel told me, "has a talent for blending in anywhere. The ability to mimic the dialect of a specific region has proved useful in the past. Particularly in a time when people rarely went farther than the next village."

This aspect of being Gabriel's sentinel had never occurred to me, but I could appreciate the value of such a talent. "But what about now? People travel all over the world, so being able to speak a certain way doesn't matter as much. Of all the accents in the world, why pick Scottish?" I could think of at least a half dozen that would be much easier on the tongue, to say nothing about the ear.

"Ah, that's my fault," Gabriel confessed, looking a little sheepish. "We were having a discussion about humans we admired."

"Humans?"

"Yes," Gabriel barely missed a beat. "I told him I had a great deal of respect for William Wallace."

"*Braveheart?*"

"A dreadfully inaccurate depiction of his life," Gabriel corrected with a grimace. "Nonetheless, Tomas watched the movie and has adopted a Highland brogue ever since."

"He doesn't wear a kilt, does he?" Imagining Mr. Rogers in a tartan skirt was mind-boggling, to say the least, especially as I recalled a particularly memorable scene from the movie. Whether or not Mel Gibson actually showed his ass is completely beside the point. There were plenty of others who didn't shy away from their chance to moon.

"Tomas is a stickler for authenticity," Gabriel said dryly, observing the slight flush on my cheeks, "and does not possess the birthright to wear a clan tartan."

I was oddly grateful. If the sentinel was that adamant about being genuine, then had he been able to wear a kilt I knew exactly what he'd be wearing underneath it. It was hard enough knowing I'd been completely naked, but Mr. Rogers with no underwear? No way!

"What can I do for ye, lass?" Tomas said, interrupting my train of thought. The slight hesitancy in his voice made me think he too was a little anxious about seeing me.

I decided to cut to the chase. Looking him straight in the eye, and trying to ignore the sudden warmth creeping up my neck and face, I said, "I want to thank you for putting me to bed." Oh jeez—that sounded even worse.

"Ye should nae be ashamed, Miss Rowan." He took my hands and lowered his voice to a whisper, making sure Henry couldn't hear him. "I carried ye in a blanket."

"Oh . . . thank you, thank you so much for telling me that." Touched by his kindness, I surprised both of us by kissing him on the cheek. His skin was freshly shaven, and he smelled vaguely of Old Spice. It was nice, and made me think of my dad.

"Och, get away with ye!" Despite the gruffness of his tone, I could tell he was pleased.

Anasztaizia kept touching me, as if to reassure herself it really was me sitting at the table, pouring maple syrup over a blueberry waffle. I sighed when she jumped up to refill my mug. She'd freshened my coffee three times already. It would be a lot easier if she just brought the pot to the table. But I couldn't get irritated with her. Gabriel had let Aleksei know that I had something to tell him, something to do with my abduction, and now both he and Anasztaizia were walking on eggshells. I had considered running it by Gabriel first, but it was his suggestion that I wait until we were all present. That way I'd only have to say whatever it was one time.

It was obvious there had been some discussion among the three of them. Anasztaizia and Aleksei kept exchanging meaningful glances, and the big Russian looked frequently at Gabriel. As if he already sensed there was a lot more to my kidnapping than just having the really bad luck to be in an accident with a pair of opportunistic rapists.

Anasztaizia had barely taken a bite of her food, and her eyes were sparkling in a way that told me if I didn't say something—soon—she was going to dissolve into a puddle. "It's okay," I said, putting my hand on her arm and giving a gentle squeeze. "It wasn't your fault, and I'm really, really sorry about your car."

She made a fist with her hand, bringing it to her mouth so she could stifle her sobs. It took a few moments, and a couple of deep breaths, but I was proud of the way she pulled herself together. "I keep telling myself it was just a stupid accident," she said in a shaky voice, "that it could have happened to anyone. Five minutes, one way or the other, and they would have crashed into someone else, taken someone else . . ." Her voice trailed off.

I looked down, fiddling with the spoon I used to stir my coffee. I could feel three sets of eyes on me. "Did the police find anything at the scene?" I asked. "A registration or anything in the vehicle that hit me?"

It was Aleksei who answered me. "No. The truck was clean. Too clean, I am thinking."

"Perhaps that's because I'm pretty sure it wasn't an accident," I blurted out.

"It was deliberate?" Gabriel said, his eyes turning dark. I could tell from the look on his face that, had he known this earlier, Gus might still be alive. In agonizing pain and wishing he wasn't, but still alive. "Why didn't you tell me this?"

"Excuse me? Who was it who suggested I only needed to say this once?" Irritated by the mild accusation in his tone, I was snappish. "Besides, you've kept me kind of busy."

There was no doubt in anyone's mind just what keeping me busy entailed. Reaching for my hand, Gabriel squeezed my fingers in apology. Up until this point everyone had assumed the initial collision had been nothing more than a wrong-place-wrong-time type of deal. Hell, I'd thought the same thing until Petrov set me straight.

"I don't understand," Anasztaizia said, giving me a quizzical look. "You're saying those men waited for you to cross the intersection and then . . . ran into you on purpose?"

I threaded my fingers through Gabriel's and gave his hand a small squeeze of my own. "Yes, that's what I'm saying."

"Why?"

"Actually, it wasn't me they were after. They didn't know until it was too late that they'd made a mistake and got the wrong girl."

"What wrong girl?" Aleksei pulled his brows together, making a sharp vertical line between his eyes.

"They meant to snatch Anasztaizia," I told him, knowing that everything had just gone from bad to worse. "They got the right car...just the wrong girl."

Aleksei's eyes flashed to the lovely Magyar. His face suddenly turned pale, making the scar that ran down his cheek a bright line marking his skin. "Are you saying they wanted Anasztaizia?"

I nodded.

Anasztaizia began to tremble, the big door-knocker diamond on her ring finger tapping its own little SOS on the table surface. She looked totally stunned. "But what would they want with me?"

"Who are these scum?" Aleksei demanded, banging his fist down hard enough to make me jump.

The description Gabriel gave of Rat Boy and Gus was far more detailed than anything I would have provided. His powers of observation were far superior to mine. I hadn't even realized Rat Boy had a tattoo on his neck, much less that it was a drunken leprechaun.

"And you have never seen these men before?" Gabriel asked Aleksei. "Anyone you might have known in your past?"

The big Russian shrugged his impressive shoulders. "I would remember anyone looking like that," he said confidently. "And these men are dead, yes?"

"One is, and the other wishes he was," Gabriel said.

"So no more problem," the big guy stated with a satisfied snort.

He was wrong; he just didn't know it.

I could tell from the look on Aleksei's face that he was beginning to doubt my "wrong girl" account. I'm sure he didn't think I was lying, I had absolutely no reason to, but I had been through a pretty traumatic experience. It was possible I was confused. I didn't blame him for thinking that. In his place the thought would occur to me also. With the oddest sensation that my next words were going to make everything go from bad to worse, I took a deep breath.

"You're not out of danger," I said, addressing Anasztaizia directly.

"I'm not?" She arched an elegant brow and looked confused.

I shook my head. "Petrov is going to use you to get to Aleksei. I know because that was his plan all along."

Chapter 11

I never saw the big guy move, but I heard Anasztaizia scream, "No, Aleksei, don't!" at the same time Gabriel grabbed the back of my T-shirt and yanked me out of my seat, putting himself in front of me. My leg caught the edge of the table, lifting it and throwing a momentary obstacle in the path of the Russian vampire. And even when my puny brain caught up with everyone else, and I realized he actually was trying to get to me, I knew it was never Aleksei's intention to hurt me.

Yeah? Did you happen to notice his fangs were out?

He was simply reacting to hearing Petrov's name. Kind of like one of Pavlov's pooches, it had triggered a response in the big guy. Unfortunately, I think I can honestly say it wasn't quite the response any of us had been expecting, although Gabriel might have had an inkling because he was pretty damn quick on his feet. Seeing one vampire move faster than the eye can follow is pretty impressive. Seeing two of them, especially when one is moving to intercept the other, is more than impressive. It's mind-blowing.

My hands clutched at thin air, looking for something, anything, to stop me from going backward, but gravity was already pulling me down so my butt could do a meet-and-greet with the kitchen floor. You would think that my ass would provide some cushioning. Then again, with all the bedroom calisthenics I'd been doing recently, it wasn't quite as well-rounded as it used to be. And I'd thought dropping a size in jeans was a good thing. Thankfully there was nothing behind me but open space, and even though my back and shoulders smacked the floor pretty hard, I managed not to let the back of my head do the same. I'm sure my brain was grateful.

I struggled to my feet with a groan, noting that the kitchen table was now lying on its side, across the room. In trying to stop Aleksei from reaching me, Gabriel had simply thrown it out of his way. Now I watched as he slammed the Russian vampire up against the restaurant-sized stainless-steel fridge. The impact was forceful enough to put a large dent in the door and create an almost musical cascade of breaking bottles from within. Having already replaced the elevator mirror, it now looked as if Tomas was going to have to get a new fridge. I didn't think he would be happy about that.

I stared across the room. Gabriel had his back to me, so I couldn't see his face, but Aleksei was looking right at me. Glaring was more like it. Both of them were pushing against each other, and the strain was beginning to show on Aleksei's face. He didn't look anything like the vampire I had come to know. His eyes were black holes in his head, and his lips were drawn back, fangs on display. He snarled at me, which earned him a head bang, creating another dent in the fridge.

Gabriel was holding Aleksei in place with nothing but the strength and muscle of his own body. With one hand around the Russian vampire's thick neck, he pressed his massive chest forward, keeping Aleksei pinned, and in a strange echo of something I had done earlier, I noticed he'd wedged his leg between Aleksei's thighs, using his hips to anchor the big Russian's lower body.

The tremendous force being exerted by both of them made the air crackle with electricity, and I felt the hair on my arms rise. Shirt seams began to give as muscles strained. I knew, without having to see his face, that Gabriel was using nowhere near his full strength. I watched as he tilted his head down, placed his mouth next to Aleksei's ear, and began talking to him in a low voice that carried like a soft hum throughout the room. Gabriel's right hand was a fist, and it moved across Aleksei's chest, the knuckles making small circles as if he was massaging the big guy's heart. Once he had finished speaking, Gabriel looked into Aleksei's eyes. Whatever he had said was having a profound effect on the Russian.

There was a sudden popping sound, followed by a yelp of surprise, and the strong aroma of coffee made me jump. The glass coffeepot had shattered, startling Anasztaizia. The electrical charge in the air had found a weakness in the carafe. Thankfully there was no flying glass. The pot had pretty much imploded, but hot liquid now flowed unchecked over the counter and dripped onto the floor, forming a puddle. I grabbed a kitchen towel and began mopping up, taking care not to cut myself on any broken glass.

Aleksei let out a frustrated moan. Anasztaizia wasn't hurt, but she might have been, and that was enough to deflate what was left of his anger. His body slumped, and for the second time in less than twenty-four hours, I saw Gabriel use his own strength to hold a man upright.

"Come, Rowan, let's give them a few moments," Anasztaizia said in a quiet voice as she took the kitchen towel out of my hand.

"I really should clean up this mess." I didn't want the coffee to stain the tile grout.

"We can get that later," she said, her voice becoming firmer as she took my arm. "Trust me, dahlink, it will be better for Aleksei once we're out of the room. He needs to be alone with Gabriel."

I looked at her face, knowing I was missing something. Aleksei's reaction might have been practically a Pavlovian response, but something had changed. The sudden violence on Aleksei's part had been frightening. Anasztaizia smiled at me—a wan attempt at reassurance that missed the mark by a mile. Which meant I wasn't the only one Aleksei had scared.

"Here, drink this." Gabriel held out a glass, a bottle of Hennessey VSOP cognac in his other hand.

"I thought you knew I'm strictly a bourbon girl," I said, taking the glass from him.

"It doesn't hurt to try something new every now and then."

I shrugged and took a healthy swallow. It was good. Very, very good. Anything that doesn't have me coughing up a lung is okay in my book. Not that I've had much experience with such things.

Really? I distinctly recall that time you were persuaded to try moonshine . . .

Suggesting my inner bitch go take a hike, I marveled as the cognac slipped down my throat like silk. A wonderful glow began radiating from the center of my chest, gathering all my fraught nerves and wrapping them in a cocoon of alcoholic oblivion. Now I understood why, in a crisis, you're always given brandy to drink. I could get to like this. Very much.

Gabriel brushed his lips across mine and lifted the corners of his mouth. "I think it's safe to say you're now a bourbon and cognac girl." He grinned.

Movement in the hallway made me glance over his shoulder. "Is Aleksei going to be all right?" I knew better than to ask what had happened. That was a discussion Gabriel and I would have later, when we were alone.

"We shall see," he relied cryptically. "Another?" He pointed to my now almost-empty glass. Jeez! When had I done that? So smooth I'd just kept on a-drinking and never even noticed. No wonder I was feeling so good.

Infused with a wonderful mellow feeling, I was already under the alcohol's effect. Unfortunately, I hadn't yet told Aleksei about Petrov, but I was confident the conversation would go a lot easier now that I had a slight buzz on. Still, I needed to make certain brain and tongue remained on good terms. "Better not," I said, refusing Gabriel's offer. "Maybe after we're done."

Aleksei and Anasztaizia came into the room together. The looks on their faces made me think they'd been standing in the hallway eavesdropping (not really necessary on Aleksei's part), waiting for an appropriate lull in our conversation to come in.

I took a seat in one of the deep club chairs, tucking my feet beneath me. Anasztaizia had changed her clothes, and the big guy had changed his shirt. Now the slogan across his chest read *Semper Fi, always faithful*. Yeah, I was feeling a definite connection between Aleksei and the Corps. He stood just inside the doorway, studying the herringbone pattern of the hardwood flooring. Anasztaizia was rubbing her palm gently up and down his arm, giving him moral support.

He cleared his throat, "Rowan, I—"

"No, Aleksei, please don't say anything," I interrupted. "I think it would be better if you heard me out first. All of you."

Aleksei glanced down at Anasztaizia, before looking over her head at Gabriel. My boyfriend answered him with a nod of his head that seemed to say, *First, last, it will all get told*. I smoothed my hands over the arms of the club chair, the soft Italian leather silky beneath my palms. Deep inside I knew that once I started speaking, I wouldn't be able to stop. And I couldn't be selective about what I told them either. This was all or nothing. Leaving anything out could be dangerous for Aleksei. Even more so for Anasztaizia.

I took a breath, felt a sudden burst of cognac glow, and told them everything from the time I'd left Anasztaizia at the restaurant with my box of Esterházy torte, to when Gabriel had rescued me. I recalled each moment of the nightmarish incident with as much detail as possible, stumbling only when it came to describing Gus's intimidation tactics as he prepared to rape me.

I could feel Gabriel's eyes fixed on me the whole time I spoke, almost feel the dull ache he was giving himself from clenching his jaw. If he wasn't careful, he was going to crack a molar. I couldn't look at him. I knew it wasn't my fault, but I couldn't look him in the eye and talk about another man unzipping his pants and masturbating in front of me. I was grateful when my narrative was over.

Nobody said anything. I don't think they honestly knew what to say, and then Anasztaizia cut to the heart of the matter. "But the drugs didn't work because Gabriel was able to find you and, well"—she gestured with her hand in my direction—"you're obviously not dead, unless—" She broke off abruptly.

"Unless what?" Aleksei encouraged in a soothing rumble.

"Well, Petrov"—she gave a little shudder as she said his name—"may have known you're involved with a vampire, but I doubt he knows you're a Promise."

"I'm pretty sure he had no idea," I agreed.

"There's no way to know if Rowan's being a Promise made any difference," Gabriel said thoughtfully. "I can tell you the first drug was somewhat effective. It definitely compromised my ability to sense her." He gave a brief rundown on the quicksilver feeling he'd had, and the frustration of almost not getting to me in time. "As for her not dying . . . I wasn't taking any chances. I put Rowan in my sarcophagus, and I do know her being a Promise was the only reason I could do that." He gave Aleksei a knowing look. "Until we have found this bastard, you must take precautions and be vigilant."

When Gabriel spoke, it wasn't as a friend or mentor offering advice, or even as a parental figure guiding an offspring. This was something different. An Original Vampire reclaiming his role as maker, instructing his progeny on a specific course of action.

Anasztaizia frowned, her fingers playing with the big diamond on her ring finger. "But do you really think he'll come after me now? Surely he will realize that Rowan will have told us everything?"

"Assuming he knows I'm alive," I murmured.

"Oh, he knows," Gabriel said confidently. "He would have gone back to make sure you were dead. But finding you gone and seeing what I left behind, well"—he shrugged—"I'm certain he knows his own existence is no longer a secret."

"But how do you know he would have gone back?"

"I don't," Gabriel said, "not for sure, but it's what I would have done."

Aleksei, who had been curiously silent during this exchange, was staring at me. I raised my brows. It seemed obvious he had something on his mind, and if he was waiting for an invitation to speak, I decided to hand it to him on the proverbial silver platter. Getting to his feet, he crossed the room and embarrassed the hell out of me by dropping to his knees before me. Even kneeling, he was still almost a head taller than me, although I was sitting in the club chair.

As if suddenly realizing this, and deciding it might be disrespectful or something, he took my hands in both of his, bowed his head and rested his forehead against them.

"I humble myself before you," he said solemnly. "You are my maker's Promise, and I beg you to find it in your heart to forgive me." He paused, and I watched a slight tremble move his shoulders. "What I did . . . what I did . . . was-was—"

"No, no, no, Aleksei—don't!" I yanked my hands out of his grasp, horrified by his display of contrition. If he wanted to apologize for scaring the shit out of me, fine. A raised hand followed by a *Sorry for scaring the shit out of you, Ro* was more than enough. But this? Going down on his knees? This was too much. Waaaay too much.

He didn't move or try to get up. And he didn't look at me, which I found really disturbing. This was the vampire who delighted in flashing me his fangs every chance he got.

It might be better not to remind him about that just now. He was the one who sat through the movie *Titanic* with me, not at all embarrassed about showing his appreciation of Kate Winslet's assets, and who teased me in fractured English. So why the hell was he on his knees? Surely he knew I would hate that.

Maybe it's because it's what he has to do? Some sort of vampire rule?

I looked over at Gabriel. His expression was stoic, revealing nothing, and yet he didn't seem surprised by Aleksei's actions. And, though

Anasztaizia looked as if she was holding her breath, she also didn't seem shocked by her man's penitent display.

The only one taken aback was me.

Aleksei remained on his knees, keeping his head bowed and dropping his hands to his massive thighs. It occurred to me that perhaps snatching my hands away might have been the wrong thing to do. It might send the message that I was still scared or angry. I patted him tentatively on one shoulder. It was like stroking a rock. "Aleksei, please, you have to look at me."

Slowly he raised his face. The look in his eyes said that if I wanted him to wrestle live alligators, all I had to do was ask.

Better be a pretty big 'gator, else it won't be much of a contest...

I stared at him. Studying his face and seeing, perhaps for the first time, his features as they truly were.

The comic-book square jaw, the dark brows shading burnt-umber eyes, a broad nose with a wide, generous mouth. It was a good face, even with the jagged, vicious scar that ran from temple to jaw. One day I was going to ask him how he had got it. And why. Gabriel had said if I asked, Aleksei might be willing to tell me.

The big guy blinked and looked up at me. His eyes were honest and true. He didn't struggle with questions over principles, scruples, or ethics. He didn't have to, because the moral code ingrained deep inside of him was strong and unwavering.

He would never hurt you.

No... he never would.

"You want my forgiveness?" I asked, cradling his face in my hands. I imagine we all heard the sharp intake of breath as Gabriel had his own Pavlov pooch moment. Aleksei's wide shoulders slumped, and I had the ridiculous urge to run my palm over the spiked bristles that passed for hair. Not certain how good Gabriel's self-control currently was, I resisted, and then took one hell of a risk. "Then tell me who this man—this Petrov—is."

Aleksei looked up at me, dark brown eyes filled with sorrow. "He's the man who destroyed my family," he said and then gestured to his face, "and the one who gave me this."

Chapter 12

Russia—1710

Count Nikolayev Vasily Petrov stood naked in front of the large mirror and stared at his reflection. His lower lip was swollen, and there were scratches across his chest and shoulders. A wicked bruise discolored his upper thigh. He leaned forward and stuck out his tongue, examining the welt left by his own teeth. Biting it had been accidental. The girl had been going for his eyes, but thwarted by his hands locked around her wrists, she'd brought her head up beneath his chin. Nikolayev counted himself lucky she hadn't been taller. She might have broken his nose.

She'd fought like a wild animal, trying to keep her virginity. Stupid girl! Didn't she realize she had given it to him the moment she crossed the threshold to his room—no, before that even. It was lost the moment he made the decision to take it. She ought to have been honored that he would even consider putting his cock inside her to begin with. He had expected a token show of resistance, nothing more, but she had refused him with a violence that he'd been unprepared for. A violence that he found . . . exciting.

Lulled into the role of a lazy lover, Nikolayev was used to women who meekly lifted their skirts, spread their legs, and gave themselves to him. But this girl—this peasant girl—actually believed she had the right to refuse him! Her insolent defiance had dazzled him, made him want her more, and heightened his passion into a brutality he'd not felt before.

He walked over to the bed and stared down at her. In the pale light of early dawn, it was hard to imagine such a slight figure offering anything in the way of defiance.

The girl lay on her back, sprawled across the furs. The sharp, acrid mix of blood and sweat and sex hung in the air. It was a scent Nikolayev found intoxicating. Feeling no remorse, he continued to gaze down at the slim figure. He felt no sense of shame at seeing the livid, purple welts that discolored her pale skin. No disgrace at knowing the bruises that marked her face and neck and arms and legs were from his hands. No guilt stirred his conscience at the blood and semen now dried on her slender thighs. Why should it? She was a peasant and, as such, his property. He could do with her as he wished, save take her life, but even if that was his pleasure, who would dare to stop him? And who would question his account if she were to perish at his hand?

Idly, Nikolayev ran his fingers over the marks on his chest where she'd raked her nails. In the end, his superior strength had worn her down. A more experienced woman might have recognized the connection between the struggle and the swell of excitement rising within him. A more experienced woman might have become passive, stopped fighting, and submitted to the inevitable. A more experienced woman would not have fought him to begin with.

But this girl was not experienced, and Nikolayev had never been so aroused. Even now his cock was stirring at the memory of how it had felt throbbing inside his clothes, wanting to be free and buried inside her.

He had finally been forced to knock her to the floor, pinning her beneath him. His breath had been nothing but a series of ragged, uneven gasps. Blood was smeared across her lips, making them unnaturally red; a bruise was beginning to discolor one cheek, but the light of rebelliousness continued to burn in her eyes. Even then, knowing that she could not prevent what was going to happen, she refused to submit willingly.

Placing his hands around her slender throat, Nikolayev began to squeeze. Small fists pummeled frantically against his arms, but he easily ignored them. She clasped her hands around his wrists, trying desperately to break his hold, but the attempt was futile. As he steadily applied more pressure, Nikolayev felt her movements grow weaker until finally she went limp beneath him.

Quickly he stripped off her clothes, revealing a body dancing on the cusp of change. She was younger than he'd thought. Her breasts were small and pink-tipped, and her hips, though showing a hint of feminine roundness, were still boyishly slim. Coltish legs splayed out before him, and what little hair grew at the juncture of her thighs was fine and silky. Nikolayev wondered if she was yet to have her first bleed, and then quickly brushed the thought away. Such matters were of no concern to him and made no difference. For what he wanted, she was old enough, and knowing he would be her first filled him with an almost brutal excitement.

The girl regained consciousness when he got on top of her, and he watched as awareness and fear darkened the pale blue of her eyes. Pushing himself between her legs, Nikolayev roughly stretched her wider in order to accommodate him. She tried to punch him in the throat, but he slapped her back with enough of a sting to momentarily daze her. Power surged through him as he reveled in her helplessness. She tried to roll away when he lifted his hips, but the weight of his body bearing down on her prevented it.

She screamed when she felt him push his fingers inside her.

Shrill and piercing, her terror merely served to enhance the thrill running through him. He took his hand out from between her legs, positioned himself at her entrance, and drove himself into her, violently shattering her innocence.

Her screams were desperate, agonized cries. Her face, awash with tears, became contorted with pain. Each brutal thrust must be excruciating, but her voice only inflamed his lust. Stretching her wider, pushing himself deeper, Nikolayev continued to pound into her small, frail body. Splintering her with the violence of his onslaught until his spine clenched, he exploded, sending himself to ecstasy and throwing her into the bowels of hell.

Barely aware of his actions, he was not sure how many more times he took her. Everything around him merged into a red haze, but he made certain she bore the marks of his displeasure for having the temerity to defy him. And now he was done.

Nikolayev sighed. His father would have been displeased. Not that taking the girl's virginity wasn't his right, but the previous count had always insisted on compensating the family for the loss of a daughter's maidenhead.

"Our fortune is tied to the land, and those who work it," his father had told him. "Better the loss of a few rubles to a girl who has stirred your lust than have the harvest suffer because of shame and dishonor."

But Nikolayev was not his father. He saw no need to pay for something that was his to take by right. What did he care if a girl's value as a bride was diminished because she was no longer a virgin? Wasn't it preferable for a husband to have a wife already familiar with the expectations of the marriage bed? And having found favor with a member of the nobility was its own form of status.

Pay for taking her virginity? The idea was preposterous! And just how was he supposed to compensate her anyway? Give her a pearl necklace? Ruby earrings? A gold bracelet set with precious stones? Would she even understand the value of such a gift? No, the more he thought about it, the more convinced Nikolayev was that his father's thinking had been wrong in this regard.

Opening the door, he beckoned to his personal manservant, who waited outside.

"I want a hot bath and something to eat," Nikolayev told him as he slipped on a robe embellished with his family crest and trimmed with luxurious fur at the collar and cuffs. He poured himself some wine, wincing a little when he pressed the goblet to his bruised mouth. "And get rid of that," he ordered, waving his free hand at the figure now moving beneath the bed coverings.

Standing before the window, Nikolayev observed the view through the glass. It had snowed in the night, and now the land was covered by a blanket of white. If he were a poet he could no doubt find some fanciful symbolism between the girl's loss of virginity and the unspoiled landscape. But he abhorred poetry and found no meaning or beauty in the transformation of the world beyond his window. To him it was a monotonous landscape, broken only by the trees stretching their stark limbs upward. He glanced at the sky. The somber color was a promise of more snow to come. If he was going to survive the bitter cold of winter, he had better travel to St. Petersburg, where the distractions were wide and varied. Besides, he had left his wife alone for long enough. It was time she did her duty and provided him with an heir. Only her connection to the tsar had prevented him from breaking down her bedroom door when she'd barred it to him. Perhaps it was time to teach her that he didn't need a bed to claim her body. How else did the woman think she was ever going to give him a son?

He paid no attention to the noises coming from behind him. The manservant, long accustomed to his master's habits, was dressing *the girl with a practiced, efficient hand. Experience had taught him that keeping the girls warm was the key to recovery, which explained the blanket he had thought to bring with him and which he now draped across her shoulders.*

They were almost at the door when the girl stopped. Shaking off the manservant's hand, she addressed her rapist. "You will pay for this," she said in a voice that was filled with contempt. "You will be made to answer for what you have done to me."

"And who is going to make me answer?" Nikolayev smirked. Like all the peasants it had been his misfortune to come across, she was no doubt fervently religious. "Do you imagine God will strike me down? If he didn't save you last night, why should he bother with you now?"

"No, not God." Something in her voice said her faith had been shaken and would never be as strong again. "My brother will make you pay."

"Then perhaps you'd better tell me his name so I will know him when he comes."

"Aleksei . . . his name is Aleksei."

Aleksei was more than halfway down the rutted track when he saw Konstantine coming in the opposite direction. Though the path was wide enough for two men on horseback to pass each other, it did not offer the same accommodation when one of them also had a cart. At another time, he might have chanced it, but not today. His horse had already stumbled in the newly fallen snow, and Aleksei was silently praying he could get the animal back to the barn without completely laming it. So he stood to one side, waiting patiently for the old man and his cart to pass him, as both he and his horse blew clouds of steam into the cold air.

"Good day to you, Konstantine," he called once the man was close enough to hear him. It was as much self-preservation as any-thing else. Everyone in the village knew Konstantine's horse had the better eyesight these days. Seeing the old man jerk his head up at the sound of his name, Aleksei frowned.

"Aleksei?" The old man's voice was querulous and his lined face troubled. "What brings you home so soon?"

"Stumbled in a rabbit hole," he answered, lightly jingling the reins he held. "You would think, as often as we have traveled that

path, this old nag would not only know where all the holes are, but would have the sense to avoid them!"

"Everything looks different in the snow," Konstantine offered, to which both Aleksei and the horse snorted. Each for different reasons.

"So, you had business with my mother?" Aleksei asked conversationally. There was only one reason to explain being on this particular path.

"Yes," Konstantine said, hesitating a little, "I brought Larissa home."

Aleksei pulled his brows together and sighed. "What did she do this time? Put too much salt in the count's soup?"

Beneath his thin coat with its frayed collar, Konstantine's shoulders shrugged. "I cannot say," he mumbled quietly, keeping his old eyes fixed firmly on the rough board between his feet.

"Has she been dismissed?" Aleksei asked. Seeing the old man's apparent reluctance to offer any further information, he softened his tone. "It's all right, you can tell me. Lord knows, I never wanted her to go to the dacha in the first place."

"Then why give your permission?" the old man snapped uncharacteristically.

Aleksei blamed age and the fact Konstantine lived alone for the sharpness of his tongue. When you had no one to converse with, it was easy to fall out of practice. Feeling charitable, he forgave the accusatory tone.

"I couldn't fight both her and my mother," Aleksei said with a heartfelt sigh. "The opportunity presented itself and, well . . ." He brushed the bottom of his ears with the tops of his shoulders.

In truth, Aleksei had never been at ease with the idea of Larissa serving at the dacha. When she had first asked his permission to work at the country home of Count Petrov, his first instinct had been to say no, using her age as his reason for doing so. His mother, ignoring his ridiculous statement that Larissa was too young, reminded him about the poor harvest. One less mouth to feed at their table could make all the difference if the winter turned harsh. Aleksei didn't know it was possible for a winter to be anything but harsh, and unable to fault his mother's argument, he reluctantly agreed.

But now it would appear that Larissa had been dismissed. He had been joking about too much salt, but it wouldn't surprise him. Whatever the reason, he was secretly pleased. Of course, he couldn't let his sister know that, at least not right away. He would have to put on a show of being disappointed, angry even, but then when they had all forgotten she had ever been away, he would forgive her. Poor harvest or not, there would be no hungry bellies at their table. He would make sure of that.

"So . . . has she been dismissed?" Aleksei asked again.

"I don't know," Konstantine said, picking up the reins and clucking his tongue against the roof of his mouth so his horse would walk forward. "But remember, Aleksei, no matter what is said, Larissa did nothing wrong."

"Wait!" Aleksei called as the cart rumbled past him. "What is going to be said?"

But even though he knew Konstantine heard him, the old man kept on going, refusing to stop or offer any further clarification.

"So, what do you suppose he meant by that?" Aleksei asked, rubbing his hand over his horse's nose. The animal answered with a toss of its head. "You don't know either, hmmm? Well, we won't find out standing here."

Blowing into his hand to restore some feeling to his cold fingers, Aleksei took one last look over his shoulder at the ancient cart as it rumbled down the track. It was getting colder, and that, he told himself, was the reason he had seen tears in the old man's eyes. After all, what other reason could there be?

The first thing Aleksei heard was his mother's voice singing a tune he recalled from his childhood. One that would scare away the monsters who sometimes stole into his sleep at night, frightening him awake. He paused, listening to the almost forgotten refrain. His mother had a lovely voice, and part of him thought it was a shame she didn't sing more often.

"Mama?"

The singing stopped abruptly as Aleksei entered the large open space that was the main room of the house. His mother, attending to a blanket spread across the table, looked over her shoulder at him. Her expression was a mix of fear and anguish. In her hand she held a piece of linen, and a large bowl of water had been placed on the table. He could see the water was a dirty rust color. The color of blood.

Aleksei felt his stomach turn. The last time his mother had been standing so, it had been to wash the body of his father before his burial. That had been eight years ago, when he was fifteen. The image of Konstantine driving his cart away suddenly filled his head. It hadn't been the cold—the old man had been weeping!

In a moment of absolute clarity, Aleksei became aware of everything around him. The aroma of soup simmering on the stove complementing the lingering smell of fresh bread. The soft rustle of mice in the rafters, and the sound of crows cawing in the field behind the house. He heard the voices of his younger brothers carried on the cold air. They were in the barn, playing with a litter of boisterous puppies.

He felt his brows pull together. How had he not seen the boys when he'd put the horse in its stall? Because they'd been hiding from him, he realized. Hiding because they did not want to be the ones to tell him about Larissa. And perhaps because they did not know what to tell him. Were they hiding because they were afraid? Afraid to face him until he had seen . . . what?

The prickle of unease he had felt on opening the door now sank its teeth into the back of his neck, disquieting him. His mother reached for his hand, holding it with both of hers. The rough skin and callused palms were a testament to the hard life they lived. Aleksei frowned at the feel of her fingers tightening. He could not recall the last time she had held his hand. Had it been when his father died? He had a vague recollection of embracing her when the priest and the men from the village brought his father's lifeless body home. But that was him holding her. In the eight years since that night, had his mother ever found a reason to hold his hand? If she had, he was unable to call it to mind.

Now he looked down at her lined face. A stoic woman from good peasant stock, she had borne eight children, burying three as well as her husband with barely a murmur. But now her features were filled with grief, and she let go of him so she could use a hand to stifle her sobs. Her distress was painful to see, but it was the fear in her eyes that worried Aleksei more than anything else. He had never known his mother to be afraid of anything.

He looked at the table and, knowing who lay beneath the blanket, carefully stepped around his mother. Keeping his gaze fixed on the still, unmoving figure, he forced himself to say her name.

"Larissa." It came out on a ragged breath, and seeing the bruises

on her face, Aleksei felt a rage rise within him. Too afraid to put his ear to her lips in case there was no breath to be heard, he asked, "Does she live?"

"She breathes, but she has not yet awakened," his mother told him. "We should be grateful that she still sleeps."

And he was, especially as he saw more bruises around his sister's neck and on her shoulders and arms. His hand brushed over the edge of the unfamiliar blanket. Even he could tell the wool was of high quality, and finer than anything he could ever hope to have.

"Where did this come from?"

"She was wrapped in it," his mother told him.

Nodding, Aleksei lifted the edge higher, shocking his mother with his action.

"No, Aleksei, you mustn't—it isn't proper!"

"And you think what has happened is?" he challenged angrily.

The fear in his mother's face was now replaced by resignation. As head of the family, it was his responsibility to bear witness to the brutalized condition of his adored sister. Across Larissa's shoulders and around her wrists were bruises from where she had been held down. There was a bite on her left breast and a livid discoloration marking the ribs below, as if she had been punched. He applied a light pressure with his fingertips, and though still unconscious, Larissa winced in pain. A rib was broken, perhaps more than one.

Pulling the blanket back further revealed the very worst. Ugly purple blotches sullied the pale skin of her legs, and her hips bore more evidence of finger marks. His mother, he noted, had not had time to wash away the dried blood that stained the inside of each thigh.

Carefully he pulled up the blanket and patted his mother on the shoulder. She had turned her back while he took in the full measure of his sister's shame. "Did Konstantine say who was responsible?" he asked quietly.

His mother looked shocked. "Konstantine? How would he know?"

"I saw him earlier. He said he had brought Larissa home. I thought someone might have said something to him."

His mother shook her head. "No. If they had, he would have told me." Which meant it could be any one of a number of males who served at the count's pleasure. As she held him by his arms, he could see his mother shared his frustration. "Be patient, Aleksei. God will-

ing, Larissa will be able to tell you who attacked her, and then you can go to the count and ask for justice."

He nodded. Even if he knew the man responsible, it would be up to the count to dispense whatever punishment he saw fit. All Aleksei could do was pray Nikolayev Vasily Petrov held the same sense of justice his father had. He took a deep breath and waited as his mother finished with her task, turning his back so as not to cause any further embarrassment.

When his sister was clean and dressed in her own clothes, Aleksei picked her slight body up in his arms. "Burn that," he instructed his mother, nodding at the fine blanket. He wanted nothing beneath his roof that had come from the dacha, nothing to remind Larissa of her ordeal.

After laying the still-dazed girl in her bed, Aleksei picked up her hand and pressed her pale fingers to his lips. Her eyelids began to flutter, and her lips moved. She spoke a single word, but it took him a moment to recognize his own name in the rasping croak that was her voice. The hoarseness of her voice told him she had screamed for a long time, and knowing that, he felt a sudden tightness in his chest.

Larissa opened her eyes at the same time Aleksei became aware of the slight pressure of her fingers squeezing his hand. Her lips moved again, and he lowered his head to better hear her. "Hurt . . . me . . ." she told her big brother as tears slipped from her eyes.

A fierce surge of protectiveness rushed through Aleksei. "Who hurt you, Lissa?" he whispered, using the familial endearment he had given her as a baby. "Tell me his name, and I will make sure he never hurts you again."

She licked her lips, wincing as the tip of her tongue made contact with her bruised, split lip. Though it was hard for her to speak, to form the words, it was even harder for Aleksei to hear. But if she could find the strength to reveal the name of her defiler, then he could do no less than be her avenging angel. Leaning down once more, he put his ear close to her mouth.

The rage that he had been trying to keep subdued tore free of his control, and the flame that had ignited at the sight of her injuries was now fanned into a roaring fire. There was no mistaking the name of the man who was responsible for her disgrace and shame.

Chapter 13

The moonlight reflecting off the snow illuminated the dacha as brilliantly as if it were the middle of the day in high summer. Aleksei, his presence hidden by the shadow of an ancient tree with gnarled limbs, watched for any sign that might suggest someone within the grand country house was not yet abed. The hour was late, but it would be prudent to avoid anyone who served the house. They had no part in his retribution.

He strained his ears, listening for any sound that was out of place, but the only thing he heard was the hoot of an owl warning him he would have competition if chasing rodents was his objective. Keeping to the shadows as much as possible, Aleksei made his way to the rear of the house. Heeding Larissa's advice, he gave the stables a wide berth. The chance of disturbing a high-strung, nervous horse or stable boy was too great.

He was surprised to find the stout outer door that would take him inside the house was neither locked nor barred. Chance or design? He didn't know, but the thought occurred to him that most of the household would be aware of Larissa's shame. Perhaps someone was expecting him to pay a midnight visit, and perhaps that same someone had arranged for the door to be left unlocked.

Or perhaps it was a trap.

Aleksei paused and then shook his head at the foolishness of such a notion. More likely no one had bothered to secure the door because it was unnecessary. The idea that someone would be stupid enough to enter this particular house uninvited, especially with the count in residence, was preposterous. If caught, the penalty would be swift and severe, but to Aleksei it was a risk worth taking as long as he got to Nikolayev first.

"Aleksei—think about what you are doing!" his mother had cried, clinging to his arm. "What will happen to us when you are caught?"

He was saddened to realize she had already decided his endeavor would end badly. "What will happen to us if I don't?" he asked as gently as he could. "Will you let him take Sofia the next time? Or perhaps he may decide he wants the twins."

"But they are boys!" his mother protested with a gasp of horror.

"Do you think that makes any difference to a man like that?" Aleksei had peeled her hands from his arm. "With the old count, there were rules. He would never take a girl as young as Larissa." Aleksei couldn't tell if the look on her face was because she didn't believe him, or because she did. "Mama, I am not a child anymore. I know what it meant when a young girl spent the night at the dacha, but the old count was generous—and no, this is not about wanting anyone to pay." He sighed deeply. "What he did was brutal . . . and if he's not stopped, then the next time it will be worse."

Seeing he would not be swayed, even though he put them all at risk, his mother let him go. It was in God's hands now, and there was nothing she could do but pray.

Stepping through the doorway, Aleksei took a few moments to allow his eyes to adjust to the gloom and his hammering heart to calm down. The room he was in was pitch-black, with no light to show his way, but he sensed it was a small space, leading to something bigger. Using his hands to guide him, he carefully felt along the wall until he came to a place where the bricks ended. Expecting to be grabbed by the collar of his coat at any moment, he carefully stuck his head out and peered beyond the darkness.

The banked fire gave off enough of a glow that he recognized he was in the grand house's kitchen. But even if the fire had been put out, the lingering aroma of cooked meats and bread would have told him where he was. His nose twitched in appreciation, and his mouth suddenly filled with saliva. A low grumbling in his belly reminded him he had not eaten since morning, but he pushed the feelings of hunger to one side as he committed the layout of the room to memory. He needed to be certain he could find his way out again.

"You must be the brother," a male voice said suddenly from the darkness. Startled, Aleksei froze. To his ear, the voice did not belong to their village nor any of those close by. However, it carried enough

of a rough edge that Aleksei knew it was not Nikolayev Petrov who addressed him from the shadows. "She said you would come."

A flicker of light in his peripheral vision told him a candle had been lit, and slowly Aleksei turned around, curious to see who it was that waited for him.

He thought the man looked older than the sum of his years. Shadows in his eyes said he had seen many things he wished he had not. "Who are you?" Aleksei asked.

The man shook his head. "My name is of no concern. It's yours that is important. You are Aleksei, are you not?"

He nodded without thinking, and immediately cursed himself for his stupidity. If there had been any doubt about his identity, he had just wiped it clean away. But the man dismissed his unease with a gesture of his hand. It was obvious that he knew who Aleksei was and why he was here. Which still didn't explain why he was waiting for him.

"I won't be stopped," Aleksei said in a belligerent tone that practically dared the man to try. "I don't want to hurt you," he added, "but I will if I have to."

"You think I'm here to stop you?" The man seemed surprised by the notion and made a point of staring at Aleksei, noting the physical disparity between them. "My dear Aleksei, forgive me, but it is not my wish to stop you. I am here to make sure you don't get lost."

Nikolayev was in the throes of a terrible nightmare. Strong hands grabbed his arms, yanking him from the warmth of his bed and throwing him bodily to the floor. Shocked, he barely had time to catch his breath before the same hands seized the front of his fine linen nightshirt and rudely jerked him to his feet. The garment, not meant to withstand such rough treatment, sounded far too loud as it tore.

Nikolayev gasped as he was pulled against his attacker's chest, their faces mere inches apart.

"Is this where you took her?" the voice snarled. "Couldn't find a woman, so you forced yourself on a child?"

Count Petrov's stomach lurched sickeningly as he realized this was no dream and there could be no doubt as to the identity of his attacker. "You're the brother?" he croaked, his voice sounding more astonished than terrified. Never in a hundred years had he imagined the girl's threat as something to be taken seriously. "You are"— what had she said his name was?—"Aleksei?"

The man seemed surprised that he would know his name. That he would know the name of any born in servitude. "I am Aleksei," he growled.

Nikolayev was stunned. Not only had the sister fought him, but here was the brother possessed of apparently the same idea. It was preposterous! The man was a peasant and could be hanged simply for touching a member of the nobility. In fact, he'd already imposed his own death sentence. Was he an imbecile? One of those slow, dullwitted creatures incapable of following more than the most rudimentary of commands?

"Do you know who I am?" Nikolayev demanded, suddenly finding his voice.

"You're the bastard who raped my sister."

"No," Nikolayev snarled back, "I took what was mine to take."

Aleksei hit him across the face with enough force to send him sprawling.

"You will hang for that!" Nikolayev shrieked as blood poured from his nose.

"Then I'd best make it worthwhile," Aleksei said, coming toward him with his hands curled into fists.

A strange kind of rage had come over Aleksei. It wasn't the same hot fire that had threatened to consume him on seeing his sister's broken body. This was a cold, intense passion that allowed him to see exactly what was happening but refused to let him alter the course of his own actions.

Nikolayev, by virtue of his birth, had received the very finest of instruction as a pugilist. Unfortunately, his instructors had never considered that he might be forced to defend himself against an opponent who didn't fight by the rules. An opponent who had no idea there actually were rules. Suddenly Nikolayev was overwhelmed. Aleksei fought like all peasants did. Which meant he didn't box so much as brawl. Nikolayev was on the receiving end of murderous skill carried in the fists of a man with centuries of injustice in his heart.

Momentum was swinging in the peasant's favor. Perhaps it was because Aleksei felt he had nothing to lose. Perhaps it was because he felt true outrage over the assault on his sister. Whatever the reason, it was immaterial; only the effect it was having mattered. Nikolayev had always known he would meet his end violently. It was the curse of the Petrov men. Even his father, thought by many to have escaped such misfortune, had succumbed to his fate. His horse, startled during dismount, had bolted, and with his foot caught in the stirrup, the previous count had been dragged to his death. If that wasn't considered violent, Nikolayev didn't know what was.

But for him to be beaten to death at the hands of a peasant farmer? Because he had raped the man's sister? The very idea was outrageously absurd!

With the prospect of such ignominy looming over him, Nikolayev found the strength to strike back. His sudden attack took Aleksei by surprise, but not quite as much as the blow to the back of his head did. As he sank to the ground, heading for an insensible state, Aleksei glimpsed the shocked face of the girl who had been sharing Nikolayev's bed and who now held a large piece of firewood in her hands.

Aleksei couldn't feel his hands. He was kneeling on the ground, arms outstretched and held by two men he had never seen before. Apparently not everyone who worked at the dacha had ties to the village. He ought not to have been surprised. Of course the count would have his own personal retinue that served him. He kept his head bowed, peering through the strands of his dark hair, as he tried to get his bearings.

He could hear terrified sobbing—female sobbing—that was sickeningly familiar. Keeping his eyes downward, he looked at the snow-covered ground. It was hard and stony, and if he had any feeling in his legs he would probably be grimacing, because the snow beneath his knees was also blood-stained. Being dragged across the rough terrain was the only explanation he could find for such a thing. The weeping woman—women?—suddenly broke off, and the crying was replaced by the noise of tearing fabric. Something else he was becoming too familiar with. This time the ripping cloth was followed by the ringing slap of an open hand striking bare skin.

Aleksei had no choice—he had to lift his head.

He wished to God he never had.

He was no longer at the dacha, but kneeling on the ground outside his home. He could smell the rich earthy scent of the barn animals, the blaze of lit torches, and the faint aroma of borscht in the air. In a line kneeling before him, with their hands tied behind their backs, was his family. All of them were trembling, but whether it was fear or the cold night air that gripped them, Aleksei couldn't tell. The boys and Sofia, his other sister, were staring at him with a look that said they knew he wouldn't let anything bad happen to them. He was their big brother, and he would protect them.

His mother and Larissa both wore expressions that said they knew otherwise. The worst was yet to come for them. His mother knew what men did to satisfy their bloodlust, and now his sister did too. And neither expected Aleksei to save them.

Petrov had torn open Larissa's dress, exposing the mottled bruising on her arms and shoulders, the fingerprints that circled her neck, the angry mark of his teeth on her breast. And now she carried the added insult of a fresh handprint on her face. It wasn't enough to have already violated her; now Petrov wanted to humiliate her further by showing his men the results of his perversity. Aleksei wanted to tell her how sorry he was, that this additional humiliation was his fault and his alone. His face burned with his own shame.

The nicker of horses cut through the air. It was getting colder, and Count Petrov's prize stallion was weary of standing still. A gloved hand gripped a handful of Aleksei's dark hair and viciously yanked his head up.

"I could hang you just for touching me," Nikolayev said, looking down at him, "and no one would stop me."

Unable to stop himself, Aleksei smiled. His fists had done considerable damage to the arrogantly handsome face, and he prayed that some of it might be permanent. Aside from the colorful bruises around the count's eyes, Aleksei saw a nose that was broken and a mouth so grossly swollen it was a miracle anything Nikolayev said could be understood.

"But I decided that would be too easy," Nikolayev continued. "I want you to suffer like the piece of filth that you are. I never want you to forget that your decision alone is responsible for what will happen this night. I want you to carry it with you every day of your miserable life, and"—he yanked Aleksei's head back even farther—"I want to make certain you never forget who brought you to this state."

The blade of the dagger in Nikolayev's hand caught the moonlight, reflecting the lunar glow and almost hypnotizing Aleksei with its brilliance. He didn't feel any pain as the blade moved in a downward arc. The night air was too cold for that; pain would come later, but he could feel something dripping off his chin. The sensation was so strange he automatically looked down and saw the snow beneath him turning red. The rapidly spreading stain was a measure of how deep Nikolayev had cut.

"Is that the worst you can do to me?" Aleksei said scornfully, his question infuriating the count.

"No," came the reply, "this is the worst I can do." And before Aleksei's horrified gaze, Count Nikolayev Vasily Petrov, using the dagger that still dripped with Aleksei's blood, slashed the throats of his brothers, his sisters, and his mother.

He didn't realize the count's men had released their hold on him until he fell over, his wounded face striking the hard ground. But by then it was too late. They were all dead. And as the dark came to claim him for the second time that night, the air was filled with the screams of dying animals. Petrov's men had set the barn ablaze, ensuring there would be nothing Aleksei could claim as his own.

Chapter 14

Numbing silence filled the room, and it wasn't until I saw Anasztaizia take the handkerchief from Aleksei's hand and wipe her eyes that I realized she was hearing her lover's history for the very first time.

"My God, Aleksei . . . your entire family . . ." My brain did its best to assimilate what I'd just heard, and I clutched Gabriel's hand, needing the physical connection to help me keep my emotions in check. "That bastard—that fucking bastard—*murdered* your entire family!" I began to shake so violently that Gabriel put his arms around me, holding me close until I managed to regain some semblance of control.

"Yes, I lost everyone," Aleksei agreed solemnly. "Perhaps if I had listened to my mother . . ." He shrugged his shoulders and let out a sigh filled with regret.

"Oh no," I countered, "don't you even think about going there!"

Would-a, should-a, could-a were all branches on the same *What if?* tree, and telling yourself things would be different if only you'd taken the other color pill was a waste of time and energy. What was done was done. The past couldn't be changed, and even if it could, there was no guarantee the outcome wouldn't be the same. Or possibly worse.

"You don't think my beating Petrov was the reason my family was killed?" Aleksei asked me.

"I think that, no matter what, Petrov would have found a way to hurt you all," I said slowly. "The man who abducted me is completely amoral. Knowing he had the wrong person"—I sent an apologetic glance in Anasztaizia's direction—"he still injected me with a drug he believed would kill me, before turning me over to his men so they could do whatever they wanted." I spread my hands. "What else is there to say?"

"But he's not a man anymore," Anasztaizia pointed out. "You were abducted by a vampire."

"You think becoming a vampire made him lose his sense of morality?" I asked her.

The lovely Magyar shook her head. "I don't know, but don't you think being a vampire could have changed him?"

"No," I said flatly. "I don't think his fundamental nature changed."

"Why not?"

"Because when Katja tried to kill me, she opened a door into her past, and let me see what her human life had been like." I didn't realize I was trembling again until I felt Gabriel squeeze my hand. "It wasn't pretty; in fact, her life was quite awful, and I'm not sure how she even survived it to begin with, but those human experiences are what molded and shaped her. Vampire or human, she still would have been one psychotic bitch." Anasztaizia tilted her head slightly, conceding my point. "Besides, don't you think there's a reason I've never been afraid of Aleksei?"

"You haven't?" He had the grace to look somewhat deflated by my statement.

"Well, you did give me one or two heart-stopping moments," I admitted with a small smile, "but that was before I really got to know you."

"So you're saying you're not afraid because he's a good vampire?" Anasztaizia seemed slightly perplexed by the notion.

I wasn't kidding myself. I was pretty sure Aleksei had been guilty of making some questionable choices since becoming a vampire. But just because someone does a bad thing, it doesn't necessarily mean they're a bad person. "Yes, but in order to be a good vampire," I said, answering Anasztaizia, "he had to be a good man first."

"A good man who got my family killed," Aleksei muttered remorsefully.

"We will get him this time, Aleksei," Gabriel told him. "I promise you that."

"This time?" I was puzzled. "You had a chance to get this Count Petrov before?" I couldn't imagine Gabriel letting someone guilty of such a heinous crime slip through his fingers. "What happened?"

"Kartel," he said gravely.

I was confused. I knew what a cartel was when you were talking about drug rings south of the border, but I wasn't sure how it applied to the murder of a Russian peasant family in the 1700s.

"Kartel? Who's that?" It wasn't me who asked, but Anasztaizia.

"Someone with a connection to Petrov."

"Okay, but *who* is he?" I asked, slipping my hand out of Gabriel's grasp and making a questioning gesture.

"Another Original Vampire," Gabriel said.

From the tone of his voice, I could tell that he did not regard this Original Vampire with the same respect he did Ryiel. Which meant having Kartel around wasn't a good thing. And it also gave me a good idea who had offered Aleksei's nemesis a shot at immortality. Or the closest thing to it.

"So how did he know about Aleksei? Was he in Russia with you? Did he know Petrov before you did? Has he—" The rest of my question was silenced by Gabriel's finger on my lips.

"Let Aleksei continue with his story."

Somewhat chastened, I shut up.

The pungent odor of animal dung pulled Aleksei back to a conscious state. The smell was strong but not unbearable. Vaguely he recalled hands pulling at his arms and legs, stripping off his clothes. Good. It was no less than he deserved. Steal his clothes and let the wolves have him. But instead of feeling the cold bite of winter's breath, he felt sweat breaking out on his body. Was he already dead and in hell? Surely not! It was hot, but he expected the fires of damnation to be unendurable. This heat, this warmth, was something he was certain he could get used to, only he didn't think it was supposed to work that way.

Fingers touched his face. Hard and bony, they pinched the ragged edges of his cheek together before something sharp pierced the flesh. Aleksei sucked in an involuntary breath as a tightness pulled at his skin. In and out, in and out, stitching his cheek closed. From the rough feel of it, the result would not be pretty; but what did that matter? And why did he care? The priests always said those souls destined to spend an eternity in hell had bodies with open wounds and bleeding sores. So why would they care about his face? Perhaps the priests were wrong.

His head now filled with strange images as the fever that gripped him ran its course. For two days and two nights he battled against the nightmares that plagued him. Caught in the throes of his delirium, he screamed and wept, and didn't even try to fight off the bony fingers when they pried open his mouth and poured liquid down his throat. If he was lucky, it would be poison.

And then his fever broke.

Aleksei opened his eyes. He was lying on the ground covered by an animal skin. The rough texture of fur scraped over his body, and he ran his fingers across the pelt, trying to identify the hide. He wasn't sure, but it felt like wolf. He blinked his eyes and stared above him at the ceiling. Animal bones and small skulls hung suspended from the soot-stained rafters. Now he understood. Now he knew where he was. He had been given into the care of Old Magda. He could either live or die; it mattered not which one he chose.

Part healer, part witch, the old woman could concoct a potion for whatever ailed you, whether it be a matter of the head, the heart, or the bowels. It was said she knew more about poison than the Italians, but like most of the village, Aleksei didn't know what Italians were, so the boast was meaningless.

"So, finally you are awake!" The voice that greeted him was hoarse with age and little use, and it spoke to him from the shadows.

"They should have left me to die," he muttered sourly.

"I'm sure they wanted to, but, alas, they could not." Aleksei felt his brow furrow as he narrowed his eyes, trying to see the old woman in the gloom. "The count decreed that were you to die, everyone in the village would suffer."

"Since when do you care what a count says?"

Old Magda stepped out of the shadows, and Aleksei was surprised to find she was not as old as he had imagined. Though her hair was long and iron-gray and her face was lined, he could still see the shadow of the beauty she had once been.

She spat into the fire, making it sizzle. "You're right. I care nothing for that crawling maggot."

"Then why not let me die?"

She turned her head and looked at him. Her eyes suddenly filled with a strange light. "Because I was told not to."

"By whom?"

"There is a priest waiting outside," she said, ignoring his question. "He wishes to speak with you but is afraid to cross my threshold. Superstitious fool!" This last she muttered under her breath.

"If what you say is true, then I doubt he needs more than to see with his own eyes that I still live," Aleksei told her. "He is a priest and will be believed. The villagers will know they have nothing to fear."

"No," the witch said, giving him a thoughtful look. "That is not why he has come."

"Then why?"

She answered with a shrug of her bony shoulders.

"Then perhaps I should speak with him." Getting to his feet, Aleksei lost the wolf skin covering him and blushed. Old Magda might be a witch, but she was also a woman, and she wasn't so old that the sight of a naked young man wouldn't be appreciated. She handed him a rough woven blanket, and his embarrassment intensified.

"Stay where you are," she clucked irritably. "I will tell the fool to come inside."

There followed a series of shrieks and screams as priest and witch cursed each other from outside the door, but eventually a compromise was reached. Still, it did not sit well with Aleksei to know the priest was risking his own soul just to speak with him. What could be so important?

Magda—Aleksei couldn't think of her as "old" anymore—came in first and immediately went to the farthest corner of the room, where she concealed herself in the shadows. Concealed or not, Aleksei could feel her eyes upon him.

The priest, clutching his crucifix in his hand, fell to his knees as close to the door as possible and began praying fervently. Aleksei wondered if the man realized that the sooner he stated his business, the sooner he could leave.

Although he attended church as both a dutiful son and as the head of his family, Aleksei didn't think of himself as being particularly religious. He had never felt a spiritual connection to God, and so he neither believed nor disbelieved. And knowing Count Petrov prayed to the same God only served to solidify Aleksei's doubts. How could a God that was benevolent and all-forgiving allow his sister to be violated in such a way by such a man? The idea made him feel more estranged than ever from the church and its teachings—something the man now praying so ardently would be disappointed to know.

As the priest paused to take a breath, Aleksei seized his moment.

"What do you want with me?" he asked, grabbing the man's fore-arm. "Has the count sent you?" It was a possibility. Given time to re-flect on his actions, Nikolayev might have had a change of heart regarding his order that Aleksei live a long life.

The priest stared at him in confusion, shaking his head before peel-ing Aleksei's hand off his arm. "I am here because of the demon," he said in a frightened whisper.

From the shadows, Magda laughed softly.

"What demon? Are you talking about the count?"

Something in the priest's eyes told him they weren't thinking about the same thing.

"What demon?" Aleksei asked, repeating his question with more suspicion a second time.

"The one that waits for you, my son." The priest dropped his voice to a whisper, as if he was worried the demon might be listen-ing. "The one that has come for your soul."

Aleksei didn't know whether to laugh or cry. It made perfect sense that, if someone wanted to claim his soul, it would be one of Satan's minions. "And have you seen this demon, priest, with your own eyes?"

The man bobbed his head up and down a number of times. "In-deed I have, my son."

"And how does he look? Are there horns on his head? Does he have cloven feet and a forked tail?"

The priest looked disappointed as he shook his head.

"Then how do you know he is a demon?" Aleksei demanded, sus-piciously.

"Because he looks like an angel."

Aleksei decided the priest had definitely partaken of someone's homemade brew. A demon that looked like an angel? The man was talking nonsense!

"I see the doubt in your face, my son," the priest continued, "but you must believe me when I tell you though he may look like an angel, God has shown me the darkness that hides in his heart."

Nonsense or not, it was obvious the man believed what he was saying to be true. "Where is he now, this demon of yours?"

"Not mine!" the priest shrieked in protest, springing to his feet and making the sign of the cross with such vigor, Aleksei thought he

might sprain his shoulder. "It is your soul he has come to claim—and he holds the others hostage!"

Alarm threaded its way through Aleksei. "What others? What do you mean?"

It was difficult to know who the priest feared more, the demon or Aleksei. "Your family," he said with a terrified roll of his eyes. "The demon holds your dead family hostage."

Aleksei was outraged. "My family? Do you mean—are you saying no one has attended to my family?" He might be ambivalent about God, but his mother and siblings had not been. The idea that no one had seen to their bodies, prepared them for burial, was horrifying to him. "You call yourself a priest!" He spat on the floor.

The cleric wailed pitifully in his defense. "The demon . . . the demon will not allow any to approach!"

Aleksei narrowed his eyes and stared at the priest. A young man, he wasn't much older than Aleksei. Why would a demon show himself to a man of God with so little experience? "And you say this demon is at my home? Waiting for me?"

The priest nodded frantically and resumed crossing himself. If Aleksei had doubts about God, then it seemed hypocritical of him to believe in the existence of demons. But the damn fool of a holy man wasn't going to leave him alone until he had seen this supposed evil spirit with his own eyes. The temptation to shake his fist in condemnation was a strong one, but then Aleksei decided that perhaps this meeting would be a good thing. It might resolve his uncertainty about God one way or the other.

"You will come with me," Aleksei ordered the priest.

Aleksei was certain that, having relayed the information to its intended recipient, the priest wanted nothing more to do with the matter. Or him. He waited, fully expecting to hear some flimsy excuse for not making the journey, but the priest did no such thing. Closing his eyes, he began to pray, muttering under his breath and pausing only to kiss the crucifix he wore around his neck a good many times. But he did not refuse to accompany Aleksei. Perhaps his inexperience was a blessing.

The priest yanked the door open. "I will wait for you . . . outside," he called back over his shoulder before closing the door behind him.

Wearily, Aleksei looked around for anything that might resemble clothes. He took a few steps and staggered a little. The feel of a hand pulling the rough blanket from him said Magda had emerged from the shadows. She put her hand around his waist to steady him. No doubt the priest would have been shocked to see her touching his naked body in so familiar a way, but now that he was over his embarrassment, Aleksei found he didn't care.

The witch handed him a bundle of clothes that were not his own. They smelled of another man, another farmer, judging from the faint aroma of manure. "Yours could not be saved," she said by way of explanation. Aleksei dressed, surprised when she handed him his own boots. "Only your clothes could not be saved," she grunted by way of explanation. "These are good boots with many miles still to be walked."

"So what do you think?" Aleksei took the boots from her and put them on. He was curious to know her opinion. "Do you believe there's a demon waiting for me?"

Sticking two bony fingers into a bowl, Magda began coating the aching wound on his face with a thick salve. "It will help with the pain and the healing," she told him, "but I don't think the girls will find you quite so handsome anymore."

Aleksei grunted. Attracting the attention of a woman was the last thing on his mind.

"Still, it might be that you will find a woman who will not care about such things." She pressed her hand to his chest. "A woman who can see what is here."

There was nothing else to say, and although he was disappointed that she had deliberately ignored his question about the demon, Aleksei stepped back and bowed. It was the only way he knew to thank her for her kindness. And he didn't do it out of fear of her anger. He did it out of respect and because it was the right thing to do. A sudden frown creased his brow as he recalled the man in the dacha's kitchen. He had thanked him as well. Had that been a mistake?

Magda's hand on his arm stopped him as he turned to leave. "It was nothing but water, Aleksei, pure water from a secret spring that was birthed by the mountains. That is what I used to soothe your raging throat." He felt his face flush that she knew he had thought it might be poison. "And it is no demon that waits for you. Do not fear him, Aleksei. Take what he offers . . . or not. The choice is yours."

Outside, Aleksei was surprised to find Konstantine and his cart waiting. The old man gave him a toothless grin, and Aleksei knew who was responsible for bringing him to the witch. The priest was already settled in the back of the cart, but not wanting to share the journey with an unending recitation of prayers, Aleksei seated himself next to the old man.

It was a long journey, made even longer by the slow, plodding gait of the horse, but Aleksei minded neither the distance nor the cold. Something was waiting for him, and, in case it was a demon, these might be his last moments on earth. It was a sobering thought.

As they rumbled through the village, Aleksei could feel the eyes of every single person who lived there watching him. But no one came out to offer any condolences. They were all too terrified he would bring the wrath of the Petrov family down upon them. At the place where the dirt track turned off toward what had once been his home, Aleksei stopped Konstantine. The smell of burned timber mixed with the aroma of charred hide and hoof and flesh still hung heavy in the air.

"No farther, old man," Aleksei said softly, patting him on the arm. This time there was no mistaking the tears that ran down either side of Konstantine's nose. He opened his mouth but, unable to find words, closed it again. Aleksei nodded. Sometimes the best words were ones that were not spoken. "Take him back to the church," he said, nodding at the priest seated in the back. Not having taken the initiative to get down from the cart, the priest had plainly gone as far as he was willing to go. It was enough. Whatever waited for him, Aleksei would face it on his own.

Chapter 15

Gabriel watched the exchange of words between the driver and his companion before the man got down from the cart. He was pleased to note that the priest had no intention of joining the man, who now continued on foot. In fact, the priest's frantic arm waving seemed to be the cleric's way of urging the driver to put as much distance between themselves and the fork in the road as possible. Gabriel could have told him he was wasting his time. The horse had only one speed. It took a while, but eventually the priest stopped waving his arms.

Gabriel grunted softly. It was exhausting watching the priest flail about like that. If only he would put as much effort into tending to the needs of those he proclaimed to serve. With the cart and its passengers no longer a concern, Gabriel turned his attention to the figure making its way through the snow.

In truth, he was surprised to see him. Others in the past had abandoned their loved ones rather than face him, and it made him wonder what the priest had said to persuade Aleksei to return. Perhaps he hadn't had to say anything at all. It might be that the man would have returned of his own accord. Seeing Aleksei stumble, Gabriel narrowed his eyes. He would know the measure of his character soon enough, and that would decide everything.

It wasn't the scent of spilled blood that had brought Gabriel to this place. It was the loss of innocent lives. Even though over the course of the centuries he had taken more human lives than could ever be counted, he never took the truly innocent. He never took the life of a child.

After examining the bodies lying in the snow, their throats slashed in a fit of pique by a man who believed it was his right to do so, Gabriel felt compelled to stay. Someone had escaped the grotesque tableau.

Separate splashes of blood in the snow, away from the bodies, told him there was a survivor. A man, judging from the depth of the footprints left by those who'd carried him away. And he was curious to know what kind of man could so inflame another's rage that he would slaughter an entire family. So he stayed that night, watching as the buildings burned to the ground. Then, as other predators were drawn to the carnage, he let them know one far more deadly had already claimed the bodies.

Gabriel had observed many rituals involving human burial. From the simplest to the most elaborate, there was one commonality linking them. The cleansing of the deceased body. So when the priest appeared at first light, he assumed it was to perform that task. But the cleric had come only to satisfy his own morbid curiosity as to the cause of death, and after investigating the vicious slashes across each throat, he turned to go without so much as offering a single prayer.

"Is it not your custom to bury the dead?" Gabriel asked, stepping from the shadows of the burned-out house.

Startled, the priest lost his footing and slipped on the packed snow. One hand immediately disappeared inside his coat, emerging a moment later tightly clasping a crucifix, which he held out in front of him. "W-w-what are you?" he stammered in a voice that wavered.

Gabriel frowned. His feelings of outrage at the priest's apparent indifference toward the dead had made him careless, allowing the man to see a hint of his true nature in his face. Why else would he have asked "What are you?" instead of the more customary "Who are you?" Ignoring the man's words, Gabriel repeated himself. "Is it not your custom to bury the dead?"

The cleric nodded his head, the grip on the crucifix turning his bony knuckles white.

"Then why are you not preparing the bodies?"

"We c-cannot—the c-count has f-forbidden it!" The priest's voice rose in agitation.

"Forbidden?"

"H-he has d-decreed that any who set foot on this land will f-forfeit their own and b-be b-banished." It was hard to know if it was fear or cold that made the priest stammer.

"So you are defying him?"

The man on the ground shook his head. "The ch-church is exempt. Even the c-count fears f-for his soul."

"His actions would seem to proclaim otherwise," Gabriel commented. The priest scrambled to his knees and crossed himself a number of times. He then clasped both hands around the crucifix, locked his elbows, and thrust his arms into the air. He also began praying. Loudly. Dropping to his haunches, Gabriel placed one hand over the crucifix and grabbed the front of the priest's coat with the other. "Where is the one they left alive?" he asked.

The priest appeared shocked that the demon before him could touch the blessed item in his hand without any ill effects. "They t-took him to the w-witch."

"A priest and a witch in the same village? How convenient."

"If he d-dies under her h-hand, the c-count will not hold us responsible."

Gabriel narrowed his eyes and pulled the priest closer. "Make sure he returns, priest."

"For w-what p-p-purpose?" the man wailed.

"Someone needs to see to the dead."

As he made his way through the heavy snowfall, Aleksei was forced to conclude he was weaker than he realized. Either that or the path had somehow become much steeper since the last time he'd walked it. The fire in his lungs and the tremors in his legs forced him to stop more than once. And when he did, he noticed the only sound he could hear was his own labored breathing as he blew clouds of vapor into the frigid air. The silence unnerved him. He should have been able to hear the cawing of crows, but all that surrounded him was a blanket of ominous silence. Had the birds been scared off by the demon or Count Petrov? Was there any difference between the two? With a grunt, he continued on his way. The cold numbed his face so he could no longer feel the dull, throbbing ache of his cheek. So far it was the only good thing that had come of his effort.

The house and barn were nothing more than blackened timbers, and despite the layer of snow, Aleksei felt certain that it would take only a few kicks to uncover smoldering embers. Another heavy snowfall, however, would take care of that and, hopefully, the terrible smell that lingered. He'd never thought the smell of burned animal flesh would turn his stomach, but perhaps it was the circumstances that made him feel so nauseous.

The sun, such as it was, had begun to slip toward the horizon, marking the end of the day. "Idiot!" Aleksei muttered to himself. He had not thought to bring a light, and it would be dark soon. He might need to revisit the idea of finding some embers in the hopes of building a fire. If nothing else, it would keep the predators at bay. Just because the crows had abandoned his land, the same wasn't necessarily true of other creatures. Like wolves.

The thought filled him with alarm. If, as the priest had said, his mother and the children were still lying where they had fallen, then it stood to reason that predators might have already found them. The idea made him feel wretched, and he fell to his knees, making horrible noises as he vomited up whatever Magda had poured down his throat. She had told him it was water, but he doubted that's all it was. Grabbing a handful of snow, he rubbed it vigorously over his face, not caring if dirt penetrated his ragged cheek. He didn't know how he was going to do it, and cared not if it was frowned upon by the church, but somehow he was going to bury his family. Even if it meant clawing at the ground with his bare hands. Steeling himself, he made his way to where Nikolayev had murdered them.

They were gone.

He had prepared himself for the possibility of seeing partially eaten corpses, and he looked around for evidence that might indicate the bodies had been dragged away. But the snow was pristine; the only tracks visible were those left by his footprints. There was just one explanation—it was the demon! The priest had warned him, but Aleksei had thought the man a fool. Now he knew better. His mother, Larissa, sweet Sofia, and the twins had all been taken to hell at Satan's bidding.

With no bodies to bury, no family to mourn, he sank to his knees and began to weep. His chin struck his chest with each shuddering intake of breath.

"Do you mean to remain on your knees all night?"

A chill ran down his back. The voice reminded him of a fine bear skin, the thick, glossy fur hiding the menace of teeth and claws. It was also disturbingly arousing. Frozen in his current position, Aleksei turned his head to see the creature that had addressed him. If he was meant to die at this being's hand, then he wanted to look him in the eye before giving up his life.

A figure came out from the shadows, and long, elegant fingers stretched themselves out toward him. "I will graciously accept a woman being on her knees," the voice said, with a hint of sly amusement, "but only if it is her choice. A man in the same position is not something that tempts me." The fingers curled, beckoning to him. "And I can see that you are at a loss as to my meaning."

Without thinking, Aleksei grasped the hand offered and felt himself being pulled to his feet with very little effort on the stranger's part.

"Definitely weaker," he muttered under his breath.

Slight movement at the corners of the man's mouth told him his words had been heard. It was foolish to give away an advantage. Although if his progress up the steep path had been observed, then his body's limitations were already known. Was the man here at the behest of the count, sent to either finish him off or confirm he still drew breath? Aleksei looked at his clothing, which, though strange to him, seemed of a very fine quality and appeared to be more than adequate to protect against the elements. Likewise his boots appeared sturdy, and although he wore no gloves or scarf about his face, he seemed not unduly bothered by the cold.

Unsure what to do next, Aleksei stared at the man with frank openness. The stranger stood a full head taller than himself, and had shoulders that were wider and a chest that was broader than his own. Aleksei was considered one of the strongest men in his village, with the well-developed physique that came from a life of manual labor. But now, in comparison, he looked as weak as he felt. His gaze went back to the face, which was framed by hair as white as the fallen snow. Aleksei had never seen hair that color, and in the stranger's brilliant blue eyes he saw the hint of something tragic. A terrible loss. One that continued to haunt him.

Was this whom the priest had seen? Was this the demon he had been warned about? Except, now that Aleksei looked at him, he saw the stranger wasn't a demon at all. He was something else. How could the priest have made such a mistake? Hadn't his mother told him about the creatures that walked the night? But then perhaps this being had found no reason to smile at the priest and had not revealed himself as he was now.

"You know what I am." It wasn't a question, but a confirmation.

There were many names for a being such as he. Seducer of the Night, Consort of the Dead, and others that were even more poetic in *nature. But Aleksei was a simple man and didn't know how to hide the truth with ambiguity.*

"You are a drinker of blood." The head of white blond hair acknowledged the truth with a single nod, and to Aleksei it seemed the honesty of his reply was appreciated. "Did you take my family?" he blurted out.

"Take them . . . ?" The hand that had helped Aleksei to stand was now held out in protest. "Of course not. We do not feed from the dead."

"Then where are they?"

"I moved them."

"You—you moved them? Where?"

The long white hair fell like a curtain over his shoulder as the creature turned his head. "I put them inside the house. It was easier to watch over them in there," he added by way of explanation.

Inside the house? There was no house. There were no walls, half the roof was gone, and what was left was being held up by two timbers that would probably collapse in the next stiff breeze. How would it be easier to watch over his family in there?

"Even the wolves know when to fear the shadows," came the answer.

A lump in his throat robbed Aleksei of speech as he entered the ruined dwelling and looked at the bodies that lay next to each other on the floor. The priest, he realized, had been wrong about this also, because someone had taken the time to prepare them for burial. The skin was freshly washed, the hair clean and curling in soft waves around each face. It looked to Aleksei as if his mother and siblings were asleep instead of dead.

As was the custom, each of them was dressed in a clean white robe with coins resting on their closed eyelids. There was also a length of white linen wrapped about each throat. This, Aleksei knew, was not customary, but nevertheless he was glad of it. He did not know if he was strong enough to be reminded of how each life had been so cruelly stolen.

"Why would you do such a thing?" Aleksei asked, gesturing to his family. This was completely unexpected, and he could feel emotion swelling inside of him. "You do not know me, nor I you."

The vampire shrugged his shoulders. "No one else was coming to attend to them, and this is your custom, is it not?"

"The priest told me—" Aleksei broke off, suddenly too ashamed to repeat the cleric's words.

"Ah yes, the priest." He made no attempt to hide his disdain for the cleric.

Aleksei couldn't even begin to imagine what the church would do if they knew a vampire had been responsible for preparing his family for burial. A hand rested on his shoulder, and he found the weight strangely comforting. *"What did your holy man tell you?"* the vampire asked.

"He said that a demon would let no one approach." Aleksei paused and then blurted out, *"Is that true?"* An odd light shone in the depths of the other's brilliant blue eyes, and for a moment Aleksei could have sworn a circle of gold rimmed each pupil.

"We'll never know, Aleksei, because no one in your village was brave enough to defy your liege lord." The hand was dropped with a sigh.

Although confused by the vampire's words, Aleksei was certain he grasped their meaning. He also noticed the vampire called him by name. *"You know my name?"* he queried.

"I know the name of everyone in the village."

"Ah . . . truthfully?"

"Truthfully."

Aleksei absorbed this information. To his mind it would be a terrible burden carrying all those names in his head. *"When you said liege lord, you meant . . ."*

"Nikolayev Vasily Petrov. He gave orders that any who set foot on your land would forfeit their own. The exception being your holy man."

"So he came to help you?" It would also explain how the priest had seen him.

"No, he did not. Even though I did nothing to him, I knew he would not return. I told him to send you."

A sudden anger flared in Aleksei at the priest's cowardice. The hand now returned to his shoulder, its companion grasping his opposite arm, and Aleksei found himself staring into the vampire's eyes. The blue was quite hypnotic and made him think there were worse ways for a man to die. *"Do not be afraid of me, Aleksei, for I mean you no harm."*

What had the witch told him? *". . . it is no demon that waits for you. Do not fear him, Aleksei. Take what he offers ... or not. The choice is yours ... "*

"You can ask me anything—anything at all—and I promise to be truthful."

Aleksei blurted out the only thing he could think of, "What is your name?"

Chapter 16

Gabriel smiled. Of all the things Aleksei could have asked him, he'd requested a simple courtesy. *What is your name?*

"I've been called many things in my time, including demon," he chuckled, "but you may call me Gabriel." Aleksei's gasp made Gabriel silently curse the priest. No doubt the peasant was wondering how he dared call himself by such an angelic name without bursting into a pillar of flame. "It is the name I was given," he told Aleksei, easily reading the unspoken question on his face.

He could also see another question that the peasant farmer was struggling not to ask. *Named by whom? Who would dare to call him thus?* Gabriel waited, but when Aleksei turned his head, he realized he would not ask. There were some things it was better not to know. Besides, Gabriel thought to himself, would Aleksei have believed him if he had told him?

"I need to bury my family," he said. The weariness lining his face was also carried in his voice.

"I do not think your priest will allow them in your churchyard," Gabriel told him solemnly.

"Because of you?"

"Partly," Gabriel admitted, "although I think perhaps his fear of Count Petrov is far greater than his fear of me, which is foolish. But if it is important to you, then we will take them there."

Aleksei shook his head. "No. The villagers will only dig them up and put them somewhere else."

Gabriel sighed, acknowledging the truth and absurdity of such action. "The body is merely a shell," he said, offering what comfort he could. "It reminds those left behind of what once was. This rite of burial is, I think, more to console the living than the dead."

Aleksei didn't disagree. "But what about their souls?" he asked. "What happens to them if the body is not laid to rest in consecrated ground?"

"What do you think happens to a man slain in battle? Is his soul doomed if he falls on foreign soil?" Gabriel could tell from the other man's expression that he had never thought about this. Was he never curious about the world beyond his village? "I promise you the souls of your family are in a better place," he told Aleksei.

"How can you be so sure?" he challenged in a hoarse whisper.

Unexpectedly disconcerted by Aleksei's distress, Gabriel softened his tone. "I was not always the being you see before you. I know when a soul has departed and where it has gone. Trust me when I tell you that your family does not walk the paths of darkness." This time he put both hands on Aleksei's shoulders. "Lay them to rest in the ground, and you will feel better for it."

"And what then?"

"Then I will help you with Count Petrov."

"Help me how?"

Apparently Aleksei had forgotten to whom he was talking.

Gabriel dropped his hands from the other man's shoulders, took a step back, and said, "Why, to kill him, of course. Is that not what you wish for?"

There was a strange whistling sound as Aleksei sucked in a breath. Thinking of taking the count's life was one thing, but hearing it said aloud was another.

Aleksei nodded in reply, and Gabriel couldn't decide if it was shock or elation that silenced his tongue.

"Are you going to make me the same as you?" The words came out in an almost unintelligible rush, as if Aleksei was worried he'd lose the courage to ask if he spoke at a normal rate.

Though disappointed by his request, Gabriel was not surprised. "Is that what you wish for?"

"How else would you help me?"

Gabriel sighed. "The count is not a vampire, and to make you one for this purpose would give you an unfair advantage."

"Not from where I'm standing," Aleksei muttered under his breath.

Choosing to overlook the comment, Gabriel continued. "If that is

*what you want, then you could ask me to act on your behalf. I could
return before light with the count's head."*

He could feel Aleksei eyeing him speculatively, seriously considering the possibility of having the vampire kill Nikolayev for him.
"No," Aleksei said finally. "I want him to know who is taking his life
and why."

Gabriel gave his own nod, this one of approval. "Very well, then
I will teach you how to defeat him as a man."

"And after that will you make me a vampire?"

Now it was Gabriel's turn to look questioningly at the Russian
farmer. "Only with good reason."

"Is not my asking reason enough?" He sounded surprised that
Gabriel would refuse him.

"It is not something to be undertaken lightly. You know nothing
about what will be expected of you or what you will be asked to give up."

"Everything that I love has already been taken from me," Aleksei
said bitterly. "What more can I possibly lose?"

"All that you have left," Gabriel whispered.

Aleksei decided that the field behind the burned ruins of the barn
was where he would lay his family to rest. Even though it was
Gabriel who did the digging, the hard ground did not yield easily,
and it was almost dawn before four graves had been dug. His brothers, inseparable in life, were buried together. Aleksei couldn't imagine separating them now. He also noted Gabriel had made each
grave deeper than was usual. Hunger, he knew, could motivate an
animal to desperate measures, and his family would be laid in the
bare earth with no coffins to shield their remains.

Aleksei insisted on placing each body in its grave himself, taxing
what was left of his waning strength. Gabriel did not offer to help
him, understanding why it was important for Aleksei to do this alone.
When it was over, he sank to the ground, chest heaving and muscles
trembling, as he watched Gabriel cover them with a blanket of earth.
Sunrise was painting the sky when they were finally done.

"They will have no markers," Aleksei mumbled more to himself
than Gabriel.

"You know where they lie. You will always know."

"What happens now?" he asked, looking at the vampire, who
seemed not in the least fatigued by the night's exertions.

"Now we must leave this place."

For the second time that night, Gabriel helped Aleksei to his feet, leading him back toward the path he had recently struggled to walk. It was hard to believe that only a few hours had passed since then. To Aleksei it felt like years. Gesturing with his arm, Gabriel pointed to where a carriage now waited in the place where Konstantine's cart had left him. The horses, black as midnight, snorted and pawed impatiently at the ground.

"Where will we go?" Aleksei asked, sounding neither excited nor alarmed by the prospect.

"St. Petersburg." The name was not unknown to Aleksei. He recalled hearing the priest discussing the naming of the city for the tsar with the village elders.

"What is in St. Petersburg?"

"Count Nikolayev Vasily Petrov."

"He has left here?" Aleksei sounded surprised.

Gabriel nodded. *"Three days ago."*

"Three days?" Aleksei repeated, coming to a sudden halt. *"The count has been gone for three days?"* He couldn't believe that not a single person in the village had come to tend to the slain bodies of his family.

"They fear the count more than they love you. You have no place here anymore, Aleksei. You are an outcast."

Grasping hold of the other man's elbow, Gabriel steered him firmly down the path, tightening his grip to make sure Aleksei didn't fall as they continued through the snow. Before Aleksei realized it, he was seated inside the carriage with a large fur wrapped around him.

"There is nothing left for you here," Gabriel told him as he leaned inside the door. *"My man Tomas will take you straight on to St. Petersburg."* He indicated the driver, a solid, compact figure dressed to withstand the elements who looked at Aleksei with compassion. The vampire nodded at a basket set on the opposite seat. *"There's food and drink in there. Use the extra furs if you are cold."*

"You will allow me to travel alone?" Twice in his life Aleksei had traveled beyond the borders of Count Petrov's land, and in each case it had been necessary to seek permission. *"What if we are stopped? What am I to say?"*

"It is doubtful you will be stopped, but if it should happen, Tomas will speak for you." Gabriel's hair began to shimmer in the early-

morning light. "*Now I must find a place to rest until nightfall, but do not fear, we will meet again soon.*"

"*And what happens then?*"

"*Then, my friend, Nikolayev Vasily Petrov will answer for what he has done.*"

Aleksei's attack on Nikolayev had been fueled by an all-consuming rage—one that obliterated anything resembling rational thought, or even the consequences such reckless action would bring. Now, with the aftermath weighing on his soul, he was ashamed to admit he had given no thought to what might happen as a result of his impulsiveness. But even if he had stopped to consider all the ways Count Petrov might retaliate, Aleksei would never have believed he would murder his family. The loss of his own life was an event Aleksei thought more probable than possible, but to slit the throats of his mother? His sisters? His brothers? Such a horror had never occurred to him.

Had he known Petrov would strike back so viciously, he would have found another way to make him pay for his deed. But he could not change the past. What was done was done, and it had brought new challenges for him to deal with. He did not doubt that Gabriel would help him find the count. When a being such as he made a promise, it was never broken. Which was why the priests always warned about conversing with demons; they were sly and could trick a human into parting with his soul with only a few words.

But Gabriel wasn't a demon. At least not the kind the church meant. And as far as Aleksei could tell, he had no interest in his soul or anything else a poor peasant farmer might possess. But he was a creature of the night, a drinker of blood, and although he had not tried to hurt Aleksei, that didn't mean he couldn't. Or wouldn't. Perhaps there would be a price for accepting his help. Perhaps Gabriel would slit his throat and drink his blood. But as long as Petrov was already dead, then it was a bargain Aleksei could agree to. Until then, he would pass each day following whatever directives were issued by the enigmatic Tomas.

Aleksei wasn't sure how to define the relationship between the vampire and his carriage driver. He had assumed that Tomas was a servant, but after witnessing the two men in conversation with each other, it was obvious their relationship was something more meaningful. Aleksei would not go as far as to say they were equals; Tomas *deferred to Gabriel more often than not, but a definite respect existed between the two. He recalled the stories he had heard about blood drinkers, about how they sometimes would take a companion. Tomas was obviously such a companion, but the storytellers, Aleksei decided, had been wrong about the preferred gender and species of these companions. Tomas was neither female nor, Aleksei suspected, human. At least not entirely.*

He couldn't say why he thought such a thing. Tomas had done nothing to suggest he was anything other than what he appeared to be, but there was an air about him, a sense of unexplainable strength and mystical power. Sometimes, when Tomas was around, Aleksei felt a prickle on the back of his neck. It was something he did not ignore even though he had no reason to believe Tomas meant him any harm. Indeed, if the vampire's companion wanted to hurt him, he had already been given the opportunity to do so.

After arriving in St. Petersburg, Aleksei spent the first few days in a fugue-like state, unable to discern dream from reality. He vaguely recalled Tomas pressing a goblet to his lips, bidding him to slake his thirst with the contents. He drank, but the cool liquid did more than ease his parched throat. It opened the doorway to oblivion. When he next awoke, he was surprised to discover he no longer felt the burning ache of Magda's handiwork on his face. The ragged edges of his cheek had now turned into a much smoother seam.

"It was too late for me to undo the witch's handiwork," Tomas told him solemnly, "and some of the damage to your skin was beyond even my skill to repair, but when you meet the right woman she will not notice it." Magda had said much the same thing.

"It is healed?" Aleksei asked in surprise as he ran his fingers cautiously over his cheek. There was no longer any crude stitching holding the edges of his skin together. All he could feel was a slight ridge in the contour of his face. "But . . . how long have I been here?"

"Three days," Tomas told him with a satisfied smile.

"Three days? That is all?" It felt like much, much longer. Aleksei touched his face again and then stared at the tips of his fingers. There was no blood, and the wound was dry. He moved his jaw, stretching it experimentally, and felt the skin begin to pull.

"Enough!" Tomas snapped, losing his smile and turning irritable. "If you tear it open, I promise I will make the witch look like the

finest seamstress in all of Russia after I stitch it back together." Alek-
sei apologized at once. "Give it a week," Tomas said, "and then you
can make all the faces you want."

Instead of hurting him, Gabriel's companion had healed him.

"You have tasked our guest with cleaning the stables?" Gabriel
raised a questioning brow and turned to look at his sentinel.

"He is not used to being idle," Tomas answered matter-of-factly.
It was a few days later, and even Tomas had been impressed at how
fast Aleksei had healed. "He needs to be kept busy. It will help him
regain his strength."

"The horses seem to like him," Gabriel noted.

"That's because he sings to them." Seeing the surprised look on
Gabriel's face, Tomas chuckled softly. It was good to see something
spark the vampire's interest again.

"Is he still sleeping with them?"

Tomas responded with a nod of his head before adding, "I think it
will be some time before you can persuade him to return to the bed-
room upstairs."

The sumptuous furnishings in the room given to Aleksei had
proved too much for him to deal with. He'd experienced an almost
overwhelming sensory overload that sent him reeling. On hearing
that the massive piece of furniture dominating the room was in fact a
bed that he was expected to sleep in, he succumbed to his very first
anxiety attack. Dazed and confused, he'd stumbled from the room,
trying to put as much distance as possible between himself and the
monstrous bed.

Tomas understood immediately why a peasant farmer would be-
come agitated. He waited until Aleksei returned to his normal self
before asking him where he would prefer to sleep, and showed no
surprise at his answer, agreeing that the stables were a good choice.

"It will take time," Tomas told Gabriel. "Your farmer does not
yet fully comprehend that his life now belongs to him, that he is free
to make his own choices. When he decides he no longer wants to
sleep in the barn, it will be an important step for him, one he must be
permitted to make in his own time."

Gabriel sighed in agreement. He had tried explaining to Aleksei
that he was a guest in his house, but the concept was too alien for the
peasant to grasp. Born and raised a serf, as his father had been be-

fore him, Aleksei was the property of his landowner. It never oc-
curred to him that what had happened could change the dynamics of
this relationship. Being born into servitude was not something easily
dismissed. The idea that he was now answerable to no one but him-
self, that he could make decisions about his life, was hard for him to
comprehend. Particularly when the person telling him he was no
longer answerable to Count Petrov was the vampire who would help
him kill his former lord and master.

As difficult as it might be, Gabriel was forced to accept that, for
the time being at least, Aleksei felt more at ease with someone telling
him what to do.

"I think it is time you engaged him in a different form of instruc-
tion," Gabriel said, turning to his sentinel. "Although I can person-
ally attest to its usefulness as a weapon, I think Aleksei should
prepare to meet his adversary armed with something other than a
pitchfork."

"So you do intend for them to meet?"

Gabriel regarded his sentinel with a look of surprise. "You think
it should not happen?"

"I wondered if you might change your mind," Tomas admitted
with a slight shrug of his shoulders. "You appear in no hurry to find
the count."

"That's because I already know where he is," Gabriel said, re-
vealing the tips of his fangs. "His location has never been the issue.
I needed to be certain that the desire to act on words spoken in grief
still remain true."

"The farmer has not changed his mind," Tomas assured him.

"Indeed," Gabriel said, his fangs lengthening. "He appears un-
wavering in his desire for vengeance."

"And what makes this the time to strike?"

"An opportunity has presented itself, one that will work in our
favor. The count and his wife are giving a winter ball to which I will
be invited. It should be a simple enough matter to let Petrov know
Aleksei will be waiting to meet him in order to settle their differ-
ences."

"Meet him where?" Tomas suspected Gabriel had already deter-
mined the exact location, ensuring the circumstances would be in
their favor.

"There are a great many empty rooms in the count's house. One located near the back hallway will afford Aleksei the greatest chance of leaving unseen."

"So you anticipate he will be victorious."

"With your tutelage . . . yes."

Looking out the window, vampire and sentinel observed the subject of their discussion now engaged in grooming one of his stable mates. There was no doubt that Aleksei possessed the physical strength for his purpose, but fighting this time would be different. Petrov, no doubt expecting a country brawl, would be prepared. The odds had to be changed to give Aleksei the advantage. To teach him a different way to fight. To teach him to win. The best any of them could do was hope Aleksei was a quick learner. As if eager to demonstrate their faith was not misplaced, the horse tried to nip his groomer in the side. Aleksei evaded the large teeth with a deft movement that hinted of untapped grace.

"Does he really sing to them?" Gabriel asked, sounding slightly bemused.

"Yes," Tomas replied, *"lullabies mostly, but I suspect they're all he knows."*

"And I thought there were no surprises left in the world."

Tomas muttered something indistinguishable under his breath.

"Begin the training tomorrow," Gabriel instructed. *"I think I'd like to hear for myself what lullabies are sending my horses to sleep."*

"I doubt he'll be so forthcoming if he knows you are listening," Tomas warned.

"And what makes you think he will even know I am there?" Gabriel smiled at his sentinel, his eyes shining with an iridescent glow.

Chapter 17

The sound of classical music suddenly filling the air made us all jump. Thanks to Gabriel's determination to broaden my musical horizons, I recognized "Ode to Joy" from Beethoven's Ninth Symphony. It took me a minute or two to realize where it was coming from. "Is that my phone?"

"You said you didn't really care for the ring tone, so I reprogrammed it," Gabriel confessed. I couldn't deny it. Katy Perry *had* been driving me batty for a little while now. "I thought it would be a nice surprise."

I took the mobile from his outstretched hand, my irritation with him forgotten the moment I checked caller ID. It was Laycee. I got to my feet and headed out of the room. "I gotta take this." I said it as a general apology. It seemed wrong to have any type of normal conversation within the same four walls where Aleksei had just described the slaughter of his family.

"Is everything all right?" Gabriel asked when I returned five minutes later.

I nodded. "It was Laycee. She's had the baby."

"Oh, how wonderful!" Anasztaizia exclaimed, squeezing Aleksei's hand and looking genuinely pleased by the news.

"She wants to see me," I said, looking at Gabriel.

He knew how much this meant to me. I hadn't been sure that Laycee would ever reach out to me again, not after refusing to invite Gabriel into my old house once she and Jake became its new owners. Laycee didn't want vampires in her life, and though I could understand her reasons, I was also saddened by her decision to exclude Gabriel. Now I was overwhelmed by his generosity at buying me the apartment, which was the perfect compromise. He understood—better, I think, than either Laycee or I did—just how important we were to each other. And how difficult and unnecessary severing our friendship was. And now she had reached out to me with an olive branch.

"Of course she wants to see you," Gabriel said, putting his arms around me and brushing his lips over mine. "And you must go to her. I'll drive you and I'll stay in the waiting room while you visit."

It was going to be a long time before I was allowed to go anywhere by myself. I couldn't blame Gabriel for being protective, and truth be told, I felt better knowing he would be with me. But as excited as I was about seeing Laycee and Jake's baby, I felt bad about leaving Aleksei and Anasztaizia.

"No, you must go," Aleksei said. Sensing my reluctance to leave, he got up from his seat and came to me. "I think this would be a good time for Anasztaizia and me to spend some time alone." He swallowed up my hands in his. "This has been difficult for her to hear, so I'm thinking a time-out, yes?"

I nodded my head in agreement. That sounded like a very good idea.

Laycee's new daughter almost made her entrance into the world in the back of her father's police cruiser. Her mother, however, had other ideas. Hell would freeze over before Laycee would let her child slide out onto a seat that had last been graced by the butt of someone with possible criminal tendencies. Needing no other incentive than the threat of never having sex again, Jake hadn't taken any chances. Hitting the cruiser's siren, he'd committed more than a few traffic violations on his way to the hospital. Thirty minutes and a half dozen hard pushes later, his daughter greeted the world.

Laycee had waited until after the rest of her family had all left before calling me. She said she wanted to make sure I wasn't going to be pestered by any awkward questions about Gabriel. I knew her intentions were good, but I wished she hadn't felt it necessary. I could deal with questions about Gabriel, awkward or otherwise. Of course, I had no intention of telling her that.

Propped up in bed, hair brushed, lashes tinted, and wearing just a hint of lip gloss, Laycee looked gloriously radiant. Like Madonna. Jesus's mom, not the singer.

"Hey you," I said, kissing her brow, "where's the proud papa?"

"I hope at home in bed, sleeping," Laycee said, giving me a smile that couldn't quite hide her weariness. "He'll be back in the morning."

"With coffee?" I had no idea about hospital food, but I doubted they were going to serve Starbucks.

"He'd better if he ever wants to sleep with me again."

"Are you sure you're up for a visit?" I asked. "Not too tired?" It was after midnight.

These days most hospitals are pretty flexible when it comes to visiting hours, even on maternity wards, but I wasn't overly confident such accommodations extended past the witching hour. I'd forgotten, however, that I'd brought a secret weapon with me. Gabriel, all charm and smiles, had convinced the nurse on duty that we just wanted to say a quick hello to the new mom and baby and then we'd be on our way. Scout's honor, cross my heart. I don't know why I was even worried. The guy could pretty much get anything he wanted, and the gushing nurse only touched his arm three times.

"Nah," Laycee replied, "but if you do see me nodding off, just give me a poke. I might as well start getting used to it."

I chuckled and let the feel-good moment wash over me before asking, "So, how bad was it?"

At any gathering where Laycee's female relatives were present, the conversation inevitably got around to childbirth. Laycee and I had listened to horror stories that covered such topics as weeklong labor, breech births and forceps delivery, unsympathetic doctors aided by concentration camp nurses, and everyone's favorite—drunk husbands. It was a miracle that any female in her family actually agreed to procreate in the first place, much less do it more than once.

"I don't really know," Laycee told me with a sigh. "I mean, I know it was painful, especially as there wasn't time to give me an epi or anything—"

"Epi?"

"Epidural." I nodded as though I knew exactly what it meant to forgo this procedure. "But it was all worth it," she finished, glowing like one of those big old lights they use for Hollywood premieres. Which was probably how she felt.

At that moment, the door opened, and the nurse who had been

gushing over Gabriel now wheeled in a bassinet that was filled with a bundle of adorable pink. She parked it by the side of Laycee's bed.

Once the nurse had left, I pointed to the bassinet. "Can I?"

Laycee nodded. The emotion at seeing her daughter, accompanied by the enormity of the moment, rose up to temporarily rob her of any form of speech. Carefully, I scooped up the bundle and stared down at the wondrous sight in my arms. "What happened to Baby Jake?"

"Guess you can't trust everything you see in an ultrasound." The beatific smile she gave me only further enhanced the Madonna impression.

"I think you took your mama and papa by surprise," I cooed at the small face looking up at me from the crook of my arm. "They were expecting you to be a Jake, but I know they'll enjoy having a little girl first so much more."

At the sound of my voice, Laycee's infant daughter scrunched up her tiny face, yawned, and promptly went back to sleep. I stroked the back of her hand with my pinkie, marveling at the perfection of her tiny fingers, her nails, the intoxicating new-baby smell she had.

"Jake and I decided to name her Jenna Rowan DuPree," Laycee said softly.

It took a couple of swallows before the lump in my throat shifted enough so I could speak. "Can you do that? I mean is it okay to use DuPree before you and Jake are married?" This was not a point I was well-versed in, never having had a reason to give it much thought before now.

"Um, actually we already are."

Laycee might not have had an epi-whatever, but I wondered if they still gave women in labor some sort of gas. "Are what?" I asked, confused.

"Married." I couldn't tell which was worse, her guilt or her embarrassment. "I'm sorry, Rowan, but it all kind of happened so fast. Jake's divorce came through, and we went ahead and had a civil service two days ago."

"Oh." My feelings were hurt, but I tried to understand where Laycee was coming from.

"Look, we're going to have a proper church do in a few months, once I've got my figure back," she said, the words almost falling over themselves in her haste to apologize. "And I promise it'll be an evening ceremony, or at the very least a late-afternoon one." She reached for my free hand and squeezed it. "Please say you forgive me."

Of course I did. How could I not? She was my best friend and had been since grade school. And because of me, she had been through the most horrific experience a person could possibly have. I would forgive her anything. Even getting married without me.

"There's nothing to forgive." I squeezed her back. "And you don't have to make wedding plans to accommodate us. I can be there whenever, and Gabriel can always swing by after dark as long as you're okay with that. I'm sure we can come up with a plausible excuse to explain his absence to Jake." I dropped my voice to a conspiratorial whisper for the last part.

She looked relieved, actually more than relieved, but it occurred to me this might be the result of fluctuating hormones more than needing my forgiveness. I gave what I hoped was a reassuring smile and then turned my attention back to Baby Jenna in my arms. Although I felt an instant connection to Laycee's baby, I knew in a moment of absolute clarity that I would always be one of those women who make a much better "aunt" than mother. That's not to say that I didn't feel a pang of reluctance when I returned the small pink bundle to her mother.

"Speaking of Eye Candy," Laycee said conversationally, "I don't suppose he came with you . . . did he?"

I nodded. "He's out in the waiting room."

"Oh." She gave me a disappointed look. "Does he have a problem with babies?"

I stared at her. Um no, it's more like you have a problem with vampires, or have you forgotten? Of course I didn't say that to her.

Do you think it's hormones?

Yeah, actually I did. I mean why else would she ask if Gabriel had a problem seeing her baby? Her hormone levels were definitely out of whack.

"No," I said slowly, thinking how best to answer her question. It was something Gabriel and I had actually talked about on the drive to the hospital. "I think he was more concerned about how you would feel having a vampire around your baby."

A newborn, her mom, and a vampire . . . it sounded like the start of a really bad joke.

"Well, that's just silly," Laycee said, giving me my first taste of her mom-logic. "Besides, there's something I want to ask him."

"And what would that be?"

She told me, and I swear to God, it was the last thing I ever expected.

Chapter 18

Laycee had used my absence to re-comb her hair and freshen her lip gloss. Something that ordinarily I wouldn't think twice about but now I found strangely annoying. Did she think primping was going to have an effect on Gabriel? If he refused her request, assuming that he could do what she wanted in the first place, then no amount of champagne-pink pearly lip gloss was going to persuade him otherwise. I was about to say something sarcastic, but the sudden feel of strong fingers tightening around my hand stopped me. Gabriel's firm reassurance prevented me from possibly hurting the feelings of the one person who, until recently, had been the most important in my life.

I watched as Gabriel took Laycee's hand and kissed her chastely on the forehead. "I think motherhood agrees with you." I could hear the smile in his voice. "The birthing went well?"

"Um, yes, very well, thank you." Flustered by the intimacy of Gabriel's greeting, Laycee was as startled as I was by his question.

I couldn't speak for her, but I know my astonishment wasn't so much at the odd phrasing as the fact he'd even asked the question in the first place. The kiss on the forehead I could accept, but asking about the birth process seemed inappropriate to me. But maybe I was overreacting and it was no more than vampire politeness.

"Would you like to see her?" Laycee asked. One hand fluttered nervously around her throat while the other pointed to the bassinet.

My astonishment changed to stunned silence as Gabriel parted the blanket with his long fingers for a better look. He murmured appreciatively, and while his voice didn't have quite the seductive tones that could liquefy my spine, I wondered if he would have used the same modulation had Baby Jenna actually been Baby Jake.

He can't help himself; it's the way he responds to the female aura. Just be thankful you're the only female who can bring him to his knees.

My inner bitch, who was keeping me company less and less these days, sounded slightly amused by my nascent feelings of jealousy.

Is that what you think I do to him, I snorted back inside my head, *bring him to his knees?*

Oh yeah . . . every single time he looks at you, and trust me, honey, he wouldn't have it any other way.

"She is very beautiful," Gabriel said, "and obviously favors her mother." His compliment made Laycee blush. Returning to my side, he pressed his lips against my temple and linked his fingers with mine. Sometimes my inner bitch gets it right, and knowing I was all Gabriel would ever want gave me the confidence to smile at Laycee with genuine warmth. "Rowan tells me there is something you wish to ask of me." His voice was suitably solemn.

Laycee licked her lips, taking off most of the shine, which told me she was nervous, and rightly so. I now had to wonder if this was the real reason she had waited before calling me. A reason that had nothing to do with saving me from her family's version of the Spanish Inquisition regarding my love life. What she wanted from Gabriel was something she would never share with her family . . . or her husband. My only concern was which worried her more. That Gabriel wouldn't be able to fulfill her request . . . or that he would.

"How safe am I from that crazy bitch?" Laycee asked in a low voice.

I was leaning against Gabriel's chest and felt him stiffen. "I assume you mean Katja?"

Laycee nodded and narrowed her eyes. "I know you told me she was taken away by . . ." She frowned as she struggled to recall the dark-haired vampire's name.

"Ryiel," Gabriel said softly.

"Yes, that's right . . . by Ryiel."

There was a slightly dazed look to Laycee's eyes as she repeated his name, which I found a little disturbing, but I was willing to blame it on postpartum whatever rather than any real desire.

"Why are you asking about Katja?" I asked, refocusing Laycee's attention.

"Well, surely you of all people can understand where I'm coming from? If she comes looking for you, there's a good chance she's going to find me first, and somehow I don't think she's going to want to friend me on Facebook." There was a slight frostiness to Laycee's tone as she chided me. "Only it's not just me anymore, and I don't want to spend the rest of my life looking over my shoulder every time I leave your house. Especially at night."

"It's not my house anymore," I muttered under my breath, but not low enough.

"I doubt that crazy bitch actually knows that, and even if she did, do you think she's going to give a damn?"

Of course not.

"But Katja is with Ryiel—" I began.

"I know that!" Laycee snapped irritably. "Stuck somewhere in the Himalayas or wherever the hell it is," she paused, taking a breath and putting aside her exasperation. "But can you say, with absolute certainty, that she will stay there until me and my kids and grandkids are all dead and buried?"

She was upset, and I wanted to calm her fears. I opened my mouth to speak, offer some meaningless platitude, but Gabriel interrupted me.

"No," he said in a voice that was firm and decisive. "There are no guarantees, Laycee. The only certainty is death, which comes to us all. Even vampires."

"Strangely, I don't find that very comforting," Laycee told him, doing a poor job of hiding her disappointment. Baby Jenna, sensing her mother's change of mood, suddenly wailed, and Laycee went into immediate maternal mode. For the next few minutes, no one said anything while the fractious newborn was soothed. When Laycee did look up again, she seemed apprehensive.

"What is it you think I can do for you, Laycee?" Gabriel asked, his hands moving to rest on my shoulders.

"I want you to protect my baby from Katja . . . and any other vampires." Saying the word made her shudder and caused an unexpected tremble to sweep through me. I held onto Gabriel's arm. Even though she had told me what she wanted to ask him, it was still a shock hearing her say the words. Especially after what she'd been through with Katja.

"What you ask is no small matter," Gabriel said quietly.

His words startled me. "You mean you can do this?" I blurted as I glanced up at him over my shoulder. His expression was serious, but the uncharacteristic downturn of his mouth said that whatever he

could do to ease Laycee's state of mind, there would be consequences. The kind that Laycee might not want to know about. But she
was my friend, and even though our relationship was moving in a new
direction, I would always care about her and her family. Something
that was even more important after hearing how Aleksei had lost his.

"I can't un-see what I've already seen, and I can't pretend you
guys don't exist. If all vampires were like you, and Ryiel and the big
Russian guy, then we wouldn't be having this conversation." She
paused and gently rocked the baby in her arms. "But I know what an
unhinged, crazy vampire can do, and take it from me, it wasn't
pretty. And as for the creepy guy—"

"It wasn't his fault he was like that," I interjected, coming to
Oscar's defense. "It was because Katja had deliberately starved him."

Oscar had been as much a victim of Katja's scheming as both
Laycee and I, and even though I knew that, given the chance, the
starving vampire would have drained me dry, it made no difference
now. Of course, it's easy to be magnanimous when the threat to your
life has been decapitated.

"You know, I still can't decide which was worse," Laycee continued. "Seeing Ryiel remove creepy guy's head with his bare hands, or
watching psychotic Vampirella rip my best friend's neck open."

"Oh my God, Laycee . . ."

"Like I said, the view from your bedroom window is pretty
good." After repositioning the blanket in her arms, Laycee addressed
Gabriel directly. "If crazy vampire bitch could do something like
starve another vampire, then there's no telling what else she's capable of." I watched as she unconsciously began to flex her wrist. The
same one Katja had broken and Aleksei had fixed. "Look, I know
I'm not supposed to know about vampires, and all I can do is give
you my word I won't tell anyone about you, not even Jake"—I felt
rather than saw Gabriel smile at her promise—"but please understand I don't ever want to be that scared again, or have my kids that
scared."

"It's against the law for a vampire to take the blood of a child," I
told her.

"And what law would that be exactly?" She didn't try to hide her
sarcasm.

"It's vampire law," Gabriel said.

"Well, did your vampire law say it was okay for Katja to starve creepy guy—"

"His name was Oscar." Annoyance made my words sharper than I intended.

I don't think Laycee was being deliberately disrespectful, but even so. She blinked, and the expression on her face told me our friendship had just received a hairline fracture. It wasn't huge, it wasn't a crack or gap or even a fissure, but it was a definite weakness.

"—or rip Rowan's neck open like she did?" Laycee continued as if I hadn't spoken. "I don't think someone capable of doing that really gives a damn about the law, no matter who made it."

She had a point, and if it were I with an infant in my arms, I would probably be asking the same thing. A small wail suddenly erupted from the pink blanket, and Laycee began shushing and cooing, apologizing to her daughter for upsetting her. Taking advantage of her distraction, I turned to face Gabriel. "Can you really do something?" I asked in a low voice.

He looked down at me, his eyes darkening to a shade that made them unreadable. "Yes, but what you are asking comes at a price."

"But can it be done?"

"Of course, but—"

"Outside, now," I said, taking him firmly by the hand and marching toward the door. "We'll be back in a minute," I told Laycee, who gave me a distracted wave and occupied herself with Jenna.

"Don't you want to help her?" I hissed once the door to Laycee's room had closed and we had the semi-privacy of the hall to talk in. "It's not like she's asking anything for herself. This is for her baby." I put an unfair emphasis on the last word.

Gabriel let go of my hands and put his own on his hips as he dropped his eyes and looked down at the floor. I'd seen him adopt this posture before, usually when he needed me to see his point of view and didn't want to lose his temper over it. "There are consequences to be considered, Rowan. What you are asking—"

"I'll pay it," I said suddenly. "That's the reason you're stalling, isn't it?" He stared at me, his eyes glittering in the low light, his hair shimmering. I saw the tips of his fangs behind his upper lip. "Whatever the cost of this protection you can give, you're worried that I won't like it. Well, let me tell you something: Laycee is as important to me as Aleksei is to you. If you could have saved his family—

saved his mother, his sisters, and his brothers—wouldn't you have done it?"

"Rowan, that's not the same thing."

"Isn't it? The specific circumstances might be different, but you can't tell me the feelings aren't the same. We're talking about protecting someone who can't protect themselves."

I wasn't playing fair, but I couldn't let him turn his back on a helpless child, not when it was in his power to help her. I grabbed hold of his hand and brought it to my mouth, pressing my lips against his knuckles. "Do whatever you need to do, Gabriel, to give Laycee peace of mind. Do it for her. Do it for her baby. Do it for me."

He stared at me long and hard, and I could feel the conflict within him . . . and knew the moment he capitulated.

"I understand there are terms, and it doesn't matter what they are. If it's up to me to pay them, then I will and gladly, I'll—" The rest of my words were shut off as Gabriel covered my mouth with his, effectively silencing me.

"Don't say anything else," he instructed when he finally let me go.

"But you'll do it, won't you?" I completely ignored his directive, adding, "You'll help Laycee and her baby?"

"Rowan—you have no idea what you ask of me!"

"It's a lot, I know, but . . . please?"

"The consequences . . ."

"Are they really so terrible?" I asked. C'mon, this was a baby we were talking about protecting. How awful could it be to agree to do this? I reached for his hand, holding it and rubbing my thumb across his knuckles. "I'll do whatever is asked of me, Gabriel, but please do this."

He twisted the hand I held and pulled me up against his body, kissing me with a fierce kind of desperation. I could feel the pounding beat of his heart, feel the blood rushing through his veins. And when he let me go, he looked strangely grim.

"Thank you," I murmured as he pulled open the door to Laycee's room.

Chapter 19

This time Laycee had not freshened her makeup. Instead she was starting to look a little frazzled, a combination of little to no sleep and worry. She began to chew on her lip, smearing what was left of her lip gloss, and for the first time I realized just how scared she truly was. "So . . . can you help my children?"

Going to the end of her bed, Gabriel looked at her solemnly. "What you are asking is not possible for Jake's older children," he told her in a voice that carried the weight of centuries. "Such a request can only be asked, and granted, within the first twenty-four hours of birth."

She sighed with relief. "So you can protect Jenna?"

"You are absolutely certain this is what you want?" Gabriel asked, his voice calm and steady, his focus completely on Laycee.

She shook her head. "No, what I really want is to have a do-over where I know nothing about vampires."

"But you can't put the genie back in the bottle," Gabriel said, giving her a tight smile.

"A genie I might be able to deal with," she assured him. "But seriously, yes. Whatever protection you can give my daughter is what I want."

"And you ask this of me with a free will?" She swallowed convulsively a couple of times, and then nodded her head rapidly like a bobblehead doll that was possessed. "Very well," Gabriel said. "I agree to give your daughter my protection."

The look he gave me said he was doing this for no one but me.

"Will it be enough?" Laycee asked, her china-doll eyes opening wide.

Gabriel gave a humorless laugh. "It always has been before. Any vampire who gets close to your daughter will recognize my scent and know that touching her in any way will result in his—or her—immediate death." He raised a brow. "This is all I can offer. Are you satisfied?" Laycee closed her eyes for a moment and then nodded. "And you," Gabriel said, turning to face me, "are you also satisfied by this agreement?"

"Yes," I said, wondering why he was asking when he already knew it was what I wanted. "Wait a minute, though." I put my hand on Gabriel's arm and asked the obvious. "Just how is this done?"

"With blood, of course," Gabriel answered, surprised that I hadn't already guessed this. Nearly all rituals of any importance in the vampire world were bound by blood.

"Okay, but whose blood?"

His dimple winked at me, and now he brushed his lips lightly over mine before saying, "Only mine, sweetheart, no one else's."

Oh well, that was okay then. The momentary fear in the pit of my stomach went back to sleep. From the look on her face, Laycee had been given a similar jolt of terror at the thought that Gabriel was going to need her baby's blood to do whatever he was going to do. I gave her a reassuring smile as the sound of rustling silk filled my ears. I turned my head to see Gabriel pulling his shirt free of his pants.

"Don't tell me you've gotta be naked to do this," I mumbled as he began undoing buttons. Over the years I'd shared a lot of things with Laycee, but I'd never planned on her seeing Gabriel in the buff. I'm a generous friend, not a stupid one.

"Don't worry," he said with a teasing grin that would have put an exotic dancer to shame. "I only need to remove my shirt. Skin-to-skin contact is vital."

"Holy Mary, Mother of God . . ." Laycee murmured from her bed. The fact that she had given birth less than twelve hours ago did not stop her appreciation for a well-muscled torso. "And to think you can see that anytime you want," she added with enough envy in her voice that it made me preen.

I saw tiny beads of perspiration break out across her upper lip as Gabriel stood by the side of the bed and held his arms out. If Laycee was going to change her mind, now was the time to do it. All she had to do was refuse to hand over Jenna and Gabriel would put his shirt back on and none of us would ever mention this again. And for a moment, I thought that's exactly what she was going to do. Let's face it, what mother would willingly put her newborn infant into the outstretched hands of a vampire? And not just any vampire, but an Original Vampire at that. Laycee may have had some hesitation, but Baby Jenna did not.

"Would you look at that?" I murmured, slightly awe-struck. "Not even twenty-four hours old, and she's reaching for him."

And it did appear as if that was exactly what she was doing.

A small chubby fist rose up from the cloud of pink, accompanied by a soft cooing sound, and grabbed a handful of Gabriel's long hair as he took her from her mother's arms. Cradled against his chest, Jenna lay nice and easy, her small body resting along the length of his forearm. It seemed to me that Gabriel had never looked so big, or perhaps it was just that the newborn looked so tiny dwarfed by his broad chest and massive shoulders.

Holding her in one arm, her small body pressed against his bare skin, Gabriel smiled down at her. She waved her arm and made baby gurgling noises, and I saw his smile widen as she tugged playfully on the strands of hair caught between her fingers. Not taking his eyes from the tiny face that looked up at him, Gabriel murmured to me, "You might want to hold Laycee's hand."

I understood the need for his instruction a moment later, because Laycee almost broke my fingers seeing Gabriel drop his fangs. Concerned that she might launch herself at him, I put my free arm around her shoulders and offered a comforting squeeze. Gabriel had assured me the only blood to be used was his own, and I had no reason not to believe him. I watched as he scored his free wrist and then held my breath as he held his hand over the baby's face.

A single drop of blood, no more and no less, fell with exact precision between the open lips of a tiny rosebud mouth, staining her tongue a brilliant crimson before being absorbed by her own genetic material. Making a single sweep of his tongue across his wrist, Gabriel sealed the wound. Then he pressed his lips against Jenna's forehead and placed her back in Laycee's arms.

"That's it?" Laycee asked. "She's safe now?"

"Yes. Any vampire will know she is under my protection."

Gently Laycee passed her forefinger across her baby's lips, as if worried some of Gabriel's blood might escape. "Thank you. I can't ever—oh, holy shit!"

The sudden outburst startled me, and Gabriel, who had been putting his shirt back on, paused for a moment before giving a shrug. Laycee may have had nothing but glowing admiration for his front side, but she was having a completely different reaction at the sight of his back. I knew it wasn't his tattoos that were responsible for her sudden outburst, but the cruel thick scars that curved along each shoulder blade. She covered her mouth with her free hand, mumbling an apology for her tactless eruption.

Slipping the shirt the rest of the way on, Gabriel pressed his lips against my forehead before saying, "I'll wait for you down the hall."

Once the door closed with a soft whoosh, I turned back to meet Laycee's stare. I hadn't thought it possible for her eyes to get any bigger, but apparently I was wrong. If she wasn't careful she'd look like one of those female anime characters. Nothing but eyes and boobs.

"Oh God, Rowan, I'm so sorry. Why didn't you tell me?"

"Tell you what? About his back?" She nodded, her expression stricken. "I guess I've just gotten used to it," I said with a shrug. "I find his tats very sexy, and I honestly don't notice the scars anymore."

It was a lie, but Laycee didn't need to know that. Just as Gabriel was reminded of what he had once been every time he looked in the mirror, I was reminded every time my hands passed over the ropey, thick scar tissue. And every time I had to force myself to push aside my anguish and despair.

"But they look like . . ." I watched her brows pull together. "It sounds silly, but it's almost as if he'd once had wings."

"Yeah I know, I thought the same thing the first time I saw them."

"What happened to him?"

I shrugged. "I don't know exactly." It was kind of, sort of the truth. My memories had been returning, but with no reference point to guide me, they remained a jumble of images. Some were pleasant, some not so much. I couldn't say on which side my recollections of Gabriel's cruel disfigurement would fall, but I was inwardly bracing myself for them to be in the not-so-pleasant category.

My sense that I had been a witness to that cruelty was strong, and it explained why I was hesitant about telling Gabriel I was starting to have such recollections. When the memory was complete, and I had a better understanding of my own involvement, then I would tell him. At least that's what I told myself. Truthfully, I was terrified what such a remembrance would bring with it.

"It's not something he likes to talk about," I said, answering Laycee's question.

"Oh. I'm sorry I asked."

A sudden wail broke the tension. "I think someone's hungry," I said, feeling a smile tug at the corners of my mouth. "Remember to send me pictures, lots and lots of pictures. A daily update would be good." I slipped out of the room before Laycee had a chance to say anything else.

Chapter 20

I waited until Gabriel slid Francine into her parking stall between Lola the Lamborghini and a Dodge Viper he called Velma. The silence between us on the drive back from the hospital was strained because Gabriel was brooding about something.

"Why is it that all your cars have names better suited to B-movie actresses from the fifties?" I asked in an effort to break the tension. I certainly didn't want to take this mood of his back to the apartment. God knows the atmosphere up there was sensitive enough with Aleksei opening old wounds while exorcising his past. One slightly unstable vampire with a short fuse was all I could handle right now.

"I liked the era," Gabriel answered. "Things seemed less complicated back then."

"Really? No civil rights, no equal rights, substandard health care, and let's not forget raving paranoia generated by McCarthyism."

"I didn't say it was perfect," he chided gently. "Just that I liked it."

"I guess you had to be there."

"Yes, well, you were."

"You mean . . . in one of those lives I don't remember?" I stared at him, feeling a sudden dryness in my mouth as he nodded.

If it was his intention to shut me down, he succeeded admirably. I sighed and leaned back on the comfy bench seat. He turned off the engine but kept the key locked so the radio stayed on. Something classical with a piano and violins was playing. It was very soothing, and Gabriel seemed in no hurry to get out of the car. But this could only mean one thing. If we were going to hash out whatever was wrong, then he was going to make me work for it. Which I also took to mean he thought I was somehow at fault. Shit.

"Gabriel?" He turned to look at me, his face highlighted by the soft glow of the dashboard panel's lights. Perfect bone structure complemented by intriguing hollows made the breath catch in my throat. It was like seeing him for the very first time and falling in love with him all over again. Except I hadn't realized I was in love with him then. I put a hand on his arm. "Look, I'm sorry if you feel like I railroaded you into helping Laycee, but it was important."

"Was it?"

"Of course it was." If it was important to Laycee, then it was important to me . . . and he knew that. From the other side of the car I heard a grunt and then the soft drumming of his fingers on the steering wheel. I folded my arms, and my irritation began a slow burn. "If you didn't want to do it, you should have said so," I snapped.

The hand that had been keeping time on the steering wheel flashed out and caught my chin, forcing my head around so he could look at me. His eyes were dark and furious.

" '*Do whatever you need to do, Gabriel, to give Laycee peace of mind. Do it for her. Do it for her baby. Do it for me.*' "

Hearing my own voice come out of his mouth was unnerving, to say the least. I had no idea he could imitate me that well. Jerking my chin out of his fingers, I gave him a look of my own. "This is about the stupid consequences, isn't it? You think I'm going to renege when it comes time to pay the piper."

"Not intentionally."

I was insulted by his lack of faith in my integrity. Did he really think so little of me? "I gave you my word, Gabriel. Surely that counts for something?"

"Of course it does." He sighed. "I'm not worried about that."

"Then what is it?" I snapped. "You've been like a bear with a thorn in its paw ever since we left the hospital."

"Seldom is our help asked for, at least not so directly or for such selfless reasons. Perhaps this is why words carry more weight with a vampire. Why we do not make promises lightly, nor do we break those promises without good reason."

"You still could have said no. I wasn't exactly twisting your arm."

Are you kidding? The guy would stake himself out in Death Valley if you told him you were just thinking of asking for it.

I was pretty sure my inner bitch was exaggerating.

"No, I couldn't," he said firmly. "Once Laycee asked, I was honor-bound to help her." He gave me a quirky smile. "My get-out-of-jail-free card lay in her not accepting the terms of my protection, which as Jenna's mother was her right. But—"

"—she didn't get the chance because I butted in and took responsibility for it?" It was a guess, and the correct one.

"Yeah . . . you did."

"And your honor code or whatever allows me to do this?"

He nodded, his long, silky hair moving over his shoulder. "Anyone who is present can agree."

"That's a little reckless, isn't it?"

"Most people don't agree until they know what it is they're agreeing to."

I wanted to ask him what had him so worried, but I was stung by the reproof in his voice. I was on an emotional seesaw, and at that moment I didn't need to deal with anything negative. And I had a sinking feeling I might have overstepped my limits, but my euphoria at seeing my best friend embrace motherhood and wanting to help her protect her child had taken over. So, no, I hadn't given any thought to whatever consequences came with asking Gabriel for his protection. Whatever it cost, in the long run, it would be worth it.

And while a part of me was still reeling from hearing Aleksei's story, another part was recalling the mess I'd been when my dad died. How was the big guy able to survive the devastating loss of his entire family? And that too had played a part in my decision, because nothing was more important than family.

You have a really bad habit of diving in the deep end before checking to see if there's actually any water in the pool . . . you know that, right?

"But, Gabriel, there were only the two of us in the corridor and three in the room," I pointed out. "Well, three and a half if you count the baby. No one else knows what you agreed to."

He reached out and caught a curl that had escaped the confines of my ponytail holder and twirled it around his finger. "Do you honestly think the Dark Realm isn't watching the events in our lives?"

Something else I needed to beat myself up about. There was at least one inhabitant watching that I knew of. Perhaps Gabriel and I were his equivalent of a Dark Realm reality TV show. However, the knowledge that I had my very own demon taking a personal interest in our love life was something I tried not to think about.

Maybe you ought to. I sent mental daggers to my inner bitch. *Okay, okay . . . just saying!*

"Well, it's done now," Gabriel said with a sigh of finality. "She has my blood in her."

"How does it work exactly? Does a vampire have to sniff her to know she has your protection?" Having had my own share of neck sniffing, it seemed a reasonable assumption to make.

"They'll never have to get that close."

That was good. No chance of teenage Jenna making out under the bleachers with the new hot guy in class who's also a vampire. "So do you have to, I don't know, check to make sure your protection is still in force?"

He shook his head. "My protection stays until it is removed, but I think, given Laycee's feelings about vampires, it would be better if I had minimal interaction with the child. Obviously I cannot go to your old house, and Laycee will not come to the penthouse, so just make sure you let me know when she plans to visit you at your new apartment. That way I won't accidentally surprise her."

Despite his concession, he sounded irritated, and I really couldn't blame him. I'd put him in an impossible situation, asking him to do something that might damage a lifelong friendship if he refused. "Gabriel . . . what did I agree to?"

"Nothing we can't deal with when the time comes," he said with a shrug. "Besides, there is another question that troubles me."

"Oh, what's that?"

He slid across the bench seat and pulled me into his arms, covering my mouth with his. His kiss was hungry and demanding, and I melted against him as his tongue pushed its way inside my mouth and danced with mine. Velvet softness combined with fiery heat made my body tremble and my head swim. This was Gabriel's way of forgiving me.

Moving his lips from my mouth, he put them next to my ear and whispered, "Who told Laycee she could ask for my protection to begin with?"

Chapter 21

It was mid-morning, and I was standing in front of the big sliding-glass doors that led onto the terrace. The sky was sullen and overcast, and it had started to rain. Normally I don't mind the rain. Gabriel had once made love to me in a particularly memorable downpour, but night rain is different from the stuff that falls in the day. Don't ask me how or why, it just is. And this rain looked miserable. A miserable morning to suit my equally miserable mood. Not even the mug of coffee I had my hands wrapped around could change my mood.

The sound of throat clearing made me turn around. I was expecting to find Tomas, the only other person who should be awake at this time of day, but instead I was surprised to see Aleksei, who was holding a mug of his own. Someone else who appreciated a good cup of joe as much as I did.

"Are you okay with this?" I asked, gesturing to the glass panel behind me. While the light outside was gray and gloomy, it still was daylight.

"Is okay as long as I don't have any direct contact with the sun." He took a step past me and looked outside. "No chance of that, I'm thinking."

Gabriel had had a special film coated on all the glass doors and windows, allowing him to see outside even when the sun was shining. But Gabriel was an Original Vampire who was able to tolerate even direct sunlight for a short while. I didn't want to take any chances with a vampire who was a juvenile three hundred years old. Looping my arm through Aleksei's, I steered him back toward the "living" area of the main room. He plopped himself down in one of the oversized club chairs across from me.

"How is Anasztaizia?" I asked, rearranging the cushions behind me.

"Tomas gave her something to help her sleep." Ah, one of Tomas's home remedies. The lovely Magyar might be down for the count for a while, but it would be a very therapeutic knockdown. "And Gabriel?" An arched brow accompanied the question.

"In the panic room." Saying he was comatose in his sarcophagus was too bizarre for me to actually verbalize, even if it was an accurate account of his current state. "I don't think he got much benefit when he had me in there with him."

"Oh, I think you'd be surprised." The corner of Aleksei's mouth twitched.

"So why aren't you asleep?" I asked, deciding to let his comment slide.

"Too many memories."

"I'm so sorry, Aleksei." I felt a huge responsibility for making him dredge up the past because I wasn't sure it was something he'd been ready to do.

He gave a resigned shrug. "I was going to have to talk about it sooner or later."

I hesitated before asking, "Are you and Anasztaizia going to be all right?"

The big guy looked at me thoughtfully and then gave a slow nod. "Da, I think so. We both cried a little, held each other, and then cried some more. It was hard for her to hear such things about me."

"You never told her any of it before now?"

He shook his head. "She never asked about my past."

No, and why would she? I had problems getting my head around the fact that I was in love with a vampire, but at least I could turn to Anasztaizia when things got too weird. She'd had no one to confide in. No one to explain vampire behavior or customs to her. I could only imagine how hard it must have been dealing with Aleksei during the normal day-to-day course of their relationship. The last thing she needed was any additional drama.

"And you, Rowan," the big guy said, derailing my train of thought. "Why are you not sleeping?"

"Too much on my mind."

"Want to tell me about it?"

Let's see . . .

I'd misunderstood Gabriel's reasons for buying me an apartment, followed by a spectacular, if one-sided, quarrel about lingerie. I'd been involved in a car wreck, was subsequently kidnapped, drugged, and threatened with rape and murder, all of which, it turned out, had been orchestrated by an old nemesis of Aleksei's, who was still out to get him. Then I'd listened to a heart-wrenching account of how Aleksei had lost his family to this same vile individual. And if that wasn't enough, I was now feeling guilty at having coerced my boyfriend into giving his protection to my best friend's infant child. An offer that seemed to fill him with resignation more than anything else.

It had been a busy week.

"Living with a vampire can be . . . challenging," I said, figuring Aleksei had enough on his plate without me adding to it.

"So Anasztaizia is telling me, especially when I don't put down toilet seat."

"That's not because you're a vampire, Aleksei," I told him with a laugh.

He looked at me in surprise. "No?"

"No. That's because you're a guy."

It was good to see him smile, even better to hear his deep, rumbling laugh. The big Russian vampire was many things, but stupid wasn't one of them. He knew there was more going on with me than I was letting on, but he also knew not to push me. Accepting my glib answer and making us both laugh was his way of saying *"It's okay, I understand."*

"So," he said, settling back against the chair's comfy cushions, "you can't sleep, I can't sleep . . . You want to hear rest of story?"

"Don't you want to wait until Gabriel and Anasztaizia can join us? I'm sure they want to hear it as well." And it didn't seem right that he should have to relive his nightmares more than once.

"Is not necessary. Gabriel already knows what happened, and Anasztaizia . . ." He paused and ran the flat of his hand across his military-style short hair. "It is better perhaps to tell her only what she wants to hear, and in very small pieces, yes?"

The love he felt for the beautiful woman shone from his eyes like the beacon of a lighthouse, illuminating the gross unfairness of their situation. How could two people love each other so much and have barely any life together? Anasztaizia might live to be eighty or more, but it would be nothing compared to the years Aleksei would continue on without her. "Are you absolutely certain she can't be changed?"

He ran his palm over the bristles that covered his head. "Yes. Humans are born with the marker already in their blood; it is not something they can grow over time. Anasztaizia does not have such a marker."

"It's so unfair! I wish there was something I could do."

"Well," he began slowly, "you could be bridesmaid."

So not what I was expecting to hear.

"Be . . . what?" I was astounded. No one had ever asked me to be a bridesmaid before. Of course I'd always assumed I'd be one of Laycee's—maid of honor, actually—but I didn't think that was going to happen now. Even if she and Jake did have another ceremony later, it wouldn't feel the same. "Anasztaizia wants me to be a bridesmaid?" Aleksei moved his head in the affirmative. "But . . . why hasn't she asked me?"

"Because she thinks you will say no."

I was stunned. "Why would she think that?"

"You haven't seen dress you will have to wear."

I snorted. Anasztaizia had impeccable taste in clothes, and the idea of her choosing a dress horrendous enough to give Aleksei the heebie-jeebies was unimaginable.

"Is like stuff on lemon pudding," he said with a glum look.

"Lemon pudding?" I asked, thoroughly confused.

"*Da.* White stuff, meringue, only dress is pink." He leaned toward me and dropped his voice to a conspiratorial whisper. "But I am wearing tux. Hugo Boss. Very stylish."

I confess I was pleasantly surprised. I'd been imaging he'd wear one of his army greatcoats and spiff it up with gold buttons and braided epaulets or something. But matrimonial attire wasn't what I really wanted to know about. "So you're actually going to do this then—get married, I mean?"

"Of course. Anasztaizia wants it, so I want it. And it will make it easier to be in same grave."

The mug I was holding fell from my fingers. Thankfully Aleksei's lightning-quick reflexes caught it before it hit the low table between us and broke. *Grave?* What was he talking about? Was the big guy intending to sleep on top of Anasztaizia's coffin in the ground? During the day? After she was dead? How was he going to be able to conceal the fact the earth had been disturbed?

"Wouldn't a crypt or mausoleum be more convenient?" I asked faintly.

Now it was his turn to look confused. "For what?"

"For you, of course. I understand you wanting to stay close to Anasztaizia, but you'll still need to eat, and digging your way out from on top of her coffin every night isn't very practical."

He stared at me for a full minute, or maybe two, before saying, "Trust me, Rowan. Inside I am laughing so hard I am busting gut!"

I frowned and shook my head. One of us was not only on the wrong page, we weren't even reading the same book. "I guess I must have missed something . . ."

I could feel an embarrassed flush heating my cheeks, although I had no idea what I had to be embarrassed about. Aleksei got up and came to sit down next to me. Taking both my hands in his, he stroked my knuckles with the pad of each thumb.

"When my darling Anasztaizia dies," he explained, "I have asked Gabriel to take my life also. I won't be going anywhere—at least not in this body." He gave me a few moments to absorb his words before continuing. "Rowan, you love Gabriel very much, yes?" I nodded. "So you understand how I cannot live without Anasztaizia."

I didn't know if I understood or not. I told myself I did. My nodding head told Aleksei I did. But until I was faced with the reality of it happening, I had no idea how I was going to react. At least I had the next sixty years or so to come to terms with not just losing Anasztaizia, but Aleksei as well.

"I am glad Gabriel found you," Aleksei continued in a somber voice. "This will be hard on him when time comes, but it will be easier to know I am not leaving him alone."

As far as I knew, Aleksei was the only human Gabriel had ever turned. Or at least the only one that was still living. And as a vampire Aleksei could only die at the hands of an Original Vampire. I wondered, if he was so concerned about the impact this would have on Gabriel, why he didn't ask Ryiel or maybe another Original Vampire to do the deed?

"Gabriel wouldn't allow it," Aleksei answered in a low voice, reading my face all too well.

"Of course he wouldn't." I couldn't say with any certainty if my lack of emotional response was due to incomprehension or was more proof of my waning humanity. In any case, I just nodded like some bizarre toy whose head was attached to the body by a spring.

"Are you okay?" Aleksei asked worriedly as he leaned back to look at me.

He was still holding my hands, so I squeezed his fingers and gave him my most winning smile. "I don't care if I look like a cream puff or meringue. You tell that girl of yours I'd be honored to be a bridesmaid."

He positively beamed, and that, more than anything else, lifted my mood. "So do you want to hear story?"

I'd be lying if I didn't say I had a vested interest in finding out how such a truly horrible person came to be made a vampire. I also considered that it might be cathartic for Aleksei to share the story of his life with someone he considered a relative stranger.

"Something went wrong, didn't it? Something that prevented you from killing Nikolayev."

"Not so much a something, more of a someone."

"Who was it—the count's wife?"

Aleksei shook his head. "No, it was another vampire."

I frowned. "But if Gabriel was there, why would another vampire be a problem?"

"Kartel is not just another vampire."

No, he wasn't. He was another Original Vampire. One Gabriel didn't trust, and I could suddenly see how that might be a problem.

Chapter 22

Aleksei swallowed and licked his lips, something he'd been doing repeatedly as his nerves got the better of him. Did a soldier approaching a battlefield get a dry mouth? he wondered. He'd never known anyone who was a soldier, but during his training sessions, Tomas had shared some stories about military life and its expectations. Whether these were his own experiences or tales told by others, Aleksei couldn't say. Tomas spoke as if they were his own recollections, but if they were, then he was the oldest soldier still standing. And that might not be as far-fetched as Aleksei might think. Still, the question of longevity aside, Aleksei could not deny being intrigued and finding a certain appeal in the military life. If only his mouth wasn't so dry!

"You can admit to being scared," Gabriel said softly from the other side of the carriage. "Being scared can be a good thing."

"It can? I thought you wanted me to be bold and brave."

"Those are two very fine qualities, but they can sometimes mask foolish behavior. If you expect to come out of this alive, then it would be better to be scared than overconfident."

"So you are expecting me to win this fight?" Aleksei noted in a colorless voice.

Gabriel stared at him, his expression unreadable in the gloomy interior. "Have you given any thought to the future, Aleksei? To what you might want to do with your life once this is over?"

He shook his head slowly. In truth, he'd thought of nothing beyond having Petrov on his knees before him, begging for mercy, something that Aleksei had no intention of giving. He didn't care if he did burn in hell for it. His gaze flickered to Gabriel, who was staring at him with such intensity, he was forced to look away. He noticed the vampire had not answered his question, but perhaps, he told himself, that was answer enough.

Despite Tomas's vigorous efforts, it soon became apparent that Aleksei was not cut out to wield a sword, and they might need to rethink the pitchfork. At least he was familiar with the feel of it in his hands. But stabbing the count, even through the heart, was no guarantee of the quick death necessary to facilitate Aleksei's escape.

"The best thing for you," Tomas had told him, "is to get in close, and cut here." He placed his hand on Aleksei's neck, showing him where he meant. "Do it properly and he will be dead before he hits the ground."

"What would I use?" Aleksei asked.

"This." Holding out his hand, Tomas showed Aleksei the dagger that had miraculously appeared there.

Utilitarian in appearance, it might have easily been overlooked as a weapon. No jewel adorned the guard; there were no fancy markings on the blade, and the handle looked heavy. As if it had been designed for a large hand. The hand of a peasant farmer. Reaching out, Aleksei curled his fingers around the grip, nodding his head in satisfaction. This was a weapon he could use. His training resumed, but with a different technique now.

Tomas showed Aleksei how to get close enough to slice deeply across his enemy's neck, making him practice again and again, until Aleksei felt confident he could do the job blindfolded. But Aleksei was no fool. Slicing through a gourd that was standing in for Nikolayev's head was one thing. Doing it to a living, breathing man—one who would most likely be armed and fighting back—was another. His only hope, he told himself, was that Petrov would be so affronted by his challenge, he would drop his guard for a moment. And that would be all the time Aleksei would need—a moment when he could slip inside the count's defenses and mortally wound him. Hopefully before being wounded himself.

It was the height of arrogance to assume Aleksei was going to come away from this encounter unscathed. He had serious doubts about his chances of surviving the encounter at all, but this was something he kept to himself. And now Gabriel was asking about his future, which could only mean the vampire expected him to survive. Did he know something Aleksei did not?

"What if I can't do it?" Aleksei said suddenly. "What if, at the last moment, my hand fails me, and I can't kill him?"

Gabriel leaned back against the plush upholstery of the carriage. "This is not like killing a rabbit for your dinner. Taking a man's life is no easy thing. The first time you do it is always the hardest. It will change you, Aleksei, make no mistake about that. You will not come away from this unscathed."

"Change me in what way?"

"I've seen it happen in one of three ways," Gabriel told him. "Some men find the experience so unsettling they never raise a hand against their fellow man again for the rest of their lives. Other men find the violence thrilling, making them yearn to repeat the experience, so much so that they have to be forcibly stopped."

Gabriel fell silent, prompting Aleksei to ask, "And what is the third way?"

"Men who understand that killing is sometimes necessary but refuse to allow the action to define who they are," Gabriel paused, and Aleksei felt the weight of his stare intensify. "I have known but a handful of such men, and all of them have earned my respect."

"But what if I can't kill him?" Aleksei repeated, his question betraying his lingering uncertainty. "Then don't," Gabriel said quietly. "There is no shame in admitting you cannot kill, and no one will think any the less of you for it." In this case "no one" meant himself and Tomas. "Should you find yourself unable to complete the act, for any reason, then I will take his head for you. All you have to do is ask . . . or not. If the count still draws breath at dawn's light, then he will know to whom he owes his good fortune." Gabriel leaned forward, his long white hair falling past his collar, partially obscuring his features. "But look to your heart, Aleksei, and know the manner of man you are dealing with."

"You're saying if I don't kill him . . . then he will kill me."

"Yes, I believe he will." Gabriel's tone was grim. "He allowed you to live only because he never believed you would seek him out. By doing so you are setting a dangerous precedent."

"I am?" Aleksei now looked startled. He had no idea what a precedent was, but he could tell it was something serious.

"You are taking a stand, daring to stand up for yourself. That takes some balls, my friend." Gabriel pointed his finger at Aleksei's

crotch. *"And from what Tomas tells me, yours are more than adequate for the task."*

Aleksei was about to ask how Tomas could possibly know such an intimate detail when the carriage came to a stop. He turned his head, and his mouth dropped open. Aleksei had been impressed by Gabriel's house, but he was stunned by the sight that greeted him now. Light blazed from every window, a warm and welcoming glow that made Aleksei think perhaps the sun had decided not to set after all and was favoring Count Petrov by bathing his house with golden light. There were more people than he could ever remember seeing before in one place, alighting from carriages similar to the one he now sat in. He watched as they climbed the broad steps that led into the house.

"Do I have to go"—a lump lodged in his throat, forcing him to swallow it down—*"through there?"*

Gabriel shook his head. *"No, Tomas will take you around the back of the house. It will be an easy task to slip unnoticed through the kitchen."* Seeing a frown of worry appear on Aleksei's brow, he added, *"There will be so much commotion, I doubt anyone will stop you, but if they do, let Tomas speak. He knows what to say."* Aleksei nodded in relief. *"Tomas will take you to the room I told you about,"* Gabriel continued, *"and I will bring Petrov to you there."*

It had taken Gabriel just one night to make a thorough examination of Nikolayev's house. Gliding silently through the rooms, he quickly had the entire layout committed to memory, including a salon on an upper floor that, judging from its neglectful state, appeared to have fallen into disuse. It made more sense to have Tomas, rather than Gabriel, take Aleksei to the room.

"What if someone comes or is already in the room?" Aleksei asked.

"No one will come, and the room has not been made ready for any practical purpose. It looked exactly the same as when I first saw it."

"But when did you last *see it?"*

"A few hours ago," Gabriel told him.

Aleksei blew out a breath to calm his nerves. His trust in Gabriel was absolute; in himself . . . not so much. *"How long will it take before you bring him to the room?"*

"I won't know that until I'm inside, but I promise to make you wait no longer than is absolutely necessary." Leaning forward, Gabriel grinned. *"I recall there being a very fine clock above the fireplace.*

Perhaps you could pass the time taking it apart? I don't think Count Petrov will object," he added with a sly wink.

Of all the items on display in Gabriel's house, Aleksei had been most fascinated by the clocks. He had a vague idea of how time was measured, but he had always relied on the sun to judge the passing of the day. As for days and months, those he marked with the rhythm of the seasons and church holy days.

Seeing him staring at a clock, captivated by the movement of the hands, Gabriel had taken it apart, showing him how the inner mechanism functioned. Delighted by his enthusiasm, Gabriel had given him a clock of his own. *"This one does not work, and I confess I am at a loss to know why."* He placed the clock, along with a small collection of tools, on the table before Aleksei. *"Perhaps you can take it apart and find out what ails it, hmmm?"* Delighted to have something to occupy both his hands and his brain, Aleksei tapped in to an undiscovered aptitude for mechanical devices.

Now he stared at Gabriel and wondered if the vampire had not had a hand in making sure he would not spend the time fretting. Challenging his brain would settle his nerves. The opening of the carriage door made him jerk back in his seat, but the feel of Gabriel's hand squeezing his shoulder was reassuring. No words were spoken, but as Aleksei gazed into neon-blue eyes, a sense of calm washed through him. He knew that no matter the outcome of this night's events, his life would be forever changed.

All because he'd put his trust in a vampire.

Gabriel narrowed his eyes as he watched the dancers moving across the polished ballroom floor. A step here, a step there, a bow, a dip, the touch of hands, only to repeat the entire sequence with a different partner. His gaze was focused on Nikolayev and the pretty young woman he was dancing with. He had led the attractive brunette onto the dance floor three times now and followed her with an almost predatory gaze when her attention was given to another. Despite reconciling with his wife, it seemed the count had already taken a new mistress.

Gabriel allowed himself a satisfied smile. It would be a simple matter to persuade the young woman to accompany him up the grand staircase to an upper room. And to be certain the count saw them go. A man who believed he was in danger of losing such a prize to a rival *acted rashly, allowing pride—and his cock—to dictate the course of his actions.*

Disappointing the number of young women hoping to be offered his hand, Gabriel led Nikolayev's new mistress out for the next dance. It wasn't difficult to see the attraction. She laughed at his compliments, but there was also a shrewd intelligence hiding behind her pretty blue eyes. And the mildly flirtatious manner told him her role as the count's lover had yet to be solidified.

As Gabriel and the young lovely danced, he was keenly aware of Nikolayev's interested gaze. Turning his partner, Gabriel noticed a trusted confidant murmuring in the count's ear, no doubt relaying Gabriel's credentials. Though the name and lineage given would be suitably impressive, both were impossible to verify. He was surprised when Nikolayev strode purposefully from the ballroom, a look of barely concealed excitement on his face. The confidant's message, it would seem, was about something else entirely.

It was a few moments more before Gabriel was able to return his partner to her companions and take his leave. He forced himself to adopt the same casual pace of movement as those around him. Without knowing what might have precipitated Nikolayev's departure, it would be unwise to draw any unnecessary attention. He crossed into the grand entrance hall at the same moment he saw Nikolayev pause at the top of the staircase.

Gabriel followed and watched as Petrov approached the room where Aleksei waited. It was almost as if some unknown force had already revealed who waited within, and for what purpose. Gabriel saw a cruel sneer curl Nikolayev's lip and knew that the element of surprise had been irrevocably lost. He waited until he saw the door to the seldom-used salon swing open, wondering why Nikolayev hesitated. And then the sudden blur of movement was all the answer he needed.

Gabriel was not the only vampire at Count Petrov's ball.

Chapter 23

Although Aleksei told himself he was ready, the sight of Nikolayev in the open doorway took him by surprise. He was halfway out of his seat, prepared to drop to one knee in deference, when his sister's face suddenly filled his head. It was all the motivation he needed. His hand was reaching for the dagger Tomas had given him when a blur of movement at Nikolayev's shoulder distracted him. It wasn't until he felt the hands around his neck, the massive chest pressing against his own, that Aleksei realized what the blur was.

Instinctively he put out his hands, trying to ward off the danger, but it was already too late. The chair he was sitting on broke beneath him, the curved legs no match for the combined weight of man and vampire. As he fell back, Aleksei felt his shin strike the edge of the table, unbalancing it. His flailing foot completed the job by overturning the table with a crash.

"No—wait!" Nikolayev shrieked from the open doorway. The creature turned his head. "Your Grace, if you will permit"—Nikolayev paused—"I need but a moment."

Your Grace? Was that how he was supposed to have been addressing Gabriel all this time? Why hadn't Tomas corrected him? The fingers around his neck relaxed slightly as the vampire shifted. He was similar enough to Gabriel that Aleksei's senses were put on high alert. Same strength, same bearing, almost the same scent. Only the long silky hair was markedly different as it shimmered between blue and purple.

How had this vampire known he was here? And who was he? Did he know Gabriel? Surely he had to. His presence was too much of a coincidence, and they were so similar they could be brothers. Per-

haps they were. But if it had been Gabriel's intent to deliver him into Nikolayev's hands, then why go to all this trouble? He could have turned him over at any time.

Could it be that Gabriel didn't know who the vampire with the periwinkle blue hair was? Reluctantly Aleksei made himself consider the possibility. It was obvious, however, that the vampire was known to Count Petrov.

"I knew you would come," Nikolayev said, addressing Aleksei. Having closed the door, he now stared down at him. "They told me you had disappeared from the village, and I knew it was just a matter of time before you came for me."

"Then I am glad not to have disappointed you," Aleksei said, surprised at his own boldness.

The freedom to express himself had been an unexpected gift. Encouraged by both Gabriel and Tomas, it came with an unexpected audacity Aleksei had no idea he was capable of. The shock on Nikolayev's face at being addressed with such impertinence was its own reward.

Now the count narrowed his eyes in anger. "Do you know what he is?" he demanded, gesturing with his hand.

The vampire turned his head and allowed Aleksei to look him fully in the face. His features were almost identical to Gabriel's, but where Gabriel's eyes were an indescribable shade of blue, this vampire had eyes of the palest green. They reminded Aleksei of an unfurled leaf or new growth breaking through rich soil.

Seeing something in Aleksei's face, perhaps a knowledge he did not expect, the vampire pulled back his lips and dropped his fangs. Razor sharp, they glistened in the low candlelight. If the vampire suspected he was not the first of his kind Aleksei had seen, he wanted there to be no doubt that he would be the last.

Doing his best to show no fear, Aleksei said, "You are vampire."

Nikolayev, expecting Aleksei to scream with terror, stamped his foot in frustration. All peasants lived lives filled with superstition, so he should not have been upset when one of them recognized, and accepted, a vampire standing before him. Or, as in this case, lying on his chest.

The oddness was in the fact that Aleksei recognized a vampire who looked nothing like those in the dire tales from his childhood. This creature was no vile corruption of something that had once been a man. No personification of evil or a specter from a nightmare. Like Gabriel, he was also something . . . more.

"My only regret," Nikolayev said, lifting his lips in a cruel sneer, "is that I didn't get the chance take your sister again before I slit her throat. I would have liked very much to hear her scream again as she lay beneath me . . . while you watched."

The rage that swept through Aleksei was a terrifying thing. Wild and uncontrollable, it infused his limbs with a deadly strength. And he wasn't the only one who felt its force. Pale eyes narrowed and then warmed with a hint of amusement as strong fingers suddenly released their hold.

Aleksei had no idea why the vampire should let him go, or what he found so amusing, but he was not about to waste the opportunity. With a lunge, he caught Nikolayev by the ankle, pulling him off-balance and making him fall. He couldn't remember which side of the neck Tomas had said was the best place for his blade, but that was now a moot point. The dagger had flown from his fingers when the vampire had taken him down. Forced to improvise, he scrambled on top of the count and began to choke him.

For a man who was getting the life throttled out of him, Nikolayev didn't struggle nearly enough. He made a token effort, a few wild swings at Aleksei's head and shoulders, but nothing to indicate he feared for his life. It was almost as if he expected to be rescued. As the count's face began to turn an alarming shade, Aleksei saw him start to gesture frantically with one hand. The movement could have only one interpretation, and Aleksei realized the vampire was beholden to the count in some way.

In a spurt of rage, Aleksei increased the pressure of his fingers. He grunted in satisfaction as he felt a sudden bolt of urgency in the struggles of the body beneath him. And then, just as Aleksei was certain the count was starting to fade, he felt the cool silky whisper of hair across his cheek. Strong fingers that moments ago had been wrapped around his own throat now cupped his chin. His head was pulled gently to one side, and out of the corner of his eye, Aleksei saw the vampire extend his fangs.

"I would rather have taken him and spared you," the accented voice said in Aleksei's ear, "but I gave my word."

Aleksei swallowed, feeling his Adam's apple move against the *vampire's palm. "You must know whatever he said . . . whatever he did . . . it was a lie."*

"Yes, but that was a discovery made too late."

An arm wrapped across Aleksei's chest, holding him close to the vampire. He looked up, startled to see that Nikolayev was now bracing himself against the wall with one hand and rubbing his neck with the other. The imprint of large fingers was clearly visible on the count's pale skin, but Aleksei felt his brow furrow. He was certain he hadn't let the count go. The vampire, noticing the marks on the count's neck, also gave a grunt of approval. It was a strangely satisfying endorsement.

"Do it!" Nikolayev suddenly screamed, beating a fist against his thigh. "And make it painful. I want him to suffer."

The grip on his chin became a little firmer. "Do not fight me," the vampire instructed as he buried his fangs in Aleksei's neck.

Fight him? How? With what?

Completely immobilized, Aleksei had no choice but to concentrate on the sensation sweeping through him. He felt a mild burning sensation as razor-sharp points sank into his skin and pierced the thick vein below the surface. His pulse accelerated as the vampire began to suck, but instead of feeling fear, Aleksei burned with shame at his immediate raging erection. Curling his hands around the arm across his chest, he did not seek to break free, but rather to hold on. The last thing Aleksei wanted was for anything to interrupt the vampire at his neck. He gave himself over completely, knowing as he did so that this was not suffering. His family had fared far worse.

The pull at his neck was getting stronger. How many mouthfuls had the vampire taken? Three? Four? A dozen or twenty? Aleksei had no way of knowing. He opened his eyes and noticed the fading light. Either the candles were dying . . . or he was.

Nikolayev moved closer, wanting a better view of how the vampire was draining his victim, but Aleksei didn't think he would be able to see much. The fall of purple-blue hair obscured most of the vampire's face, and the count's expression became that of a man realizing he was being cheated of a great prize. Catching Nikolayev's frustrated look, Aleksei gave him a warm smile. It was the only weapon he had left with which to punish him.

The darkness was increasing, coming faster now, and Aleksei was having difficulty discerning substance from shadow. Nikolayev was turning hazy, threatening to become vapor in a few moments more.

Aleksei recalled a memory from childhood. A priest, not the same one who had braved Magda's hut, but an older, kinder man, had told him he had nothing to fear from death.

"When you die, my son, if your heart is pure, you will be carried to heaven by the gentle hands of angels," the priest had said, "and bathed in the warmth of a soft, glowing light."

It would seem the truth was somewhat different.

Death came for Aleksei on a great roar of thunder, bringing with it enough blazing light to blind him. And there were no angelic hands lifting him to paradise. Instead, he felt himself being rudely yanked free of the vampire's embrace and thrown over a broad shoulder, his throbbing erection crushed against a mass of muscle and bone. He couldn't decide which was worse, his need for release or his embarrassment at having a hard-on at such an inappropriate time.

"Life or death, Aleksei, which do you choose?"

Gabriel stared down at the cruel scar that covered half the peasant farmer's face.

He would carry the witch's signature with him for the rest of his life, no matter which choice he made. The healing properties that came with being a vampire would only restore injuries received as a vampire. They could do nothing for wounds already given.

Gabriel had been halfway up the staircase when he saw the familiar shock of periwinkle hair. Only one vampire, to his knowledge, was so brightly hued, but he could not imagine what might have brought Kartel to this house on this night. Still, there was no mistaking another Original Vampire. It had been so long since he last saw another of his kind that Gabriel was momentarily shocked. He hesitated and almost cost Aleksei his life.

He burst in through the door and realized Aleksei was only moments away from the point of no return. The moment where the amount of blood lost would be too great, giving his mortal body no chance of recovery. Humans facing the precipice of death rarely got the chance to step back from the edge, and those taken there by a vampire never were. They either became a vampire or were tossed over the edge.

In separating the two of them, Gabriel had been splashed with Aleksei's blood. It was a few drops only, but enough to reveal he possessed the element that would enable him to make the transition to vampire. Something Kartel could not have failed to recognize as he drank. There was no precedent that said the offer had to be made, but that an Original Vampire had not done so troubled Gabriel. True, the process was not as easy as was believed, and it could only happen if absolute submission was given. And relinquishing their independence was something most humans were neither willing nor prepared to do.

But Gabriel could not, in all good conscience, deny Aleksei his chance to become a vampire. He had already asked if Gabriel would change him, and his reply had been *"not without good reason."* Was imminent death good enough? It seemed to Gabriel to fall into that category, which was why, after throwing Aleksei over his shoulder, he had fled with him. Climbing upward through the grand house, Gabriel had exited onto the roof and from there moved across the city until the safety of his own home came into view.

Now, with Aleksei in his arms, he made his way to the chamber that held his sarcophagus. *"Life or death, Aleksei,"* he repeated softly, lying down with him on top of the blue marble. *"I can give you either, but you must choose—and quickly, my friend, for time is running short."*

"Does . . . Petrov . . . live?"

Gabriel could not answer with any certainty, but he recalled the look on Kartel's face when he'd pulled him away from Aleksei. Unpredictable and cruel, Kartel had cared little for the human race as an angel, and even less as a vampire. Indeed, Gabriel had often wondered what had driven the angel to stand with him on that battlefield so long ago.

With neither compassion nor any depth of understanding, Kartel had been known to change a human simply because it amused him to do so. Without proper guidance, the effects of the transition could be traumatic. The fact that no vampire changed by Kartel had ever managed to survive beyond their first year was considered by Gabriel to be a good thing.

And now he was certain the same fate awaited Nikolayev, although in this case Kartel's cruelty might be considered poetic justice.

"He lives . . . for now," Gabriel said, grimly.

Aleksei gripped his arm, surprised at the feel of bare skin beneath his fingers.

"It will save time," Gabriel told him, answering his unasked question, and wondering if Aleksei was coherent enough to realize that both of them were naked.

If he was, it made little difference because his pale tongue passed over even paler lips as he said, "Make . . . me . . . as . . . you . . ."

Gabriel, pleased by the choice, smiled at him. "You must surrender yourself to me, Aleksei. All that you are or ever will be must be given to me. Can you do this?" Even as he saw the vague movement of Aleksei's head, Gabriel felt him yield.

Using his saliva to close the puncture wounds made by Kartel, Gabriel pierced the other side of Aleksei's neck. His fangs were longer than Kartel's had been and went deeper. Aleksei, barely conscious, lay inside Gabriel's embrace, his head supported by the vampire's broad shoulder. Pulling deeper, Gabriel took only as much blood as was necessary. Enough to trigger the start of the death spiral, but still leaving enough to assure the same fatality caused no long-term damage to the delicate balance of internal organs. Drawing back his fangs, Gabriel waited.

He felt Aleksei's body as it stilled, chemical reactions triggering the natural process that would result in atrophy and decay as each organ slipped into a state of inertia. The brain's electrical impulses began slowing as it succumbed to a paralytic dream. And when all that still functioned was Aleksei's heart, moving on muscle memory, Gabriel listened and waited. The slowing beat, followed by another, and then another . . . and then Gabriel struck.

Without hesitation his fangs sliced through Aleksei's rapidly cooling skin, sliding between his ribs and into his heart. And as the organ contracted for what should have been the final time, it now began to fill with blood. Instead of siphons used to draw blood from the body, Gabriel's fangs were functioning in reverse. Filling the stilled heart with a mix of Aleksei's human and his own vampire blood. A mix that sent a shock wave through the motionless body and jolted to life a long-recessive gene.

In the normal course of events, Gabriel would have slit his wrist and fed Aleksei back his own blood, his vampire body easily holding the surplus volume until it could be returned. But Kartel had almost drained Aleksei, leaving barely enough liquid to stimulate the change. Now Gabriel needed Aleksei's own body to replace the lost amount. But that would take time.

He tightened his arms around Aleksei, watching the runes on the glassy surface of the sarcophagus as they glowed and started to move. Tasked with the responsibility of protecting and restoring him, the small black symbols now scurried like insects, realigning their positions in order to accommodate two bodies instead of one.

Having done all he could, and praying it was enough, Gabriel closed his eyes and gave himself and—God willing—his progeny up to the Dark.

Chapter 24

"So how long were you in the sarcophagus with Gabriel?" I asked, watching Aleksei get up out of his seat. An unexpected twinge of jealousy flared at knowing I wasn't the only person Gabriel had taken into his coffin. It was unreasonable, I know, and I felt horrible about it.

"I'm not sure," the big guy said with a frown. "Three days, maybe four?"

"And you looked like this when you came out?"

He nodded and grinned at me. "Yes. Even more handsome than before."

"Any regrets?" It was an unfair question, but I was curious to see if he fully understood that when Gabriel had asked him to make his choice, he was hardly in a clear state of mind to do so.

"Being a vampire has allowed me to see the world in a way I never knew was possible. That alone has made every minute of every night worth it. So no, I have no regrets about what I am." He narrowed his eyes slightly. "No matter the circumstances, Rowan, believe me when I say I would always choose to be vampire."

So now you know.

"And how bad was the transition for you?"

"For me? Not so bad, but I was lucky. I had Gabriel to help me."

"Yeah, I can imagine having to drink blood took some getting used to."

"That was not problem." He chuckled softly at my puzzled expression. "Rowan, you don't think about needing food or drinking. You know is necessary to keep body alive. When you are vampire, blood is same thing. You need it to keep body alive."

"So you never had a problem drinking blood?"

Clasping his hands together, Aleksei rested his chin on them and stared at me. "You are wanting to know if I thought it was wrong to drink blood, yes?" I suppose I was, and I gave him a small nod. "No," he replied. "I have never been confused about what I was doing or the reason why. And I never felt guilty."

"But can't a vampire kill someone by draining their blood?"

"Of course," he said with no hesitation whatsoever. "It happens. In the beginning it cannot be helped. It takes time to learn how to control the feeding and there will always be vampires who use it as a form of execution." He paused, giving me a few moments to let his words sink in.

"But you have killed people, haven't you?" I asked, with morbid curiosity. He hesitated for only a moment before nodding his head. "So . . . how?"

He held his hands out and then made a quick twisting motion in the air. "Snapping neck is faster and cleaner, unless, of course, message needs to be sent."

Message?

Yeah, like the kind of message Gabriel sent courtesy of Gus.

"Besides," Aleksei continued, dropping his hands to his knees, "blood from those people leaves bad taste."

Those people were the corrupt and depraved, and how their blood would taste was something that, in a million years, would never have occurred to me.

"But have you ever drunk from someone . . . and killed them accidentally?"

The way his eyes darkened told me I was skating on very thin ice, but I needed to know as much as I could. Aleksei was the only human Gabriel had ever turned, which made him special. And I didn't mean riding the short bus special. I could feel the link between the two of them, and in light of what Aleksei was expecting Gabriel to do when Anasztaizia died, I felt I had the right to know as much about this vampire as possible. After all, he was expecting me to help Gabriel pick up the pieces.

"Only once," he said in a voice so low I almost didn't hear him. "It was few months into my transition. As I already said, I had no problem with drinking blood, and Gabriel was teaching me how to regulate my feeding so I never took too much from one person."

"But something went wrong?"

He nodded and lowered his eyes. "You must understand that as vampire I was much bigger and stronger than before. I had to learn how to use my new body. Holding something small was challenge. It was six months before I was allowed to drink from a glass."

The difficulties were perfectly relatable, and I could understand that it took time to adjust to the new parameters afforded by the physical enhancements. "What about your senses?" I asked. "Were you having trouble with those as well?"

He shook his head. "The improvement there did not happen until after I was in more control of my body. Is too much to deal with all at once. I had to get used to the changes in . . ." He held his hands up, palms facing each other about an inch apart.

"Baby steps."

"Da, baby steps."

Okay, that made sense. "So how did that feel?"

His face lit up like the Fourth of July. "Amazing! I could smell when rain was coming, I could hear people in next house arguing, I could taste blend of grapes in wine," he paused and smiled at me. "But you want to know what the very best is?" Returning his smile, I nodded. "Seeing colors. Seeing *all* colors, seeing *colors* that make up colors."

"It sounds fantastic, but kind of one step away from a nervous breakdown," I told him.

He shrugged. "Yes, is true, and Gabriel has said some new vampires cannot deal with so much, um . . ." He screwed up his face as he searched for the right word.

"Stimulus?" I offered.

"Yes, is too much." He beamed at me, pleased that he had not succumbed to such a fate. "But Gabriel was big help. He taught me how to turn it down. How to hear everything, but not so loud and not so much."

This time he made a lowering gesture with his palms facing the floor. I understood exactly what he was saying. He needed to find a way to be aware of everything around him without letting it overpower him. Teach his brain how to compartmentalize all the information his heightened abilities were sending him.

"So what happened?" I asked softly, bringing him back to my original question of whether he'd ever killed anyone by accident.

He lowered his eyes, concerned with the dregs of coffee in the bottom of his mug. "Has Gabriel ever fed from you while you are . . ." The color crept up from below the collar of his shirt, flushing his neck and jawline.

"What? Having sex?" I couldn't decide if his embarrassment was over the subject of sex in general, or as it pertained to me and Gabriel. The blush grew deeper in color.

"Then you know how closely linked the two appetites are," he said after clearing his throat a couple of times.

Oh yeah, I knew. Did I ever.

I stared at the big guy, wondering which appetite had gotten out of control, because from the way Aleksei was now squirming in his seat, one of them had. With really, really bad consequences. I hoped it wasn't lust because having so recently been threatened with it myself, I couldn't bear it if Aleksei turned out to be a rapist.

"Tell me about it," I murmured in a low voice.

He put the coffee mug on the table between us and clasped his hands together, holding them so tightly his knuckles turned white.

"Tomas had very strict rules for the house servants," he began in a voice only a little lower than mine had been. "If any of them began to ask questions or show too much curiosity about Gabriel, then he found them another position somewhere else. The servants had no concerns about Gabriel as far as I knew, but my presence in the house was causing some . . . unease."

I could well imagine that. It would be hard to not notice this newly turned and improved version of Aleksei.

"The servants were told not to go into my room when I was in the house, and even when I was gone to never go in without Tomas. It was for their own safety. My behavior was erratic, unpredictable, which is why going through the transition without the help of another vampire is so dangerous." Unclasping his hands, he now began rubbing them together. Kind of like air-washing. "You must understand I was a peasant with no knowledge of women, so when I experienced lust—real lust—for the first time, it was both terrifying and wonderful. Please believe me, Rowan, when I tell you I never meant to harm her."

"I believe you," I said. Even if it turned out that Aleksei had assaulted this girl, I was certain he had not been aware of his actions. And the fact that whatever happened still haunted him was proof of his remorse.

"There was a new girl in the house, and she either forgot or decided to ignore the instructions about being in my room." He shook his head, recalling the foolishness of the girl's actions. "She came in alone, without Tomas, just as I was rising. Gabriel had told me that he had made certain arrangements for me"—the color began creeping up over his collar again, and I could appreciate just how difficult this was for him—"and so I assumed . . . seeing a girl alone in my room . . ." Placing a hand over his mouth, Aleksei began shaking his head slowly.

"You attacked her?"

He gave me a stricken look and nodded.

"How?"

"I fed from her." I could only imagine the terror the girl must have felt at having Aleksei grab her from the shadows, but I was relieved there had been no rape. "But with the lust so strong in me, I could not control the feeding." He slumped back in his seat, and the hand that had been covering his mouth earlier now covered his eyes. "I didn't even know what I had done until Tomas and Gabriel pulled me off her."

"Was she . . . ?"

He nodded. "It was almost ten years before they told me I had killed her that night. So yes, I do regret taking a life, but that is the only one, and I will carry it with me to my grave."

There was nothing anyone could say to ease his guilt, me least of all, but perhaps that was the way it was supposed to be. In the grand scheme of things, he needed to carry the burden of an innocent death. To remind him just how fragile we all were. Even vampires.

"You said Gabriel made certain arrangements?" Aleksei stared at me, his face unreadable, and now it was my turn to feel my face pink up. "Was it with another vampire or . . . ?"

"Do you remember your first time with Gabriel?" Remember? It was something I was never going to forget. "And you were virgin, yes?"

I was definitely feeling a five-alarm burn on my cheeks, but it seemed ridiculously hypocritical of me to refuse to answer the question. My relationship with the big Russian vampire had gone past awkward to more than congenial two pots of coffee ago, but I just hoped he never asked me anything that was even slightly intimate when Gabriel was around. I nodded and mumbled something under my breath that could have passed for a yes. In any case, Aleksei took it as such.

"But you didn't know Gabriel was vampire, true?" Not expecting me to answer, he continued. "And once you knew, you could appreciate how much restraint he used that first time, yes?" Apparently this time he did expect an answer because he waited until I managed to squeak out a faint affirmative. "Now imagine if it was Gabriel's first time, and he had no control over the impulses, the physical desire and need that drove him." Oh shit! Not good, not good, not good! "It was how I first met Katja."

I felt myself stiffen. Of course I knew he had a history with the psycho vampire bitch. I just never expected it to be a physical one.

"Is best you know all of this now," Aleksei said with a sigh. "Gabriel would not risk my hurting another girl. The best way to control my lust was to have sex with someone I couldn't kill. Bruise a little maybe, but not actually kill."

"You might have done us all a favor," I mumbled under my breath.

"Rowan!"

"Don't 'Rowan' me. You know as well as I do that girl's a serious whack job!"

He may have looked shocked, but I could see the corners of his eyes crinkle as he tried not to laugh. Ready to leave the subject of sex and Katja behind, I said, "So you got through your transition, and then what? You just hung out with Gabriel and Tomas?"

He nodded. "For a while. Gabriel taught me to read and write, and then had scholars continue my education in whatever country we were in at the time."

"And did you ever return to your home village?"

"Once it was safe and everyone who had known me was dead, Gabriel took me back. It was about a hundred years later. Of course he didn't know it at the time, but we could have returned sooner. After Petrov's disappearance, and with no son to take over, the village was abandoned. A few houses were still standing, but the dacha had fallen into disrepair. Still, I was able to pay my respects to my family in the field where Gabriel and I had buried them." He gave me a sudden, unexpected smile. "It was nice. I had, um, what's the word? Closure. Yes, that's it. I had closure."

"And what made you decide to come to America?"

He got up from his seat and gathered our empty coffee mugs and took them into the kitchen. I'd been sitting for too long, and my butt was numb, so I got to my feet and did a quick circumnavigation around the room, stopping at the sliding-glass doors that led onto the terrace. It wasn't quite nightfall but close, and even though the rain had stopped, the gloom and darkness lingered.

"America was the last place Gabriel had seen you," Aleksei said, answering my question as he returned with fresh supplies. He brought a tray of cookies with the coffee. "So it seemed the best place to look for you. And he was right. It just took a little longer than expected."

"Aleksei . . . can I ask you something?"

"Of course, anything."

"Did you ever see that other vampire again, the one like Gabriel?"

"You mean Kartel?" His pause told me he was thinking. "No, I have never seen him again. Trust me, I think I would remember."

"But if you were to see him again, do you think you would recognize him?"

"Of course," he answered with a rich chuckle. "Why do you ask?"

"Because there's a vampire standing on the terrace . . . and he's got blue hair."

Chapter 25

Ithink I'd been expecting something in the punk-rock range of bright blue with streaks of shocking purple, but the blend of colors was far more subtle than that. On the surface, his hair was blue with purple undertones, and all I could think was how perfectly it suited him. And didn't make him look in the least bit gay. Something you can't say about a lot of men who decide to sport a long blue mane.

The only other Original Vampire I'd ever seen was Ryiel, and that meeting had been somewhat stressful. Having a psychotic female vampire threatening to rip your throat out can put a damper on the best of circumstances, but I won't apologize for admiring a good set of pecs. And if that makes me shallow, so be it.

But I'd never had the chance to be as up close and personal with Ryiel as I was with this new vampire standing on the terrace. With only a thick pane of specially coated glass separating us, I could already tell he was going to pop the top of the drop-dead-gorgeous thermometer without even trying. I don't know why I was surprised by this. When you consider that all the founding vampires were angels before making the choice to embrace the Dark Realm, it stood to reason they would be handsome. Was it surprising they were the blueprint the Wraith used for his ultimate predator? And I'm sure it didn't hurt that they already came fully armed with his weapon of choice. Seduction. The human race should be thankful there were only nine of them. Any more and I'm not sure as a species we'd survive.

I could feel Kartel's pale green eyes staring through the glass at me, and I wondered how he'd gotten onto the terrace without anyone noticing, and how long he'd been out there. Had he been eavesdropping on Aleksei and me? I stared back, seeing raindrops sparkling like diamonds in his hair and across the wide shoulders of the long gray duster he wore. Whatever the reason for this sudden, unexpected appearance, it was ridiculous to keep him outside. What was I going to do? Pretend I hadn't seen him? He could easily break the sliding door, and I'd have to explain to Tomas why there was shattered glass all over the floor.

"Does he need to be invited in?" Although the penthouse was now my home, I didn't think I could technically invite a vampire inside.

My question had been for Aleksei, but it was Gabriel who answered. "A vampire does not need permission to enter the home of another vampire," he said, "but opening the door would be good."

He doesn't want to have to explain shattered glass to Tomas either.

The blue-haired vampire had stepped forward and wore an expression that was both bemused and mildly irritated. I opened the door, feeling the glass slide smoothly on its track.

"I wonder what he wants," I heard Aleksei murmur under his breath.

I'm not a big fan of coincidences, and Kartel showing up not a half hour after I'd learned of his existence seemed a little too flukey for me.

The vampire stepped inside. The look of irritation disappeared as he crossed the threshold, but I figured that was due to Gabriel's presence more than anything else. He looked down, and the smile he gave me seemed genuine enough. But he was a vampire. There was no telling what he was thinking.

"You must be Rowan," he said, presenting me with another weird accent to add to my collection. Not quite English and definitely not Eastern European. Maybe Australian or South African?

I looked pointedly at his hair. "Then you must be Kartel."

"If you say so, then I suppose I must be." He reached for my hand, clasping it with long, cool fingers that almost wrapped around my wrist. "It's a pleasure to finally make your acquaintance."

Except I knew it wasn't.

There are some people you share an instant connection with the very first time you meet them. You just *know* you're going to be life-long friends even if, on the surface, you have nothing in common. You can be separated by race, religion, social, and economic differences. You can argue over politics, disagree on Miley Cyrus twerking, and ponder the silent half of Penn and Teller—what's up with that guy? But in spite of all that, you will always be there for each other.

And then there are the other kind of people. The ones who give off a really bad vibe. They haven't done anything wrong, mainly because they haven't been given the chance—yet—but they're never going to get a Christmas card from you, assuming you're someone who still sends out Yuletide greetings. And should they ever extend an invitation to any type of get-together, you'll come up with an excuse not to attend.

Aunt Mabel's cat is throwing up hairballs.

Aunt Mabel is throwing up hairballs.

Aunt Mabel and the cat are both throwing up hairballs.

If pressed, you couldn't give any viable reason for not liking this person, but something inside you says you need to distance yourself both literally and figuratively. This "something" is your sixth sense. The one that most of us acknowledge only in hindsight, if at all. And no, it doesn't mean you're going to start seeing dead people. Haven't you ever felt a weird prickle on the back of your neck and thought, *I've got a really bad feeling about this?*

Yeah, that's right, *that* sixth sense. The only way I can explain it is to say, good or bad, the person you're dealing with left a strong enough impression that it carried over from a previous lifetime. Unfortunately, most of us have replaced our sixth sense in favor of technology, so that when it does speak we just don't hear it. Or if we do, we don't believe it.

Being with Gabriel has taught me not to ignore anything—especially not the voices in my head—and right now my own sixth sense was pinging all over the place like some malfunctioning video ping-pong game telling me to be wary. And with good reason. I could tell from the flicker of annoyance Kartel didn't hide quickly enough that meeting me wasn't a pleasure. It was an infuriating aggravation.

I wonder why?

I pulled my hand from his grasp as politely as I could, while doing my best to resist the urge to wipe it down my pant leg. But I think Kartel was fully aware of what I was feeling even as his smile remained fixed in place. He looked over my head, and I noticed the corners of his mouth twitching.

"Ah, it's the peasant farmer. You cannot know how pleased I am to see you survived our initial meeting."

Aleksei inclined his head slightly in acknowledgment before saying, "And I find it hard to believe you did not already know such a thing."

Our guest made a noise that might have originated in the land of mirth before saying, "Regardless, it does not diminish my pleasure in seeing you again. You came through the transition well. Being a vampire suits you."

"I was fortunate," Aleksei said solemnly. "I had a strong hand to guide me."

Kartel's eyes suddenly flashed a darker shade of green at the not-so-subtle criticism. "Indeed you were fortunate. No one could ever fault Gabriel's level of commitment." A trait that, according to what I'd just been told, this particular Original lacked.

I wasn't the only one getting weird vibes from Kartel. Aleksei was also dealing with old feelings, but I had no idea in which direction they were running. While Kartel was not the first vampire the big guy had met, he had the dubious distinction of being the first to take Aleksei's blood, drinking so much that Gabriel almost hadn't been able to offer Aleksei the chance to become a vampire. Did something like that leave a bad taste? Or don't guys care about such things?

Maybe if the vampire had been female? My inner bitch snarked.

"Kartel." Gabriel crossed his arms and nodded at the other vampire, who nodded back. Guess handshakes weren't a vampire form of greeting. "Can I offer you something to drink?"

"Thank you. Scotch, if you have it."

He shrugged off his wet coat and held it out to Aleksei, who seemed to immediately engage Kartel in some wordless conversation. From their body language I assumed it was one of those male don't-come-into-my-house-and-piss-on-my-shoes type of exchanges. The fact that this wasn't actually Aleksei's house was a minor detail not worth mentioning. His point made, the big guy grinned and took the outer garment from Kartel, unceremoniously throwing it across the closest chair.

"Let me," I said as Gabriel made a move toward the bar. Pouring a drink was well within my range of capabilities.

"You said scotch, right? Any particular brand?" I added as I began checking labels.

I'm a simple girl who drinks bourbon. Scotch intimidates me, mainly because there are so many different brands, all called Mac-something, Glen-whatever, or Highland-what's it.

"I believe our guest is partial to Ballantine's," Gabriel said, coming to stand on the other side of the bar from me.

"I'm honored you remember such an insignificant detail."

"Hardly insignificant when I basically had to stop you from drinking the distillery dry."

"Yes, I was determined." Kartel was definitely pleased and more than a little flattered by Gabriel's recall.

"There should be a bottle behind the Glenfiddich, sweetheart," he said, pointing to the shelf behind me.

Seeing his reflection in the mirrored wall made me want to kiss the ever-loving bejesus out of him. He gave me a flash of his dimple.

Gabriel had obviously sensed Kartel's presence the moment the other vampire stepped onto the terrace, and he had forced himself to rise earlier than he should. By my reckoning, he needed a few more hours in the protective confines of his sarcophagus. He still looked tired, but I think I was the only one who noticed. I was, however, glad not to have to deal with our unexpected guest on my own.

I located the bottle of scotch and poured a generous measure of the amber liquid into a heavy-bottomed crystal tumbler. "Where's Tomas?" I asked Gabriel, curious about the sentinel's absence. "Doesn't he know we have company?"

"He's keeping an eye on Anasztaizia . . . and yes, he knows."

The change in Gabriel's voice as he said the last part made me look up. There was a reason for Tomas's nonappearance. A reason that had to do with Kartel. First me, then Aleksei, and now Tomas. What was with this guy?

I glanced at the other Original Vampire. He appeared to be studying a painting on the wall. An original Chagall, it had been given to Gabriel by the artist himself. I shook my head and felt my brows pull together. With his heightened vampire senses, Kartel had to be aware of the negative effect his presence was having on us. Aleksei had already put him on notice, for God's sake! Still it was possible—make that probable—that he just didn't care. His concern was with Gabriel, and as Original Vampires, they had to share a common bond.

But there was one thing I was certain Kartel hadn't taken into account. If he knew who I was, it stood to reason he also knew what I was, and putting me on edge seemed a particularly stupid thing to do. If the situation were reversed, I would have gone out of my way to try to put him at ease. If only to not risk pissing off Gabriel. Whatever he'd picked up from me by shaking my hand was more than enough interaction between us. But the tension was growing. His reason for being here was important enough to risk the equivalent of a nuclear meltdown should the wrong thing be said.

I pushed the glass of scotch across the bar, as well as a separate glass of Stoli Elit. My man is a vodka drinker by choice. Sensing my overall lack of warmth, Gabriel pressed his lips to the corner of my mouth before picking up both drinks.

"I always did admire your taste in art," Kartel said as Gabriel handed him his glass. "Personally, I find anything by Dali strangely compelling."

I knew who Salvador Dali was. Gabriel had taken me to a showing of the surrealist painter's works. Compelling wasn't the word I would have used to describe his art. Clever yes, weird definitely, but if I'm honest I also found his work more than a little creepy. It didn't surprise me to hear Kartel was a fan.

As both vampires took a seat, I saw Aleksei chose to remain standing. He positioned himself behind Gabriel's chair, crossing his arms over his chest. My lover looked over at me and raised a brow. I shook my head, preferring to watch the show from behind the bar. I wanted an unobstructed view as I watched this drama play itself out.

In spite of my best efforts, Gabriel continued to make black the predominant color in his wardrobe. Not that he didn't look absolutely spectacular in it, but I had come to the conclusion that this was not accidental on his part. Black not only made his hair look stunning, it also intensified the blue of his eyes. How was I supposed to argue with that?

I don't know what color Ryiel favored, but dark leather pants and skin seemed to work well with his black hair and silver eyes, as I recall. Kartel had a fondness for gray. The muscle shirt and pants, the belt and boots were all within a shade or two of each other, and as much as I hated to admit it, it was a good choice, complementing both his hair and the pale green of his eyes.

And just like Gabriel and Ryiel, he also bore exotic tattoos.

Gabriel's ran the length of his spine, Ryiel's across his upper chest. Kartel wore his down the inside of each arm. The symbols told each Original Vampire's story, what they had once been and how they came to be what they were now. Seeing Kartel's, I had to wonder if all nine Original Vampires were tattooed in different places on their bodies. And was that by choice or design?

No one spoke for a good five minutes. Vampires don't seem to bother with small talk, or maybe they did, just communicating in a different way. Perhaps the steady staring at each other was their way of saying *Hey, how you been? How's the wife? Is Junior playing baseball this year? How about them Cowboys?* Yeah, right, whatever.

I may not have been in tune with Kartel, but I knew enough about Gabriel to tell he wasn't interacting with him the way he had with Ryiel. I don't know if Aleksei noticed anything out of the ordinary about Gabriel's response. The big guy was dealing with issues of his own, but even if he wasn't bristling, he might not have noticed. With Gabriel you had to know what to look for. Everything from his breathing to the flexing muscles of his forearm—hell, even the way he was swirling his vodka—confirmed his lack of trust in the vampire sitting across from him.

Well, well, well . . . isn't that interesting?

Actually, it was. This was my first glimpse of Gabriel interacting with a vampire he didn't like.

Aren't you forgetting Katja?

That was entirely different. I think he liked her well enough until she tried to kill me, and besides, I'm pretty sure Kartel isn't interested in getting into Gabriel's pants like Katja was.

I think, given the opportunity, she'd still like to do that.

That reminder I could have done without. I mentally shushed my inner bitch so I could concentrate on everything that wasn't being said between Gabriel and our guest.

"So what brings you here, Kartel . . . to my home?" Gabriel asked.

A blind man and his dog would be able to pick up on that one. This was a big deal. Coming to a vampire's home uninvited.

Kartel, with his Katy Perry hair, seemed to be fashioned from the irritating younger sibling mold. The kind of relative that, as a kid, had a standing weekly appointment with the principal and, as an adult, only called when he needed bail money. Which was often.

Of course I could be totally wrong. My own family dynamic hardly made me an expert, but I've watched enough daytime TV.

"I've come to tell you that Petrov is off-limits. He is under my protection, and any punishment he may receive will be both determined and administered by me." He paused before adding, "And only by me."

Chapter 26

"You do know he abducted Rowan?" Gabriel said, keeping his voice deliberately calm.

Kartel waved his hand in my direction. "And yet there she stands, alive and unharmed."

"No thanks to your boy," I snapped. "Did he tell you he actually injected me with some concoction that was meant to kill me? Did he tell you that?"

"As I said . . . alive and unharmed."

Fuming, I reached for the bottle of Jack Daniels and a shot glass.

"I had no idea you still shared a bond with him." Gabriel took a sip of his vodka. "I assumed you would have discarded him long ago." *Like all the other vampires you ever created,* he didn't need to add.

"I have my reasons, Gabriel, and Petrov has proved his worth to me."

"No matter, his actions warrant an accounting, Kartel. You know that." Gabriel's voice was grave.

"Then trust me to take care of it, but in my own time."

"And when will that be?" Aleksei asked, jumping into the conversation. "After he has persuaded you to kill me?"

"Killing you has never been his aim," Kartel said, looking over Gabriel's head at the Russian vampire. "He just wants you to suffer. Why else would he go after the female that feeds you?"

I couldn't believe what I was hearing. If they gave out prizes for the most selfish, uncaring, arrogant prick of a vampire, then this guy was a winner, hands down.

"Don't you think Aleksei has suffered enough at Petrov's hands?" I wasn't expecting an answer. I was throwing the question out there as a reminder of who the real monster was in all this. A monster with zero remorse.

"Ah, so you are familiar with the details of their little dispute, are you?"

"I hardly think rape and murder can be categorized as a *little dispute*," I snapped. He made a dismissive gesture, and I clenched my hands to stop myself from throwing something at him. Preferably the bottle of Ballantine's.

"Is this the only reason for your visit?" Gabriel asked.

Kartel was startled by the question. It seemed as if he was being dismissed, except he wasn't quite ready to go. "Yes," he said slowly before adding, "and of course I wanted to see for myself that your Promise had indeed survived."

"Take a good look, asshole," I muttered, filling the shot glass with bourbon and managing not to spill any on the polished mahogany bar surface.

"You do know your abduction was an accident, don't you? If those imbecilic morons Petrov used had half a brain between them, this never would have happened, and I wouldn't be here."

"You're wrong," Gabriel said coldly. "You would still be here as you are, but we would not be engaged in so pleasant a conversation." *This is pleasant?* "Petrov's intended victim is just as important to me. Someone whose well-being is very much my concern." Gabriel tossed down his vodka, giving Kartel a moment to grasp the full ramifications of his words. "But I am curious . . . just when did Petrov realize Rowan was a Promise? Before or after he gave her the injections meant to kill her?"

I had told Gabriel that although Petrov sensed I was different, I wasn't certain he knew I was a Promise. A fact Kartel now confirmed.

"I'm not sure he did realize, at least not until after he found the message you left behind."

What message? Had Rat Boy said something? Somehow I didn't think he'd ever be coherent again.

"He didn't know it was you," Kartel said, answering the unspoken question on Gabriel's face, "until I enlightened him. Had you simply broken the imbecile's neck, I would also have remained ignorant of your involvement, but removing the heart that way? That's quite unique, and there's only one vampire I know who kills with such ruthless efficiency. Of course the why was a puzzle until Petrov admitted the woman was also gone. After that everything became clear as crystal."

"I find it hard to believe he didn't know what Rowan is," Gabriel said in an icy voice. "Any vampire that comes within ten feet would pick up her scent and be able to identify it. And he actually spilled her blood."

"Well, he didn't know," Kartel said unconcernedly. "Blame me if you wish. Perhaps I should have told him how to recognize a Promise, and what to do if he came across one. Frankly, I never expected it to happen. Petrov told me he panicked, and I have no reason to doubt him."

"That's bullshit! He's lying, and you know it!" I slammed the empty shot glass I was holding down on the bar hard enough to crack the glass. The vampire I recalled wasn't at all panicked. He was in complete control of the situation and had no hesitation whatsoever about what he was going to do, or what he expected Gus to do to me.

Kartel turned his head and stared at me, his pale green eyes glowing oddly. "A compromise then," he said, turning back to Gabriel. "I will give him to you when I am done with him."

"No," Gabriel said, getting to his feet, indicating the discussion was over. "His life is mine. You have twenty-four hours to bring him to me . . . alive and unharmed."

"Unharmed?"

Kartel was hiding something, but if he was angered by Gabriel's decision, he hid it well. Tossing what was left of his scotch down, he got to his feet. "Tell me, Gabriel, did it never strike you as curious that both the peasant farmer and Petrov could be turned?"

Gabriel shrugged his shoulders. "Coincidence, nothing more."

Kartel stared at him, a look of mock surprise on his face. "You don't really believe that, do you?" He shook his head, making the periwinkle-blue hair shimmer across his shoulders. "Well, I can tell you it's more than coincidence."

"What do you mean?" Aleksei snarled from behind Gabriel.

"You forget, Aleksei, I have tasted your blood as well as that of Nikolayev Vasily Petrov, and I find too many similarities for mere coincidence."

"Stop talking in riddles, and speak plain!" His snarl turned a little more menacing. "What are you saying about Petrov?"

"He's saying, or rather he's implying, that you and Petrov are related by blood," I burst out incredulously.

Aleksei slowly turned his head and looked at me, and then whipped his gaze back to Kartel. "Is that true? Is that what you're saying?"

"What Petrov did to your sister? That was just a boy following his father's example. Petrov doesn't hate you because you sought revenge; that was something he understood. He even admired you for having the balls to take him on, and I know because he's told me often enough. What Petrov hates is the fact you are undeniable proof that a rumor was true." Kartel stepped out from between the seating arrangement and the low coffee table, moving into an unobstructed part of the living room. "What Petrov hates is knowing his only surviving brother—a half-brother—exists because his father took a peasant girl into a barn full of cows and straw and shit and fucked her. An unacceptable reminder that under the skin—peasant or aristocrat—you're all the same. Trust me, what he did to your sister, and subsequently your family, was no accident."

"But how did Petrov find out about Aleksei?" I asked.

"He says his father told him," Kartel replied.

"Why would he do that?"

"Who knows? You humans are consumed by guilt over the most trivial things. Perhaps a living reminder of his infidelity filled the old count with a need to confess, or maybe," Kartel continued with a grin that was pure evil. "He knew how his legitimate heir would react to such a revelation."

A howl of rage almost shattered my eardrums. The knowledge that Kartel was superior to him in strength was forgotten by Aleksei who, in a moment of sheer madness, launched himself at the Original Vampire. I told myself the surprise of his attack would surely be an advantage, but if it was, I never got the chance to see it.

Unwilling to let Aleksei commit suicide, Gabriel tackled him. Wrapping his arms around him, he took the big guy down to the ground in a movement that was so quick it was over before I had time to blink. That was the other thing Aleksei seemed to have forgotten. Only an Original Vampire could take the life of another vampire. It was something I was sure Kartel never forgot.

Gabriel snapped out a series of commands as he dragged Aleksei from the room. I didn't recognize the language, but the tone and intent were clear. And as I watched the big guy struggle in his maker's arms, I had the most absurd idea that perhaps this entire incident wasn't quite as spontaneous as it might appear.

What would possess Kartel to move to the only place in the room where Aleksei had a clear shot at him? He must have known his inflammatory comments would provoke such a reaction. Why would he want Aleksei to attack him? Was it to satisfy some warped vindictive streak, or did the Original Vampire want to finish what Petrov had started and failed to complete?

There was no doubt in my mind that Kartel had an agenda. I just wished I knew what it was. I went to reach for a new shot glass and stopped. How many would that make? Three? Four? Instead I recapped the bottle of Jack Daniels and put it back on the shelf.

Perhaps you're looking at this all wrong . . .

Huh?

Perhaps goading Aleksei was nothing more than poking an angry bear with a stick. Maybe the object was to get both Aleksei and Gabriel out of the room, leaving you all alone . . .

Shit! I never considered that.

Apparently not . . .

No sooner had this thought finished bouncing around inside my head than I felt Kartel's cold, pale green eyes staring at me. His mouth had become a grim line, and my sixth sense began pinging again, only louder this time. Maybe I'd been too hasty in putting the bottle of Jack away.

The voices in the hallway were getting louder, becoming more strident and anger-filled. It seemed that Gabriel was having difficulty convincing Aleksei not to rip Kartel a new one. He had my sympathy, and my complete support. Aleksei, that is. Then Anasztaizia's gentle voice somehow made itself heard over the brouhaha. She had more success than Gabriel in calming Aleksei down, if the low grumbling was any indication.

"What do you want, Kartel?" I asked, returning his steely stare with one of my own.

"From you?"

If he was expecting me to be quaking in my boots at finding myself alone with him, he was in for a rude awakening. I made a deliberate sweep of the room before turning my attention back to him. "Don't see anyone else here, do you?"

He grunted. "All I want from you is the answer to a question."

"Asking is free, but I can't guarantee I'll answer."

"Oh, you'll answer all right," he said menacingly.

The fact that he was openly threatening me with Gabriel only a few feet away said he'd lost his mind. There was no other explanation. Mad as a hatter. He was Johnny Depp in the middle of Wonderland but with better hair and no weird makeup. Trouble was, I wasn't Alice.

"What do you want to know?" I asked, thinking maybe the question would be a simple one and I could answer without any more drama.

"How did you survive Petrov's drug?"

Aw, shit—why couldn't he have asked me something else? "I don't know," I told him, which was true. There could be any number of reasons that would account for my still being in the land of the living. Petrov's formula might not have been as lethal as he'd thought. Gabriel's sarcophagus might have worked its mojo on me. My demonic pact might actually have come through. All were possibilities. There was just no way to know for certain.

"You're lying," he sneered.

"I'm n-not!"

"There's only one way to find out."

My mouth suddenly became the Sahara Desert, making it impossible for me to speak.

"I'm going to taste your blood," Kartel said with a chilling smile.

I took a horrified step back and hit the counter behind me with enough force that several bottles rattled. "Are you insane?" I said, my voice a hoarse whisper. "I'm not going to let you take my blood."

"I don't recall giving you a choice."

There came a soft click as the blue-haired vampire dropped his fangs. I didn't even try to hide the shiver of fear that ran through me.

"Do you think Gabriel is going to let you do this to me?"

"Of course not. Do you think I'm stupid?"

You really don't want me to answer that . . . do you?

For a moment, a millisecond in time, I actually thought Kartel was going to slap his thigh, give me a belly laugh, and tell me I'd just been punked. I waited for him to grin and say, "Girl, you should've seen your face!" while Gabriel and Aleksei came back into the room high-fiving each other, acting all frat-boyish at making me fall for their vampire joke.

But of course, no such thing happened.

Instead Kartel snapped his wrist, and I saw something black and shiny fly from his fingers. It reminded me of one of those Ninja throwing stars, although I couldn't imagine why he would feel the need to have such an object. I realized my mistake the minute I heard it hit the wall. Instead of a metallic twanging sound, it landed with a wet-sounding *whomp.*

"What the fuck?" I was going to have a permanent ridge between my eyebrows if I didn't stop frowning, but this couldn't be helped. Kartel had thrown a rune, and like those on Gabriel's sarcophagus, this one also moved. It scurried up the wall like some alien beetle until it reached the top of the open doorway and embedded itself in the sheet rock. I can honestly say it added nothing to the décor.

Anxiety and fear spiked in me, and Gabriel, sensing my snow-balling apprehension, was suddenly framed in the open doorway. The air of hostility between Kartel and me was now thick enough it could be neatly sliced with a knife and passed around on plates, but my relief at seeing Gabriel was short-lived. Taking a step forward, my lover was thrown violently up against the opposite wall. An invisible barrier prevented him from entering the room. The embedded rune above the door pulsed with a red glow as Gabriel snarled. At least from the way his face contorted, I assumed that's what he was doing because the rune was also blocking all sound from the hallway.

"You can tell him his sentinel isn't the only one who knows how to cast runes," Kartel gloated.

I watched as Gabriel got to his feet and ran his hands around the doorframe, a frown marring his brow. He looked at me and began to speak, but I put my hand to my ear and shook my head, indicating I couldn't hear him. He nodded in understanding. It was in a way unfortunate that he could see me. My fear over Kartel taking my blood, and the effect it would have on Gabriel, was growing exponentially.

I continued to watch as Gabriel placed a tentative hand on the doorframe and snatched it back almost at once, shaking his fingers as if he'd just received some type of electric shock. I looked about me for something to write on and found a pad of paper and a black Sharpie on a shelf beneath the counter. I could kiss Tomas for his efficiency.

I darted out from behind the bar, holding up the pad and the word I'd written in black marker. I pointed above the doorway and then at the pad. Seeing the word **RUNE,** Gabriel nodded, and I heaved a sigh of relief as Tomas suddenly appeared next to him. If anyone knew how to break through, surely it would be an experienced runecaster.

The sentinel ran his hands around the doorway. He didn't get shocked, but his expression quickly changed, and he grimaced more than once. The rune implanted in the wall was having a decidedly unpleasant effect on anyone who touched the doorway.

"Pathetic, absolutely pathetic," Kartel said, coming up behind me and snatching the pad of paper from my hands. "By the time that idiot is able to determine what I have cast, I'll be long gone."

My frustration boiled over, and I rounded on him, punching him wildly in the chest with my fist. "Fucking asshole!" I screamed.

He laughed at me, sounding like a hyena on crack, and grabbed my wrist, holding me off easily. "Really, Rowan, if you keep this up I shall have no choice but to think you want to fuck me." That stopped me at once. I yanked my hand from his grasp, making him laugh again. "Now where were we?" He snickered. "Ah yes, I do believe you were going to give me a taste of your blood."

"Did it ever occur to you that perhaps the formula was wrong to begin with? Maybe that's why it didn't kill me." I was stalling, hoping to give Gabriel and Tomas time to break through the door.

"Impossible. One syringe was potent enough to bring down an elephant. I know, we tried, and you had two. You should have been dead within minutes." He tilted his head to one side and narrowed his eyes. "So why aren't you?"

"I'm a Promise. Maybe it doesn't work on us?"

Kartel shook his head. "No, that's not the reason either."

I started. There was only one way he could be that certain. Had he used Petrov's concoction on another Promise? His own perhaps? The smirk on his face told me everything, so I screamed, "Fuck you!"

"What is it about humans and sex? As intriguing as I find your proposition, I'm going to have to pass. I'm not sure Gabriel would be *that* understanding."

"But you think he'll understand your taking my blood?"

"Of course not, and I don't expect him to. He can add it to the long list of unforgivable things I've done."

"What about me? Don't I have a say in this?"

He gave me a pitying look. "You don't have the strength to deny me, so . . . no. Still, if you'd like to test yourself, I'd be more than happy to accommodate you."

I was so pissed I picked up the closest thing I could find, a really pretty Murano glass paperweight with a fish design that I was quite fond of. I threw it at Kartel's head. He barely had to flinch to avoid my chronically bad aim, as the paperweight hit the back of the bar. I may have missed the vampire, but the bottle of Ballantine's exploded in a spectacular fashion.

"Enough," Kartel snapped. "I've no more time to waste. Give me your arm."

Of course I didn't.

Like a petulant five-year-old being asked to show what's in her hand, I put both of mine behind my back. He muttered something under his breath—I'm certain it was very unflattering—and grabbed my braid. In the blocked doorway I could feel Gabriel going all DEFCON 5, but I didn't dare look over my shoulder at him.

Yanking on my hair hard enough to bring tears to my eyes, Kartel used his other hand to grab my elbow and jerk my arm out from behind my back. I swung my other arm, meaning to punch him again, but he let go of my braid and somehow my fist was enclosed inside his palm.

"If you don't stop being ridiculous, I'll crush your hand, making certain you scream in agony with every single shattered bone while Gabriel watches, unable to help you and unable to stop me."

The expression on his face told me that he already knew I'd had my fingers broken recently, and he would make sure this would be so much worse. His grip tightened, making my fingers shriek from the pressure. The pain would be unbearable, but more than that, I knew as well as Kartel the effect it would have on Gabriel to see me in pain. And in the end the blue-haired vampire would just take what he wanted anyway.

"Just do what you have to," I said, turning my head so I wouldn't see him bite me.

I felt his breath fan my skin as he raised my wrist to his mouth. I closed my eyes, grateful that he hadn't insisted on going for my neck. That was much more personal. His bite was swift and sure, striking my wrist just below the heel of my hand. I felt his fangs slide through the skin and into my vein. And then I felt him withdraw.

"Well, well, well . . ." A trickle of my blood ran from the corner of his mouth, and he wiped it with the back of his hand as he stared down at me. "You are either the smartest human I've ever encountered or the most stupid." No brownie points for guessing which way he was leaning. "You actually made a deal with a demon?" He shook his head. "You don't really expect him to keep his side of your bargain, do you?"

"Yes," I snapped. "Actually I do."

"Why?" he asked, a look of stunned surprise on his face.

"Because he said so."

His laugh was cruel and mocking, and I risked a glance toward the open doorway. Gabriel was on his knees. His bowed head and his hair, falling like a curtain of white, obscured his face from me. But I could sense his suffering, and his rage, escalating with every moment he was kept from me.

Kartel had not bothered to seal the puncture holes in my wrist, and blood now flowed freely from the wounds, dripping off my fingertips and staining the carpet. He frowned and then gestured for me to give him my wrist. I guess having a leaky victim was bad manners or something, or else he figured why piss off Gabriel any more than he had already. He actually had the nerve to hiss at me when I snatched my hand back, refusing him.

"You got what you wanted," I said, backing away from him. "Now why don't you just fuck off." Hell could freeze over before I'd let him anywhere near me again.

A sudden pounding that made the walls shudder was immediately followed by the sound of breaking glass. Gabriel had hit the other side of the wall hard enough to make a picture fall. I hoped it wasn't his treasured Chagall.

I thought hearing Gabriel roar was simply my imagination, but one look at Kartel's face told me he'd heard it too. He snapped his head around, and I saw real fear in his eyes. Either Tomas had found a way through, or Kartel's casting wasn't as good as he'd proclaimed.

"Touch her again, and you'll beg me to kill you." Gabriel's growl, though barely registering as human, was nevertheless comprehensible. The rune's power was definitely faltering.

Either madness or defiance made Kartel grab my arms. Instinctively I leaned back, forcing him to lean further in to me so his periwinkle-blue hair brushed over my breasts. "You tell him the next time I put my hands on you, none of us will survive the experience."

He half-pushed me away, and I fell to my knees as he walked back across the room, heading for the sliding-glass door. He collected his long gray duster from the chair where Aleksei had thrown it and picked up a gray carryall from the floor. It was similar in design and size to those used to carry a bowling ball, but I didn't remember seeing him bring it in with him.

"I was going to give this to you as an apology, but it might be better if you gave it to Gabriel as compensation." He put the bag on the table. "And tell him he will not be getting Petrov any time soon."

I was pretty sure Gabriel had already figured that out for himself.

Chapter 27

The rune or spell or whatever the hell it was that Kartel had used to keep Gabriel out vanished the moment he did. I scarcely managed to take a breath before Gabriel was all over me, his lips marking every inch of skin within reach, and what his mouth didn't reclaim as belonging to him, his hands did. I didn't even try to stop him. Not only had his temper been severely tested, his possessive streak had been put on a rack and stretched almost to the limit.

Picking up my wrist, he ran the pad of his thumb over the open wounds left by Kartel's fangs. They were still bleeding, but I knew without his saying the words what he was asking. I nodded, murmuring a soft yes under my breath. He punched his own set of holes through my skin over the marks Kartel had left, going deeper than he normally would in order to completely obliterate any sign of the other vampire's fangs. Then he began drawing up my blood in a strong pull. Two mouthfuls, both of which he spit out into a bowl Tomas held out for him. I wasn't offended seeing him do this. I wanted to be as certain as he that my blood would carry no possible residue from Kartel.

When he was satisfied there was no taint left behind, Gabriel sealed the fresh wound. I took a deep breath, pulling in the scent of pine trees, snow, mistletoe and that other indefinable something that was uniquely Gabriel.

Tomas covered the dish of blood with a cloth and took it away. "Burn it," Gabriel said quietly to his sentinel's retreating back. I wondered if I would ever have the nerve to ask Tomas what had gone down between Gabriel and Kartel, because obviously something had. And it was bad.

"Why did Kartel want your blood?" Gabriel asked.

He sat cross-legged, Indian style, on the floor, and had pulled me into his lap. I rested my head on his shoulder, still breathing in his scent and exulting in the feel of his hard, toned body beneath my hands. "He wanted to know why Petrov's lethal injection hadn't killed me. Apparently they tested it on an elephant."

"And it was successful, I presume?"

I nodded, and then asked, "Does Kartel have a Promise?"

"Not anymore."

"What happened?"

"I heard she died."

"Do you know how?"

He placed his finger beneath my chin and turned my head so he could look at me. His eyes had darkened to a color that was almost indigo. "There's a rumor that Kartel killed her . . . deliberately."

"I don't think it's a rumor," I said, then told him about Kartel having rejected the idea that my survival was owed to being a Promise.

"So what does he think is the reason?" Gabriel asked, his voice slipping into that spine-melting honeyed tone.

"He knows about the deal I made."

Regardless of my reason for striking such a bargain, I was still mortified that I had entered into such an agreement to begin with. Even if it seemed that it had apparently saved my life. I pulled my bottom lip into my mouth, something I did when I was upset.

Gabriel put his lips next to my ear. "Don't do that or else both Aleksei and Anasztaizia are going to get a first-hand view of your tattoo."

"Aleksei's already seen it," I reminded him.

"Something I haven't quite forgiven him for." He was teasing me, and I sighed, rubbing my hand down his arm, feeling the muscles bunch and flex beneath my palm. "So what else did Kartel say?"

"He said to tell you if he put his hands on me again, none of us would survive."

"He actually said that?" Gabriel growled.

I pulled back so I could look into his eyes. "Yeah, but I'm hoping I can rely on you to make me a promise if I'm ever in that situation."

The beginning of a smile curved his mouth, and I traced his lips with my finger. "Ask me anything."

"I'd really appreciate it if you were to rip his head off for me."

"Oh, trust me, sweetheart," Gabriel said, giving me a throaty growl, "that's a promise I will have no difficulty keeping."

I leaned forward and kissed him, sliding my tongue between his fangs and into the warmth of his mouth. I'm still hesitant about making the first move, so it was gratifying to see Gabriel's eyes glaze over when I pulled back. He picked up my hand and brushed his lips across the inside of my wrist.

"Anything else?" my vampire lover asked huskily.

"You do know he's not going to give you Petrov, right?"

"I knew that the moment he came inside."

"Then why did you ask him to?"

"Because Aleksei could not."

I picked up a section of his hair, loving the silky feel as it flowed through my fingers. "Is it true? About Aleksei and Petrov being brothers?"

"Kartel would know better than I . . . but it does make sense. The gene tends to run in familial bloodlines."

"Will this change the way Aleksei feels about Petrov, do you think?"

"Only Aleksei can answer that." Gabriel picked up my hand and kissed my fingers. "I want you to know it almost killed me seeing him take your blood."

"Please don't think I just gave it to him." I placed my hand on his chest, feeling my palm vibrate as he rumbled. "Actually I did, but that's because it was better than the alternative." In answer to his quizzical look, I told him about Kartel's threat to crush and shatter my bones. Gabriel's response was to give me more mouth-to-mouth resuscitation. I leaned back in his arms, feeling definitely euphoric once the demonstration was over.

When I looked at him again his eyes were still dark, only now the golden ring around his pupils revealed the level of stress he'd been under. He needed reassurance delivered in a specific combination. Sex and blood. A pairing I was more than happy to provide, until the sound of Anasztaizia's voice reminded me that Gabriel and I weren't alone. Truth be told, we never were, but if you looked up the word *discretion* in the dictionary, it would show a picture of Tomas. It explained why, even though I could yell like a bull moose and frequently did, he'd never caught Gabriel and me having sex. Near misses didn't count.

I looked across the room in time to see the petite Magyar poke Aleksei in the chest with her finger. Like a lot of Europeans, she talked with her hands, especially when she wanted to get her point across, and right now she and Aleksei were having a difference of opinion. I wasn't even sure you could say what they were doing was arguing. It was more like playful bickering. Still, Anasztaizia had also been through a lot these past few hours, and I didn't want to see her upset, no matter how mild it might be. Reluctantly, I got out of Gabriel's lap. "What's wrong?" I asked.

"Aleksei won't let me see what's in the bag."

"Have you already looked?" I asked the big guy, who nodded back at me. Well, it wasn't a bomb then, but I asked anyway. "So is it dangerous or something?"

"Not dangerous . . . just something."

I honestly hadn't given much thought to what the carryall might contain, but Aleksei's response made me curious. I mean, how was Kartel going to make up for what he'd done to me? Especially knowing that he had pissed off one already furious vampire. I didn't see Hallmark making a card for that. Anasztaizia snapped her fingers and held out her hand for the carryall.

"Anasztaizia, please!" the big guy pleaded, "I'm only thinking—"

"Aleksei! You're a vampire, and you don't think—you react!" she snapped. "Do you suppose after hearing about your family, after seeing what Rowan has just been through with that monster—"

Atta girl, Anasztaizia!

"—that there's anything left that could scare me?"

The big guy glanced at me, and even though I heard his mouth say no, his eyes said yes, there was plenty, and he knew it. I raised a brow. "What's in the bag, Aleksei?" I asked quietly.

"Are you going to stop Rowan from seeing what's inside?" Anasztaizia asked sweetly.

I didn't enjoy being pulled into the middle of their squabble, but Anasztaizia always had an open, sympathetic ear when I had my own vampire difficulties. It would be churlish of me not to offer my support now. "Will you show me?"

Aleksei scrubbed a hand over his face before saying, "You don't want to see either, Rowan."

Oh, that is so completely, totally, absolutely the wrong thing to say.

And guys wonder why we sometimes seriously think they're morons. It's one thing to say no, but to say no without a reason? Offer no justification? Nuh-uh, the result is not going to be pretty.

"I'm sorry," I said, crossing my arms, "but from where I'm standing, what's in the bag is mine, according to Vampire Smurf."

"Vampire Smurf?" The Russian raised a brow.

"Okay, so they had blue skin, not blue hair, but c'mon, you know I wasn't going to be able to resist calling him that."

He looked confused. "What is Smurf?"

"I'll show you later," Anasztaizia told him as her anger simmered down a notch to indignant irritation.

"You might as well let them see," Gabriel said, deciding to bring the standoff to an end. "Neither of them is going to be satisfied until they do."

Aleksei looked momentarily stricken. "But Gabriel, you know . . ." He stopped and then asked, "*Do* you know what's in there?"

"Knowing Kartel, I've a pretty good idea." He nodded in Anasztaizia's direction. "Just make sure you catch her if she faints."

As it turned out, Anasztaizia didn't faint, but she did grab Aleksei's hand when she puked all over the floor.

The apology-slash-compensation was Rat Boy's head.

Chapter 28

"**E**nough of this nonsense!" Tomas said sternly, taking the suit-case out of my hand as I waited for the elevator door to open.

Gabriel had been gone for almost two weeks, and I was slowly going out of my mind. Once Anasztaizia had recovered sufficiently from her vomiting episode, Aleksei had taken her home. She wanted to be in her own bed with her man. Sentiments Gabriel readily agreed with.

He made love to me with a passion that made me wonder which of us he was trying to reassure. Either way I didn't care. After cresting yet another multiple orgasmic wave, I fell asleep or passed out. In any case, I truly believe it was an act of self-preservation, my body warning me it was possible to have too much of a good thing. When I opened my eyes again, it was past midnight. There was a spray of golden yellow freesias on the pillow next to me, and a note written in Gabriel's hand saying he would return soon, he loved me, and not to worry.

Like that was really going to work.

Now, a fortnight later, and still no word from him, I had reached the point where I believed my only option was to leave. My brain had run itself ragged imagining all sorts of horrible scenarios, leaving me to conclude that, as a vampire girlfriend, I sucked. No pun intended. My sixth sense had warned me that Kartel was bad news, and I'd allowed myself to be caught alone with him. Talk about stupid! I swear at times I'm so dumb I could wear myself out trying to stand in the corner of a round room.

And now Gabriel had taken off, leaving me with nothing more than an ambiguously worded note. To my way of thinking, *return soon* is what you say when you've run out to get coffee and muffins.

And it doesn't take two weeks to do that. Not even if you've gone to Colombia to handpick the fucking beans yourself.

I spent the morning rearranging my half of the closet, but when I got to the drawers containing my underwear, I lost it. For a Promise, I had some serious issues. After that, it was simply a matter of pulling down a suitcase and throwing some clothes in it. Thankfully I had a nice apartment where I could go feel sorry for myself. I just hadn't counted on Tomas stopping me.

Now I watched as he took the suitcase from my hand and steered me none too gently in the direction of the kitchen. The look on his face was both stern and compassionate.

"He'll be heartsick if he does nae find ye here on his return," he admonished, rolling his *r*'s so impressively, I forgot he wasn't a Scot by birth.

"And when might that be?" I asked, miserably taking a seat at the kitchen table and wondering if Gabriel had any idea how heartsick I was.

"When he's done, of course. It would nae do any good to return before then." Pulling his dark brows together, he added, "You canna leave your demons behind so easily, lass." I nearly jumped, wondering if he was referring to demons in general or my own personal ambassador to the Dark Realm. "Ye canna run from what has happened to ye, Rowan. Ye must deal with it head-on. Don't let that bastard Kartel define who you are."

"So you're saying I should stay here and wait for Gabriel to return."

"Aye, that's what I'm sayin'."

"No matter how long it takes?"

"Aye."

I stared at him. "You know where he is, don't you?"

"Aye."

"But you're not going to tell me, are you?" The laugh that erupted from him was startling. I couldn't ever remember hearing Tomas laugh before. He turned his back and began getting out some cups and saucers. "You're not making tea, are you?"

I wasn't sure if the Scots were as addicted to tea as the English. After watching *Downton Abbey* I was well aware that any crisis could be averted over a cup of tea. Unfortunately, I already knew I hated the stuff. I was pretty sure what I'd been offered in the Dark Realm was on a par with anything Carson served Lady Grantham.

"No tea," Tomas assured me. "How about some of my special coffee . . . with a wee kick?" Tomas's "special" coffee didn't need anything added to it, but who was I to turn down a wee kick?

"I let him down, didn't I? I mean with the whole Kartel thing. I should never have let him take my blood."

What were you supposed to do? Let him shatter your bones?

"And just how were you going to stop him?" Tomas said, echoing my inner bitch.

I shrugged. "I don't know, but I just feel I should have done *something.*"

"You did," the sentinel said quietly. "You gave only what was demanded of you. No more, no less."

Like all things Tomas turned his hand to, the coffee was very good. And it had more than a wee kick. We both sat and sipped in silence. Each lost in our own thoughts as a contemplative silence enveloped us.

"Can I tell ye something, lass?" Tomas asked, breaking the quiet between us.

"Of course."

He stared at me, his expression becoming serious. "Gabriel loves you something fierce, and there's nothing he would nae do, no risk he would nae take, for such a bonnie lass as you. He just canna always give you the whys of what he does, no matter how much he may want to. When he leaves you, as he has now, it's because he has no choice. You have no idea the depth of his rage, or the breadth of his impotence at feeling so helpless." He paused for a moment. "You kept him from you for a long time. Do not expect him to share everything he feels, not just yet. He wants to, but he still fears you might push him away."

Me push him away? I wanted to ask Tomas why he would think I'd do such a thing, but instead I said, "I'm not that naïve, Tomas. I mean, no one ever tells everything, do they?"

"Don't they?" He sounded surprised at my admission, and my cheeks flushed unexpectedly. I opened my mouth to explain, but the sentinel held up a hand. "Nay, lass, 'tis not my place to judge. I trust your reasons for keeping silent are guided by the love you bear for Gabriel, and that is reason enough for me."

I wanted to throw my arms around him and hug him, but as if

sensing I might give in to the urge, Tomas picked up our empty coffee mugs and got to his feet, giving the urge time to pass.

"Go visit your friend," he suggested as he rinsed our cups at the sink. "She and the bairn have been home for a few days. I daresay she'd welcome a visit."

"You think I should?" The truth was, I was dying to see Laycee and Baby Jenna, but not knowing much about new mothers with new babies, I didn't want to intrude or upset anyone's schedule.

Tomas smiled at me—an occurrence so rare I almost fell off my chair. "Dinna fash yourself, lass. Gabriel will return soon enough, just nae tonight."

Awww, fuck it! I didn't give him a hug, but I did kiss him on the cheek. "Thank you, Tomas, for everything."

I left him blushing with embarrassment and making odd harrumphing noises to himself.

"Rowan, you can't do this to me!"

I wasn't used to being scolded by anyone, let alone Laycee, at least not when I was standing on what used to be my front porch in the middle of the afternoon before I'd even had a chance to come inside and put my purse down. I took a good long look at my best friend. She was wearing flip-flops, yoga pants, and a T-shirt that was decorated with a weird stain on the left shoulder. Her hair was pulled up in an untidy knot on top of her head and secured with a large clip. She wore no makeup, not even lip gloss, and looked like she hadn't had a decent night's sleep since coming home from the hospital.

"What are you talking about?" What had I done?

The sudden eruption of tears was frightening. I pulled her into my arms, rubbing her back and making what I hoped were soothing, shushing sounds until the crying jag had run its course and turned into wet-sounding snuffles. It also gave me time to identify the stain on her T-shirt as spit-up baby formula.

"Goddamn hormones!" Laycee grumbled, pulling out of my arms and looking a little embarrassed. "I swear to God I'm never getting pregnant again."

Yeah, like I'm so going to believe that one. Wanna bet she'll be pregnant again by Christmas?

Laycee turned around and stomped off down the hall, headed for the kitchen. I followed, mystified by her reaction to seeing me, and with no idea what she was talking about. I hadn't seen her since that night in the hospital . . . so what had I done? I set my purse down on the kitchen table as Laycee unrolled a length of tissue from a roll of toilet paper and used it to blow her nose. "The way I'm crying, this is more economical," she explained, waving the roll at me before putting it on the counter.

"Where's Jenna?" I asked, looking around and thinking it was funny how all the dramas in my life seem to center around this one particular room.

"Taking a nap—thank you, Jesus."

"Is there anything I can do?"

Laycee didn't seem to be in any hurry to explain her doorstep explosion, but maybe if I offered to do something simple, like make coffee, she'd settle down and tell me.

A light shone in her eyes, and she grabbed my hand. "Yeah," she said, dragging me toward the living room. "You can deal with this."

"Wow, what did you do? Have another baby shower?"

I didn't know you were supposed to have an after-the-baby-gets-here shower as well. I satisfied my inner bitch by letting her know I was equally mystified.

There was an odd, maniacal gleam in Laycee's china-doll blue eyes, and I told myself she wasn't the only one who would be glad when her hormones stopped fluctuating.

I glanced around the living room, which now looked more like the overflow stockroom of a Babies-R-Us store. One corner was filled with stacked boxes of disposable diapers, while a chair was camouflaged by a multitude of receiving blankets. A half dozen crib sets lay on the floor still in their zippered cellophane bags, and I counted two car seats, one stroller, something called a diaper genie (I didn't want to ask), and two—no, make that three—plastic newborn baby baths. The sofa had become a display piece for clothing. All of it girly, all of it frilled, beribboned, and fit to be worn from newborn to size twelve months.

Well, at least someone was thinking ahead.

The only thing I didn't see was a crib or bassinet, but the five-foot-tall stuffed giraffe glaring woefully at me from between the fireplace and DVD cabinet more than made up for it.

"All this," Laycee said with a game show hostess wave of her hand, "is you, Rowan Marie Harper."

I stared at her, certain I had misheard. "What? No! You're kidding, right?" The look on her face said not just no, but hell no. "But . . . how?"

"*How?* Are you saying you didn't send any of this? Oh my God! Rowan, did someone hack your credit card?" She grabbed my hands as concern replaced her exasperation.

"No, of course not," I gave the giraffe a look of my own. "I know I got you all this stuff, I recognize some of it, but I just don't remember getting you so much."

"So you did send this?" Laycee asked, needing confirmation.

I nodded. "I must have."

"You don't remember?"

I shrugged. "Oh, I remember all right . . . I guess I just got carried away."

"You think?"

I certainly wasn't about to admit that alcohol might have played a part in my decision-making process, or that buying via the internet didn't really feel like shopping, or that it was during one of my not-so-good nights with Gabriel gone.

Laycee moved a pile of cute onesies from the arm of the sofa and sat down. "So you're saying this is all you, and none of it's from Eye Candy?"

I nodded. "Nope. Gabriel's been out of town for a couple of weeks." I gave her an apologetic smile. "If you want, we can send it all back, or give it away?" I picked up a carton of baby wipes. "Know anyone who could use these?"

"You would do that? Give it all away?"

I shrugged. "Well, I don't think it can be returned once it's out of the original packaging, do you?"

Laycee gave me an oddly exasperated look. "I can contact the hospital. They have a program for mothers who need help."

"That's settled then. Keep anything you want and give the rest to the hospital."

"Ro . . ." A troubled frown marred her brow. "How much did you spend on all this?"

"Umm, I'm not sure. Not exactly."

It was true. I had no idea how much I'd splurged on my six-hour spending spree, hitting every conceivable website I could think of that dealt with babies. I do know that by the time I was done, I still hadn't maxed out my credit card.

Crossing her arms over her chest, Laycee gave me a long, hard look. "You lied to me."

"I did not—I've never lied to you!" I protested hotly.

"Yeah, you did. You said that Eye Candy's money wouldn't change you." She looked pointedly around the room. "I hate to break it to you, girlfriend, but you lied."

"Yeah, well having a credit card with a limit that's six figures is kind of surreal." Her mouth dropped open, and I decided not to tell her about the Palladium card Gabriel had originally wanted to give me. At least I'd had the good sense to refuse that one.

"Just promise me the next time you get the urge to go on a spending spree, you'll call me first."

"Why? So you can talk me out of it?"

"Hell no—so I can tell you what I need!"

We both laughed, but I did give her my word not to be so financially reckless in the future.

"How mad is Jake about all this?" I asked when we were done chuckling.

"Well, he doesn't want people to think he can't provide for his own child." I winced. I could understand how that might emasculate him. "But I think he'll forgive you when I tell him this was all you. He was worried about how to refuse a gift—any gift—that came from Eye Candy."

"So is that why you asked if it was from him too?"

Now it was her turn to look guilty. "I wasn't sure if, well, if this was because of what I'd asked him to do."

Now I understood. Laycee had naturally been concerned there was a possibility Gabriel's offer of protection came with strings attached. The same sort of strings that I had assumed might be attached. I told her about Gabriel's decision not to be an active participant in Jenna's life, something that pleased Laycee, but saddened me.

Jenna would never know the wonderful gift Gabriel had given her, and he would never experience the wonder of watching a child grow up. Still, sensing Laycee's relief, I knew I should not try to reverse this decision. Of course I couldn't guarantee we wouldn't spoil Jenna on her birthday and Christmas, but that would probably be more my doing.

"It's okay," I reassured her. "He told me you still don't have to invite him in."

"Ah, I was wondering about that." She reached for a stack of receiving blankets and began to fold them into a neat pile. I could already tell she was mentally selecting which items she would keep and those she would give away. "So where's he gone?"

"Who?"

"Eye Candy, of course. You said he was out of town."

"Oh, he's away on business. Paris, I think." Laycee was right. I did lie to her. I was doing it now, and it was amazing how easily the words rolled off my tongue.

"You don't know? You haven't spoken to him?" Her problems-in-paradise radar was all plugged in and rarin' to go.

I shook my head. "Not recently."

"When's he coming home?"

"Soon."

"Uh-huh." Her eyes suddenly took on an unnatural sparkle.

"Are you going to start crying again?" I asked worriedly.

Yes! Please make that a yes so we don't have to answer any awkward questions about an AWOL boyfriend.

"Probably." Her smile was definitely wobbly as she pointed to her chest. "If I'm not crying, then I'm leaking. Either way I'm losing liquid—oh, but thanks for the breast pump. That's been a godsend."

Breast pump? I didn't remember ordering a breast pump, but the sound of Jenna wailing put a stop to any further conversation about my spending habits, missing boyfriend, or lactating mothers. I was happy to spend the next few hours holding the most perfectly beautiful thing I had ever seen.

Chapter 29

"Would you like me to contact the realtor?" Gabriel asked two nights later when he returned.

I was torn between wanting to throw myself in his arms and needing to haul off and smack him. "Do you mean that bitch who flirted with you? The one with the pretentious name?" I said instead, acting as if he'd only been gone half an hour instead of nearly three weeks. Keeping my eyes downcast, I continued with my task of pulling weeds from around the planter of evening primroses and night gladioli.

"Well, I'm sure we can find someone else to flirt with me, if you prefer. I had no idea it was that important to you."

Unable to help myself, I looked up at him and saw the corners of his mouth twitching as he tried not to laugh. "Oh, you enjoyed her flirting, did you?"

"Not particularly, but I did find your method of putting her in her place more than pleasurable."

I was suddenly back in the bathroom, feeling the cold tile against my ass. "You never did give me back my panties." There was a sudden huskiness to my voice.

"No, I didn't, did I?"

And apparently he's not going to.

I cleared my throat and turned my attention back to the planter. The lack of a real garden was, as far as I could see, the only downside to living in the penthouse, a fact I felt more acutely after my recent visit with Laycee. But Gabriel had more than made up for it by having a number of raised wooden flower beds and planters installed on the terrace. All were filled with night-blooming flowers, and the scent of Casablanca lilies was particularly fragrant in the night air.

"Why do you need a realtor?" I asked, returning to his original question. "Are you going to make me give back the apartment?" I was surprised by how proprietary I felt. Gabriel had put the apartment in my name, but since my abortive attempt to move out, I hadn't trusted myself to go there. I had, however, succumbed to the temptation of internet shopping again by ordering some new furniture and draperies, being a little more circumspect in my spending this time. As well as stone-cold sober.

"The apartment is yours, and I would never take that from you." He walked to the far wall of the building, where pink and white moon flowers climbed a supporting trellis. His fingers curled gently around one of the massive blooms, and I swear the damn thing shivered in delight at his touch. "I just thought perhaps you might want to live somewhere other than here."

"Why would you think that?"

"I don't want you to be reminded of what happened whenever you go into the living room."

"The K Incident," as I thought of it, complete with the appropriate capitalization and quotation marks, was already old news as far as I was concerned. But I wasn't an Original Vampire who'd seen his girl being snacked on by another Original Vampire.

I brushed the dirt from my hands and walked over to him, taking his chin in my fingers. "Kartel took my blood." I didn't miss the flinch when I said his name. "But I will not allow him to take anything else from me. Especially not the home I share with you. I like living here."

"But if we had a house, you could have a real garden."

"Yes, I could, and I'd have a lot more weeds to pull!" It was nice to hear the low rumble of his laugh. "Besides, you can't beat the view." Whenever possible I tried to be sure I caught the sun coming up over the city before going to bed for the day. The skyline never looked more lovely than when it was bathed in a warm golden glow. "I'm not saying I wouldn't like a house one day," I told him quietly, "just not right now."

"You know we already have a half dozen. In other countries."

"Well, one of these days you're going to have to let me see them. Each and every one."

Turning his face into my hand, Gabriel kissed my palm. His lips tickled, and I giggled at the sensation. "I've missed you," he murmured as his lips moved to my neck and began making up for lost time.

"I missed you too," I murmured, putting my arms around him. "Where have you been?"

I paused, waiting for him to give me a rehearsed excuse, not because he was hiding anything from me, but more as a way of protecting me from things I might not be ready to know about. He surprised me by saying, "I've been following Kartel."

"Because of what he did to me?"

"Yes, but also because I want to know what he's up to."

"You don't trust him, do you?"

He shook his head. "No, I don't."

"So where is he?"

"I don't know." He gave me a frustrated look. "He seems to have disappeared just outside of Nuuk."

"Nuuk? Is that even a real place?"

"It's the capital of Greenland." He grinned at me. "I promise we'll visit, and I'll take you to Kangerlussuaq so you can see the Northern Lights."

Oh boy. That was a definite on my to-do list. "So you don't know where Kartel is now?"

Gabriel shook his head, his mane of white hair forming a halo in the moonlight. I found it hard to believe that no one had seen Vampire Smurf. Someone knew where he was; they just weren't saying, and in a way I couldn't blame them. The risk of having two Original Vampires pissed off with you wasn't something I'd want. As long as Kartel stayed down whatever hole he'd crawled into, Gabriel would have no choice but to let sleeping vampires lie. Personally I didn't think the blue-haired vampire was stupid enough to try crossing paths with Gabriel anytime soon.

"Did you try looking somewhere other than here?" I made a circular motion in the air with my forefinger.

"He's not in the Dark Realm either. I know. I looked."

"Ah well, maybe he's at the North Pole. With that color hair he should fit right in with Santa's helpers."

Gabriel laughed and kissed me again. And then deepened it, pressing himself against me so I could feel just how much he'd missed me. It was a balmy night, and I had no problem with getting naked out on the terrace. My hands went for the bottom of his shirt, pulling it out from the waistband of his jeans. I slid my hands over his smooth skin, feeling the muscle move beneath my fingers and hearing his breath quicken. I had more than half the buttons of his shirt undone when the sound of discreet throat-clearing made us both freeze.

"This better be important," Gabriel murmured in my ear.

"Has Tomas ever interrupted you when it wasn't?" I murmured back.

With a sigh I re-buttoned his shirt and made sure my own clothing was as it should be before turning to face the sentinel. The remnants of a faint blush stained Tomas's cheeks.

"My apologies, but Miss Anasztaizia is here, and is most insistent that she speak with you."

"Which one?" I asked, pointing a finger first at myself then Gabriel.

"She did not specify, but I believe it would be best that she speak with both of you. She seems a wee bit agitated."

Dressed in a figure-hugging black sheath, with her hair pulled up in an elegant French twist, the lovely Magyar had obviously come here straight from the restaurant. I watched as she paced in front of the fireplace, wringing her hands and then holding herself, then wringing her hands again. Whatever was wrong, she was beyond agitated.

The moment she saw us she launched into Hungarian, speaking so quickly I wasn't sure if Gabriel caught more than every third word. She was also gesticulating wildly. Taking hold of her hands, more to stop her from accidentally poking herself or him in the eye, Gabriel listened intently as she raced through whatever it was she needed him to hear. From the tone and the number of times she said his name, she was talking about Aleksei.

When she finally stopped to take a breath, Gabriel took advantage of the sudden silence to ask something of Tomas before addressing Anasztaizia. He spoke in a low voice, his tone calm and reassuring. I saw her clutch his hands so hard her knuckles turned white. She nodded her head and then, at a slightly slower rate, she pleaded with him for something. I didn't need to understand Hungarian to know she was asking for his help, and also that something was wrong. Very wrong.

Tomas came back into the room and took hold of one of Anasztaizia's hands. He turned it over and pressed something into her palm, and she immediately became calm, relaxed, and more focused.

I looked at her hand and saw a small, black rune lying in her palm like an exotic blossom. With his arm around her shoulders, Gabriel led her to a seat. Thankfully, Anasztaizia had not been present for our little tête-à-tête with Kartel, so there were no additional recollections to upset her. Except, of course, the ones from Aleksei's past.

"Talk to her," Gabriel said in a low voice to me. "I think she might respond better to a female voice."

I pushed the coffee table out of the way and knelt on the floor in front of her, reaching for her hand.

"Be careful not to touch it, lass," Tomas warned as I turned Anasztaizia's hands over and cradled them in my own. The rune pulsed gently, but I don't think Anasztaizia was aware of it being pressed into her palm.

"Anasztaizia? What's happened?"

Hearing English, Anasztaizia answered me in the same language. "He's gone," she said, hiccupping back a sob. "Aleksei has gone."

"Gone?" I repeated, "Gone where?"

"I don't know." Her lip began to tremble. "He's just . . . gone."

Apparently this was more than the big guy popping out to pick up Thai for a dinner surprise. From her distressed state, it seemed obvious that Anasztaizia didn't believe Aleksei was coming back. "Has he ever done this before?" I asked and flashed Gabriel a look that said, *See what happens when you guys take off for parts unknown without telling us? See how badly we deal with the situation? We can handle you being gone, as long as you tell us where the hell it is you're going.*

Anasztaizia shook her head in reply to my question. "He always tells me if he's going to be away for more than a night."

Gabriel had the decency to look apologetic when I glanced at him. "Is it possible he just forgot to tell you?"

"No." She shook her head so hard I was surprised her hair remained in place. "He didn't forget . . . he doesn't want me to know."

"What makes you say that?"

"Because I can't feel him anymore." Pulling out of my hold, she tapped her temple with her forefinger. "In here. He's gone from inside my head."

I looked up at the two men standing behind her chair. Both of them wore grim expressions, and that, more than anything else, told me this was bad.

"Have you checked the gym?" Gabriel now asked, coming around to kneel at the side of the chair. "The gun range? The stables?"

She nodded yes to every suggestion he made.

"Aleksei rides horses?" It would have to be a Clydesdale or something similar in size, but even so, he didn't strike me as a horsey kind of guy.

"No, but he owns a horse farm," Anasztaizia said, taking the handkerchief from Tomas's outstretched fingers and dabbing her eyes with it. This was a woman who would never use a roll of toilet paper to blow her nose. "He usually goes there in the summer, on campfire night so he can make s'mores with the kids while they tell each other scary stories."

Don't they know Aleksei is a scary story?

"It's in Virginia," Gabriel explained. "A horse farm where kids with disabilities can go riding. Aleksei discovered a long time ago the therapeutic benefits of riding and of being around animals in general. A lot of kids will respond to animals when they won't, or can't, to humans." Yet another side of the big Russian that I knew nothing about. "But he wasn't there?" Gabriel asked gently.

Anasztaizia shook her head, tears now flowing. "You don't understand, Gabriel—*he's gone!*"

"Then I'll find him, and I'll bring his stubborn ass home."

She paused and held the square of white linen to her mouth before crumpling it in her hand and saying, "That's not why I'm here. We both know, even if you do find him, you won't be able to bring him back."

"Aw shit—are you sure?"

Anasztaizia nodded, and I watched Gabriel pick up her hand, the one without the rune in the palm, and press his lips to the back of it. Something significant had just gone down, only I had no idea what.

He turned to look at me and said, "I'm so sorry, sweetheart, but I have to go. This is important." And before I could say a *yeah, sure* or whatever, he got to his feet and left the room.

"What the fuck just happened?" I said, looking first at Anasztaizia and then Tomas. Guilt flushed the lovely blonde's tear-stained face, while Tomas turned completely stoic. If I wanted answers, there was only one place to turn, and I needed to hurry.

Gabriel was completely naked as I burst into the bedroom. Under normal circumstances, indeed even fifteen minutes ago, the sight would have brought me to my knees in a pool of take-me-right-now need. But these weren't normal circumstances. "What just happened out there?" I said, pointing to the closed door behind me.

"I have to leave." I followed his magnificent ass as it disappeared into the closet.

"Yeah, I get that, but what does this have to do with Aleksei? And why can't you bring him back?"

"Because he's about to do something very stupid," Gabriel said, pulling on a pair of black jeans.

"He's going to kill Petrov, isn't he?" Gabriel's answer was slightly muffled as he pulled a black T-shirt over his head, but muffled or not, I recognized an affirmative response. "But I thought only you could kill other vampires?"

"Original Vampires are the only ones permitted to do so."

That was a distinction Aleksei had failed to mention when I'd asked him to tell me how to kill a vampire. "So what are you going to do? Stop him?"

"If it's not too late."

"And if it is?"

Gabriel paused, pulling on a leather jacket. I noticed he'd also put on his heavy-duty biker boots. "There's a reason that only Original Vampires can take the life of another vampire."

"It's one of your rules, isn't it?" He nodded and went to the far end of the closet, stopping just before the entrance to the panic room. I watched as he punched in a code on the keypad that opened the vault containing my jewelry and his watches. What, the Rolex wasn't good enough for this? "And if Aleksei kills Petrov, he's breaking those rules, isn't he?"

I knew the answer without being told. And I also knew the penalty for such a thing was severe. Gabriel pulled out a long, flat box that I didn't remember ever seeing before. He opened the lid, and the soft recessed light in the ceiling caught whatever was inside, making it glow with an iridescent radiance.

"Oh my God," I said, unable to hide my shock and awe as Gabriel pulled the single item from its bed of deep blue velvet. It was a sword straight from the pages of King Arthur and the knights of Camelot. "Where d-did you get that?"

Gabriel took in a deep cleansing breath before looking at me, the glow in his eyes matching the lustrous sheen on the blade. "Before I was a vampire, Rowan, I was an angel . . . an avenging angel. The sword was gifted to me. It can only be wielded by my hand."

Of course it was his. It explained the massive blue jewel embedded in the pommel, and the way he handled it with such grace and ease. I closed my eyes and swallowed down the lump in my throat. "What do you need a sword for?"

His lips pressed against my forehead, and the arm around my shoulders held me tight. "You know why."

Yeah, I knew, or at least I had a pretty good idea. "Does Anasztaizia only think it's too late, or does she know?"

It was a moment before he said, "She doesn't know for certain."

"But you think he's already killed Petrov, don't you?"

"It would explain why Aleksei broke his bond with her."

"And now, because he broke your rule, you're going to go kill him."

"Better I than another," he said, moving past me, the big sword dangling easily from his fingertips.

I couldn't believe what I was hearing. "Even if Aleksei has killed Petrov, surely you can understand why. That has to count for something!"

"It does. It guarantees him a merciful death at my hand." He paused in the open doorway and turned to face me. The tip of the sword rested lightly on the toe of his boot. It didn't look real. "I have no choice in this matter, Rowan. It doesn't matter what Petrov did to Aleksei or his sister or his family. His life was already forfeit because of what he did to you. And Kartel knew that, just as he knew placing Petrov under his protection tied my hands."

"He knew Aleksei would go after him."

"Yes, he knew."

Clarity came to me like the proverbial bolt from the blue. It was all a lie! Kartel had never planned to protect Petrov; he intended to use him as bait. A sacrificial lamb staked out in the knowledge that Aleksei's sense of honor would not allow him to pass up the opportunity to right so heinous a wrong. And because Gabriel would have no choice but to enforce a law he was bound to uphold, he would carry the weight of having to behead the only vampire he had ever created. The effect would be devastating.

Don't forget . . . you were supposed to be dead too.

A double whammy, a huge cut-your-knees-out-from-under-you whammy. I closed the distance between us and put my hand on his arm. "Gabriel . . . did you ever consider that my kidnapping and Aleksei's disappearance—well, did you ever think that maybe both events are actually about you?"

A puzzled frown pulled his brows together. "What do you mean?"

I walked past him into the huge master bedroom we shared. I like to pace whenever I have a problem I'm trying to solve, and I needed room. More room than the closet, even with its generous dimensions, would give me. Funny thing was, Gabriel liked to pace as well whenever something was bothering him.

"We've been assuming my abduction was an accident, but what if it wasn't?" I recalled how my car had been deliberately blocked in, leaving me no choice but to take Anasztaizia's. "What if that was the plan all along? What if I really was the target? You'd be devastated by my death, and then, if word got out that it was the same Petrov who had murdered Aleksei's family, you know what Aleksei's reaction would be. As your only made vampire, he'd feel duty bound to go after Petrov—"

"As he has."

"—as he has," I agreed with a vigorous nod of my head. "And now his life is forfeit because of that. But tell me, Gabriel, how much time would you need to recover if you lost both Aleksei and me so close together?"

Gabriel caught me in mid-stride. "I would never recover from such a loss," he said, horrified by the very idea. He turned my hand over and kissed the inside of my wrist.

"And I'll bet not only does Kartel know that, he's counting on it," I said softly.

"Except you didn't die."

"No, I didn't." I stroked his cheek with the fingers of my free hand. "Petrov couldn't have known, not for sure, that I *hadn't* died; he only knew I was missing. Who knows what Rat Boy told him, and I figure one look at Gus had him pissing in his pants." I paused as Gabriel nodded his head. "But he still didn't know if I was dead or not," I finished.

"And he could hardly come here to see for himself—"

"No, but Kartel could." Gabriel let go of my hand so I could resume pacing. I think he just liked to watch me go back and forth. My movement appealed to the real hunter that lived inside his skin. "It would explain his need to know how you had survived, and why he took such a risk to taste your blood."

I stopped and pivoted on the ball of one foot. "He did take a hell of a risk, didn't he? To assault me more or less in front of you—it was absolute lunacy! And then the way he pushed Aleksei's buttons?" I thought back to how the blue-haired vampire had got up from his seat and positioned himself, as if telling Aleksei to take his best shot. It had all been a reckless move, a totally calculated reckless move.

"But Kartel knows why you survived, and he knows about your demon." I really could have done without the possessive reference. "So now he can only hope to get rid of Aleksei."

"Yes, but even so, I'm no threat to him. I never was. And he could certainly take care of Aleksei by himself if he really needed to. He is an Original Vampire, after all."

"Except if he were the one to kill Aleksei, I might turn vengeful."
Might? No doubt in my mind, sister.

"You'd be out for his blood."

"And that's the last thing he needs." Now it was Gabriel's turn to wear a hole in the rug. "He needs me to be so distraught, I'm of absolutely no use to anyone."

"How much do you want to bet that Aleksei got some anonymous text message on his phone, telling him exactly where to find Petrov?"

"Pushing him into a decision that would leave me no choice but to take his head."

"But now you do have a choice, Gabriel. If all of this has been orchestrated by Kartel, if he's been behind the scenes, making others dance to his tune, then it's time you found out why. What's he planning that he needs to go to such lengths to get you out of the picture? Why are you such a threat to him?"

I could see Gabriel's eyes begin to darken. He was angry, but not with me. He was livid that Aleksei and I might have been used in order to manipulate him. And now Aleksei had been backed into a corner and was a hair's breadth away from losing his life. If he hadn't already. Taking me in his arms, Gabriel kissed me hard and fast, and then turned to go.

"Gabriel!" He turned back to look at me. "Are you still intending to cut off Aleksei's head?" I asked worriedly, pointing at the sword.

"Not anymore."

"Then . . . who?"

"Kartel," he said, looking grim.

"So you think he's wherever Aleksei is?"

"If Kartel believes I have no other choice but to take the life of my progeny, he won't pass up the opportunity to witness it with his own eyes."

"But you don't know where either of them are," I pointed out.

"I have a good idea where Aleksei would go to stake a vampire," Gabriel said grimly.

Still reeling from Gabriel's words, I asked, "Are you saying Aleksei intends to stake Petrov out in the sun?"

He nodded. "Yes, and he'll make sure it's a slow burn."

I shivered. "Where would he go to do such a thing?"

"Death Valley," Gabriel told me before kissing me quickly as he left.

Of course. What other perfectly appropriate place was there to stake a vampire?

Chapter 30

Tomas drove Anasztaizia home. She didn't want to stay just in case she was totally wrong and Aleksei came home. None of us believed that, but I think it made her feel better if we pretended it could happen. Even if it was just for a little while. I hugged her and offered to stay at her place so she wasn't alone, but she politely turned me down. I think my presence was a reminder of Gabriel and worst-case scenarios. I understood, but I made her promise to call me if she needed anything.

I picked up the remote and turned on the TV, more to fill the silence around me than anything else. But all I found were sitcoms written for an average IQ in the teens or the latest crop of reality shows. Was there anyone who actually believed these shows were "real"? I turned the TV off in disgust and grabbed my purse and keys. I needed to get out of the penthouse.

I had no idea how long it was going to take Gabriel to get to California or what would happen when he got there. I'd been making a lot of assumptions, and now I was gripped by doubt. What did I really know about vampires? I might be living with one, bound to him even, but my knowledge of Gabriel's everyday world was still pretty limited. God forbid—what if I was totally wrong about Kartel?

But you're not . . . You know in your gut he's a piece of shit who'd like nothing more than to bring Gabriel to his knees.

But why?

Does it matter? Would that truly make a difference to you?

I sighed and had to confess that no, it would not. The fact that someone wanted to hurt two vampires—one I loved and one I liked enough to care about—was enough.

The problem is . . . what happens if Kartel succeeds? Will he come after you?

Not gonna happen!

I applaud your confidence in our man, and I don't think it will happen either, but there's a poem or rhyme or some similar shit about a war being lost for the sake of a horseshoe nail. You get my drift?

Yeah, you're saying I should hope for the best, but it would be stupid not to consider the worst. So, worst-case scenario—do you think Kartel will come after me?

I don't see how he couldn't. You and Gabriel, you're two halves of a whole. He would have no choice but to come after you.

My inner bitch is a pain in my head more often than not, but on rare occasions, like when it involves really important shit, she comes through for me.

Tomas had yet to return from taking Anasztaizia home. It was self-evident that Gabriel had entrusted his sentinel with my safety; he was still here and not on his way to the Mojave Desert. I wrote him a note explaining where I'd gone and why. Something innocuous enough that he wouldn't feel the need to come after me. If Kartel did put in an appearance, it would only be because Gabriel was in no condition to stop him—a fact I was certain would not be lost on Tomas. I saw absolutely no reason for both of us to suffer at Vampire Smurf's hands. Without me to protect, Tomas would have a better chance of getting away.

I packed an overnight bag, taking longer than usual because I had to stop and make sure I wasn't hearing Tomas's footsteps every few seconds. The bag served no purpose except as a ruse. After reading my note, Tomas would check the closet and bathroom. I would take my toothbrush and hairbrush as well as a change of underwear, if nothing else.

Stopping at one of Greenley Heights's two premier five-star hotels, I made a point of engaging the desk clerk in conversation, telling her I was not to be disturbed and to please hold all calls, so she would be certain to remember me. After that, it was a piece of cake to just place the contents of my overnight bag in the hotel suite I'd booked myself into. Of course, if Tomas was bound and determined to see me, then he'd just use one of his mystical runes to open the room door and come in. But I didn't think he would. I was actually safer in a hotel surrounded by a few hundred guests and who knew how many staff than I was in the penthouse with just him. Not that he couldn't protect me. Of course, he could, but vampires have an innate dislike of crowded places. It was one thing for Kartel to take me by force from the seclusion of the penthouse, but a very different matter to drag me kicking and screaming through the lobby of the Royal Arms Hotel. And you better believe there was going to be a lot of kicking and screaming.

Satisfied with my subterfuge, I used the back stairs to the hotel garage and drove across town to the apartment Gabriel had bought me, taking a circuitous route just to be on the safe side. I'm not a very good liar. Actually, I'm total shit when it comes to coloring the truth. My mouth might say all the right words, but my face turns bright red. The equivalent of having the *L* word tattooed across my forehead. But by the time I pulled into the garage and waited for the door to close behind me, I was feeling pretty good about my chances of pulling this off.

It took me nearly five minutes to unlock my door. Didn't help that I wasted four and a half of them trying to force the wrong key. Once inside, I locked the door behind me and leaned against it for a moment, letting out a sigh of relief. I had protected Tomas as much as I was able to. Of course he wouldn't be happy with me when he found out I wasn't at the hotel, but I figured by then this would all be over one way or the other. I'd either be asking his forgiveness or it wouldn't matter.

I dropped my purse on the chair and headed for the kitchen and the bottle of bourbon I'd bought as an apartment warming present to me, from me. As I got the bottle of Jack Daniels and a glass, my hands started to shake. So much so, I thought I might drop the glass or the bottle. One I could deal with, but the other would be just a shameful waste of good liquor.

I stretched my arms out along the length of the tile countertop and clenched my fists, allowing the physical reaction to my stratagem to work its way through me. Bowing my head, I sucked in a deep breath, counted to ten, and then exhaled slowly. I felt better. I held out my hands, pleased to see the tremors had subsided and I was able to open the bottle of JD with no problem. I'd just poured the generous amount I'd promised myself when a voice behind me had me clenching everything in the hope I didn't pee myself.

"I'll take one of those," my demon said.

The glass in my hand didn't fall to the floor, even though the shock of hearing those rich, dulcet tones made my fingers release their hold. Instead it paused in mid-air, with the contents splashing upward over the rim suspended just as bizarrely. Like the face of a small child seeing a magician pull a rabbit from his hat for the very first time, my mouth dropped open, and my eyes widened at the unbelievable reality I was seeing.

I was vaguely aware that he had moved and was now standing close to me. I was also aware that the only place he could have come from was the narrow sliver of space that existed between the fridge and the wall.

Had he really squeezed out from that impossible slice of darkness?

Oh yeah . . . you betcha ass he did.

Now I knew I was in trouble, because my inner bitch sounded impressed, and it takes a lot to impress her.

From the corner of my eye I saw his hand reach out and cup the floating glass in his palm, well-manicured fingers cradling the tumbler. The signet ring on his pinkie had a single stone, a ruby, and it glowed like a red-hot coal in the overhead light.

"Rowan . . . look at me."

His voice was oddly compelling, and my need to obey was strong, but I couldn't take my eyes from the glass. I knew the moment I looked away, or blinked, I would miss seeing the magic behind the trick. And I really wanted to know how it worked.

"Rowan . . ." The sound of my name came from next to my ear, although he was still holding the glass, and I never saw him move. "Look at me, Rowan."

I blinked and missed the secret to the trick. Shit.

The bourbon fell into the glass with a gentle sloshing sound, but not a single drop was spilled. I turned my head and looked at him, seeing the same figure that had invited me to take tea in a fantasy garden that existed only in the Dark Realm.

Only he'd taken more than tea. He'd taken a piece of my soul as well.

"Another Armani?" I asked, referring to the expensive cut of his dark suit. After Gabriel found out that my demon favored this particular designer, he'd asked Tomas to remove everything in his closet that bore the same name. I really hoped the demon wouldn't make Gabriel give up anyone else, especially not Tom Ford, because I liked the way Gabriel looked in his designs.

"Yes," the demon whispered in my ear, lengthening the last letter so he sounded like a snake. "I remember how much you admired my wardrobe the last time we met."

I forced myself to make a slow sweep from head to toe, taking in the stylish cut of his glossy black hair to the Ferragamos on his feet, making sure I paused and frowned every now and then. The same snowy-white shirt was a backdrop for the same blood-red tie, adorned with the same tie clasp and cufflinks, both accented with rubies. "Funny, in this light you look more like a used car salesman," I said, being deliberately rude.

"Only if I were selling you a Veyron or a Maybach." The apparent lack of brand recognition on my face made him laugh. "Still, if the Armani bores you, perhaps something different."

The sudden odor of sulfur made my nose sting and my eyes water. I coughed and reached for the kitchen roll, tearing off a square and using it to wipe my eyes. So much for waterproof mascara. Once everything was no longer blurry, I stared at him and gasped. He looked exactly like every medieval illustration of the devil I'd ever seen, complete with horns and cloven hooves.

It was fascinating . . . and disgustingly revolting at the same time.

From the waist up he looked like a man. A powerfully built man, with the well-defined muscles of his upper torso a testament to his fearsome strength. From the waist down he had the muscular hindquarters of an animal that bore a definite similarity to a goat. He was covered with a pelt of black hair from his hips down to—*are we really seeing this?*—the cloven hooves that supported him.

His sex was enormous, almost comically so, and completely unavoidable. It hung from the dark fur so the head of his cock twitched against what would have, should have, been his knees. I defy anyone, male or female, not to have stared at it. I swear it looked as if it had a mind of its own, and I'm not completely certain it didn't, but all I could do was thank God it was flaccid. I didn't even want to imagine how it would look erect.

I forced myself to look up at him. To stare at his face. His upper body might look human, but there was nothing human that I could see in the bone structure of his skull. The elongated jaw and sloping forehead told me there was more animal than modern *Homo sapiens* in their formation. His skin was charred, although I saw no blisters or obvious burns; still it did seem to be stretched tightly over his bone structure. As if he was wearing a mask that was just a touch too small, but had been forced to fit.

Perhaps it is a mask. Perhaps at the back of his skull you'll find a zipper or two pieces of Velcro holding it together.

His eyes, beneath heavy dark brows, were black-rimmed and glittered red and gold, reminding me of the flames in a fire. His ears were strange, pointed at the tip with lobes so long they brushed the tops of his shoulders. And then there were the horns: solid-black protrusions that erupted from his forehead, twisting up over his head in distorted corkscrews.

He smiled at me, a flash of brilliant white made even more dazzling because of the blackened lips that surrounded them. Only he seemed to have far too many teeth crowding his mouth. Razor sharp and glistening with saliva, they looked like daggers.

"Is this image more to your preference, Rowan?"

His voice was gravelly and harsh, but before I had a chance to respond, he held out his arms and twirled for me. A demon parody of a nervous first date seeking approval.

Well, look at that—he's got a tail too!

And he did. Emerging from the thick glossy pelt, it moved, twisting around his waist as he pirouetted, his cloven hooves making a surreal clopping sound on the tiled kitchen floor. I shuddered and knew I had to get rid of this *thing* before I vomited.

"The concept of subtlety really is beyond your grasp, isn't it?" I added enough sarcasm to make the twirling come to an end. "What are you supposed to be? Some sort of bad Halloween costume?" He leaned toward me, bringing his face close to mine. His eyes didn't just look like fires; I could see actual flames moving in their depths. "And what's worse," I continued, "you stink!"

The last thing I expected to do was make him laugh. Throwing back his head, he let out a great, belly-roaring sound that reverberated around the entire apartment.

"Not to your taste, eh?" he said as his mirth died down. "Perhaps this, then. They do say the third time's the charm."

He vanished in a puff of smoke—literally!—and materialized in the middle of the living room, and once I turned the corner it was easy to see why. His wings were enormous, requiring more room than the cramped quarters of the kitchen to open fully. The breath caught in my throat.

They were stunningly beautiful. *He* was stunningly beautiful.

Black and glossy, each feather was tipped with red and shone with an iridescent luminosity. He crossed his arms over his bare chest and stood with his legs slightly apart, balancing his weight on the balls of his feet as he watched me, assessing my reaction.

I hated myself for the way I was responding to him. His physical appearance was all male—except for the wings, of course—but even those I could relate to. How could I not? Formed from the same ball of light that had made Gabriel, he and my vampire lover were, for all intents and purposes, brothers. Looking at him, I could so easily see Gabriel standing in his place, dazzling as the angel he had once been, only with wings that were neon blue instead of glorious black.

Now my demon folded his wings, tucking them against his back as he came toward me and stopped. He smiled. His teeth, though still impossibly white, were now more human in size, shape, and, I assumed, quantity. The features of his face were similar to those he adopted with his Armani persona, although now there was a touch more of the exotic about him. Perhaps it had been there when he was Mr. Armani and I just hadn't noticed. He held his hand out to me.

Why are you on your knees? Are you praying?

I had absolutely no idea. I certainly didn't recall assuming the position of a supplicant. He bent forward, and his hair tumbled over one shoulder. It fell to his waist and had the same glossy sheen as his wings, without the red ends. His body was a healthy bronze color, a natural hue that owed its pigment to genetic code instead of a tanning bed.

I placed my fingertips in his palm, feeling the blush rise to my cheeks, and grateful to see he was wearing black leather pants. I couldn't decide if my embarrassment was because he was clothed or because in his previous manifestation I'd seen more than I expected to. My apparent look of relief at his wardrobe choice did not go unnoticed. He gave me a quizzical look and asked, "You prefer me partially clothed?"

"Well, a girl does like to be surprised every now and then," I said, getting to my feet.

"Something to remember." He widened his smile. I wasn't sure how I should take that, but I wasn't going to ask for clarification. "As is this image that pleases you."

"It's okay," I lied. The last thing I wanted was to hand him something he could potentially exploit and use against me. "A bit theatrical, with all the Vegas showgirl feathers."

"Liar," he said, as he narrowed his eyes. In his current form, they were black with shards of red and green glittering in their depths. "Your body betrays you, Rowan. Your heart is beating so fast you can scarcely catch your breath, and I can smell your lust for this image before you."

I wanted to remind him that he was the liar as well as a trickster and deceiver, but I couldn't. Not this time. I didn't love him, and I never would, but the sudden lust I felt for him, while unexpected, was also very real. In my head I wanted nothing more than to feel the physical sensation of having that body touch me . . . taste me . . . fill me.

ARE YOU OUT OF YOUR FUCKING MIND?

My inner bitch shrieking like a banshee was better than a cold shower. I snatched my hand from his and took a step back. He looked mildly disappointed.

"Almost," he murmured.

"Why are you here? What do you want with me?"

There was a rustle, a snap as if someone was treading on dry twigs, and then his wings were gone. And now I was alone with a really hot-looking guy with waist-length black hair wearing nothing but snug leather pants. I took in a deep breath to clear my head and caught the lingering scent of anise. His scent.

"I've come to give you a gift," he said.

"I don't want anything from you."

"Oh come now, don't be churlish. What kind of a groom would I be if I didn't want to give my bride-to-be a wedding gift?"

Groom? Bride-to-be? Wedding gift?

He was out of his mind, completely and totally off the deep end. Except he ruled the Dark Realm, and although I was fairly certain a good many of the inhabitants were clinically insane, I doubted the jailer was. Too risky. Then again, who knew what passed for madness in such a place.

"I don't remember discussing marriage with you," I said slowly. "And I don't know why you would think I would ever agree to such a thing." Frantically I pulled up the memory of our last meeting, running it through my head like an old 8mm movie. Had I agreed to this and didn't remember? No, I was certain there had been no mention of matrimony. I stared at him. He was too calm, too collected. He knew something I didn't. I wondered if he was trying to change the rules of our agreement, trick me into defaulting, but deep down I knew his pride would never allow that.

Even demons have a code of honor. Admittedly it might not be one most other people would agree with, but then again, how many folks have ever entered into such a bargain with the ruler of the Dark Realm? I stared at him, and he looked back at me, a half smile playing on his lips. He wasn't here to try to change something in the agreement between us in order to give himself an advantage. He was here because he already had that advantage. Something had already changed.

Gabriel!

The Master of Discord, my demon had to already be aware of the animosity existing between Aleksei and Petrov, Kartel and Aleksei, Kartel and me, and Kartel and Gabriel. If I asked, he could probably tell me exactly how far from Death Valley Gabriel was right now, or if he was already there. If he'd reached Aleksei in time, or if . . . or if . . .

"Is Gabriel dead?" I blurted out.

Don't be an idiot! If Gabriel was dead you'd be lying on the floor, eyes rolling, muscles twitching, and fluid leaking from places I don't want to think about. Oh . . . yeah.

To his credit, the look of surprise on the demon's face seemed genuine enough. As if he too had forgotten the terms of our deal.

"Dead? Why would he be dead?" For a moment I was equally surprised by his look of concern, but then he quickly covered it with a mask of sly mischief as he asked, "What is it that you think he's done?"

In as few words as possible, I told him about how Kartel had manipulated Aleksei to go after Petrov. I didn't say anything about my own abduction or my suspicions about the blue-haired vampire wanting to weaken Gabriel for some unknown reason.

"Oh . . . that!" He laughed and looked . . . relieved. "I have no interest in the petty squabbles of vampires, and to answer your question, no, Gabriel isn't dead . . . but you already know that, right?"

"Why would you think I'd ever want to marry you?"

"Well, you don't have to," he said agreeably. "I just made the offer to be polite. I know how important these ridiculous rituals are to your kind."

My kind? Did he mean humans, or was he referring to me as a Promise? "So you don't want to marry me?" A headache was germinating in the back of my skull. With any luck it would be a doozy that would knock me out.

"Your foolish rites make no difference to me, but if they make you happy, so be it." He shrugged nonchalantly.

There was something I still wasn't getting. Some nugget of information that he was deliberately keeping from me. Shit! The bastard was going to make me work for it.

"I'm not going to marry you," I said firmly. "Not now, not next week, not in the next century!"

"Very well then, we can forgo the ritualistic formality. I'll just take you when the time comes."

"What time? What the fuck are you talking about?"

He stroked his chin with his long fingers, looking thoughtful. "You don't know, do you?"

"Well, duh—what do you think I've been trying to tell you?" I put my hands on my hips and glared across the space between us as any lustful desires I might have had completely vanished. "Our agreement was for a specified amount of time, and I don't think we're anywhere near the end of that."

I knew we weren't because Ryiel, busy poring over ancient scrolls searching for a way to break my demonic agreement, would have told me if my time was up.

"No, of course not," the demon agreed with me, "which is why I was surprised that you decided to end your relationship with Gabriel so soon after our pact. What happened? Did he disappoint you, hmmm? Was it performance problems? You do know that can be fixed—"

"There's nothing wrong with his performance, either in or out of the bedroom!" I snapped hotly.

I heard the ruffle of feathers as he shrugged. "Well, if it's nothing physical, then what could it be, I wonder?"

This was going nowhere, so I decided to bulldoze right in. "Why don't you quit with the bullshit and tell me what you know. What's happened to make you think I've ended my relationship with Gabriel?"

"Well, you have to admit it's difficult to believe in the sanctity of your love when you deliberately consent to his infidelity."

"I . . . I've done no such—what?!"

"Infidelity, you do know the definition, I assume?" I was too stunned to offer a pithy comeback to his sarcasm. "Correct me if I'm wrong, but our deal was to see if the affection you have for each other was strong enough to withstand temptation, greed and lust. Gabriel's sleeping with another woman is a deal breaker, even if you have sanctioned it."

"But I didn't sanction anything of the kind—and he hasn't slept with another woman!"

"Not yet, but he will."

"What? When?"

"Twenty-five years from now, give or take a month or two."

Twenty-five years? Twenty-five . . . oh, God damn it all to hell— Jenna!

"Are you talking about the promise of protection Gabriel gave Laycee's baby?"

He arched a brow. "Of course, what else would it be?"

"Who do you think he's going to sleep with? Laycee?" I snorted at the idea.

"No, not Laycee," he said, rolling his eyes. "He's going to sleep with the baby. Once she's all grown up," he amended.

"Why would he . . ."

Aw shit—the price, Rowan, it's the price for Gabriel's protection! The price Laycee could have turned down—probably would have turned down—but that you agreed to pay.

The bands of red and green in his eyes gleamed maliciously. "You really didn't know?" he asked, amazed by my ignorance. I shook my head. "Well, if Gabriel deliberately deceived you, then he is the one who has broken the pact."

"But he didn't deceive me," I refused to let his integrity be impugned.

"If he asked you to agree to a payment without complete disclosure, then he deceived you. It's really very straightforward."

"Would that void the agreement?" I asked, grasping at what I hoped was a straw.

He smiled wickedly. "No, it just tells me where to place the blame."

"Then you have to give it to me, because Gabriel didn't deceive me." I was going to sound like a broken record if I kept this up. "He didn't tell me because I didn't give him the chance to. I agreed to pay whatever was asked without knowing what it would be." Saying it out loud like this made me feel like the biggest, most stupid moron in the world.

"So you didn't know that the price for his protection is her virginity?" I shook my head. "And Gabriel didn't tell you?"

No, he didn't. And now I knew why. I crossed my arms over my chest and stared down at my feet morosely.

But why didn't Gabriel tell you?

As if hearing my inner bitch, the demon said, "Because once the agreement was verbally accepted, no part of it can ever be spoken of again."

"Well, that's just stupid!"

I stumbled as I crossed the room and sat down on the couch. My head was throbbing, and it had nothing to do with my burgeoning headache. I was angry. Angry with myself more than anything else, because, as usual, I'd made a decision based on emotion instead of reason. Now I understood why Gabriel had looked so horrified when I'd blurted out my willingness to accept responsibility for his gift. And to think I'd accused him of doubting *my* integrity! And he hadn't told me because, by then, he couldn't tell me. The price to protect my best friend's baby from being hit on by a vampire as she was growing up was to allow her to give herself to one specific vampire once she was old enough. Holy shit!

Mistress of impulsive decisions, questionable behavior, and all foolish choices . . . had you known, would it have made a difference?

We'll never know, will we? I can't go back and re-live that moment, but I think in my heart of hearts, if I had known, I would have let Gabriel and Laycee decide.

And if the result was the same?

I don't know . . . I honestly don't know . . .

I put my elbows on my knees and my head in my hands. This was such a terrible mess. The only thing I was certain of was I had to tell Gabriel I knew as soon as I saw him. It wasn't fair to expect him to carry the secret alone. And I wasn't going to tell Laycee. How and when the shit hit the fan twenty-five years from now would be a problem to deal with then.

My demon sank to his haunches in front of me, and I felt him tug gently on a lock of my hair, pulling the curl between his fingers, and stroking it with this thumb. "You, of all people, should know the care needed when entering into agreements with supernatural beings. Words that mean so little to humans carry far more weight with us. And vampires in particular." Gabriel had said something similar, but at the time I really hadn't understood what he meant. Unfortunately, I did now. Dropping my lock of hair from his fingers, the demon said, "And it never crossed your mind to ask?"

My only concern had been to give Laycee some peace of mind and to assuage my own feelings of guilt for exposing her to the world of vampires to begin with. "No," I said, shaking my head, "and in all fairness, Gabriel did try to tell me . . . I just didn't listen."

He did a credible job of suppressing his glee, and I knew I'd pretty much just handed myself over to him. From out of nowhere a large square jeweler's box appeared. The color told me it was from Tiffany's. "This is my gift to you." His voice was rough and filled with the promise of sex. A promise I wasn't sure I'd ever survive. "When I take you, you will wear these . . . and only these."

He opened the lid, and my eyes were dazzled by a necklace of brilliant black opals, each stone striated with bands of bright red and brilliant green. Just like his eyes. I stared down at them for a few moments, admiring their beauty, and then my eye caught the red diamond solitaire I wore on the third finger of my left hand. I felt steel bolting itself to my spine as resolve coursed through me. This wasn't over yet, not by a long shot. I had twenty-five years to find a way to fix my monumental screw-up. And I would find a way . . . or die trying.

I put out my hand and closed the lid on the opals. "It's beautiful, but you can take it back. I don't want it now, not twenty-five years from now, not ever."

"Now or later makes no difference," he said, "but you will wear them the first time you lie in my bed."

Yeah, keep telling yourself that . . .

"What happens if Gabriel doesn't sleep with her?" I asked, refusing to discuss his desires any further.

"Then she dies," he said coldly.

Christ-all-friggin'-mighty! Does everything have to be such a drama?

"And if he does sleep with her?" It had never been so hard to keep my voice level, to pretend that inside I wasn't dying just thinking about this.

"With her virginity gone, the protection can be renewed or revoked by either of them. Whatever the choice, it will be lifelong and irreversible."

"But this is the only time he would have to have sex with her?"

"The price is her virginity, Rowan."

"Yeah . . . right."

He stood up suddenly and turned his head to the big picture windows that lined one wall. I loved the view they offered of the city, especially at night with all the lights twinkling. Now a light breeze made the floor-to-ceiling sheer curtains move like a graceful dancer, and I thought of the mess I'd made of things.

Except I hadn't done it all by myself.

"It was you, wasn't it?"

"What was?" he challenged arrogantly.

"You're the one who told Laycee she could ask Gabriel for his protection. Somehow you put the idea in her mind."

He didn't say anything, but he didn't need to. I knew it was true, and his raised brow was all the affirmation I needed.

"One of the things I love about humans is how open they are to the power of suggestion, as long as it is put to them in just the right way." He looked exceedingly pleased with himself.

"You're one smug bastard, you know that?" I snapped bitterly. The pale blue Tiffany box was now on the table. I picked it up and threw it at him. He caught it with one hand. "Allow me to make a suggestion—get the fuck out of here!"

He laughed at my temper. "This conversation between us is not over."

"Yeah, it is," I said, suddenly feeling more tired than I could ever remember feeling. "There's nothing more to discuss."

My demon tilted his head slightly, giving me a questionable look as if he was certain my brain was cooking up some unimaginable ruse to use on him. I only wish. He headed for the kitchen.

"No," I said, my voice stopping him. "You can use the front door like everyone else." The idea that the space between the fridge and wall was a doorway to the Dark Realm was more than a little unsettling.

"It's only a shadow, Rowan." He grinned, reading my concern and flashing those impossibly white teeth at me. "I can use any shadow to go anywhere."

"Yeah, well, go find a shadow out in the hall." I got up and marched to the door, unlocked the dead bolt, and pulled it open.

He sighed and stood next to the open door, looking down at me. "And so it begins."

"What?"

"The first of many concessions I am willing to make for you."

"I don't want you to do anything for me."

"Are you sure? Is there nothing I can give you? Something Gabriel can't . . . or won't?" The last he added in a tease.

His words pricked a bubble inside my head. "Yeah, you can tell me your name."

That startled him. Something he hadn't expected. Foolish demon, trying to ply me with baubles. Okay, very expensive and very beautiful baubles, but so very much the wrong kind of enticement. Did I look like a gal who shopped at Tiffany's?

We can but hope . . . maybe a couple of centuries from now?

"What's wrong? Worried I won't be able to pronounce it?" I challenged. "Come on now, don't be embarrassed. I promise not to laugh even if it is something off the wall like Algernon or Cuthbert."

His eyes glittered strangely as he leaned down, putting his face so close to mine I could feel the warmth of his breath on my skin. "The whisper of my name on your lips would be a promise of unimaginable pleasure."

Jeez! Give him his dues—the guy can spin a line!

"Then why not tell me?" I repeated, not swayed by his flattery.

"Because then you would have a power over me that few possess."

Shit! You don't think it's actually Rumpelstiltskin, do you?

"So I take it that's a no then," I said, hushing my inner bitch.

"I'll tell you my name," he promised, "when I'm buried so deep inside you, you can't tell where you end and I begin."

He suddenly grabbed my shoulders and ran his tongue down the side of my neck, leaving behind the faint scent of anise on my skin, before releasing me and walking out the door. It took me a full minute before I could move again. It doesn't sound like much, but those sixty seconds were the longest of my life.

My hand was shaking as I slid the dead bolt home, and I leaned against the door as I waited for my breath to stop coming in sharp gasps. I was shaky and wanted nothing more than to take a very long, very hot shower so I could wash the smell of him from me. Perhaps I should go back to the hotel and actually spend the night there. Being surrounded by so many people might not be such a bad idea.

Why? The worst is over. Your demon boyfriend has left.

That may be, but I didn't think the worst was anywhere near over. I had an awful feeling it was still to come. I stared at the coffee table. The Tiffany box was still there. The bastard had left it behind. Deliberately. What did he think I was going to do? Prance around in my undies wearing it when I thought no one was looking? If I believed anything about my demon to be true, it was that the Dark Realm was always looking.

But I refused to allow that to affect how I lived my life. If I did, then he'd already won.

I would go to the bank in the morning and rent a safe-deposit box for the necklace. I wasn't about to leave it lying around, and there was no way in hell it was going in the vault at the penthouse. Wearily I slipped off my shoes and heard a knock at the door. Maybe my no-name demon had decided to take back my supposed wedding-night trinket. Better it was with him than in some bank vault. I picked up the jeweler's case and opened the door, only to have the pale blue box slip from my fingers when I saw who was standing before me.

He looked terrible. He looked worse than terrible. His coat was missing a sleeve, and was torn and covered in what looked like oil stains, suggesting he'd either been dragged behind a vehicle or run over by one. Possibly both—it was hard to say. The skin had been scraped off his forehead, and there was a massive contusion on one cheek. His left eye was nothing but a ball of blood, while the other was swollen shut, the surrounding skin a frightening shade of purple. Dried blood caked his nose, and from the odd angle I guessed it was broken. His lower lip was split open, and I wasn't sure, but I think he was missing an ear.

I felt tears spilling down my face, and his image blurred as I stared at him. I couldn't begin to understand how he'd found the strength to drag himself to my door, or the willpower that was keeping him upright. His hands were swollen, fingers broken, knuckles bloodied and bruised, but the worst had to be his skin. It was gray, an unhealthy pallor that told me he had lost too much blood. More than his body could tolerate. He needed to feed, and soon. In fact, I wasn't sure he would make it through the next hour if he didn't.

There is a cardinal rule about not feeding one vampire when you are bonded to another, but I couldn't think about that right now. I wasn't about to have his death on my conscience. It would be more than I could bear. I pulled my hair away and exposed my skin, feeling the vein throb in my neck and the blood rush through me. There came a familiar click as he dropped his fangs, and the enormity of what I was about to do suddenly filled me.

Mistress of impulsive decisions, questionable behavior, and all foolish choices . . .

Yeah, I was all that and more. Guilty of obeying my heart more than my head. And this was going to be no exception.

No one had visited me in my new apartment, so an invitation to cross the threshold was necessary, and I gladly gave him one. Even though he was weak, I still wasn't able to support his weight. I fell backward, and he followed, his damaged hand cradling the back of my head protectively. Fangs punched through my flesh, and I felt his body tremble with shock and fear and gratitude. I couldn't begin to imagine what he had been through, or what would happen to both of us when it was known that I'd allowed him to feed from me. That was for later. All I could do right now was make sure Aleksei didn't die.

Look for the exciting conclusion to the
Vampire's Promise series next month!

A VAMPIRE'S HUNGER

Rowan Harper sacrificed her blood and her soul to keep her
friend, Aleksei, alive—and in the process, broke a bond of
sacred trust with her lover, Gabriel.

But her act of heroism wasn't enough to stop the evil bent on
tearing the world asunder. Newly turned vampires are
slaughtering innocents, and those lurking in the darkness
are threatening the people Rowan loves.

She may be Gabriel's Promise, but it's looking more and more
like Rowan will belong to the demon of the Dark Realm instead.
Time is of the essence and with her soul already tainted, will
Rowan be forced to break the ties she's forged with Gabriel?
Which of the two rivals will stand beside her as she faces the
end of the world?

"This series is highly recommended."
—*Library Journal*

"Wicked fun not to be missed!"
—*USA Today* bestselling author Rebecca Zanetti

**"*A Vampire's Honor* was a great read! Couldn't put it down.
The minute it was done I went to get the first two books in the
series. Can't wait for the next one!"**
—Lynsay Sands

Carla Susan Smith owes her love of literature to her mother, who, after catching her pre-teen daughter reading by flashlight beneath the bed covers, calmly replaced the romance book she had "borrowed" with one that was far less risqué, and much more appropriate! Though she was encouraged to include different genres in her reading tastes, romance—paranormal romance in particular—has always been her first love.

Born and raised in England, she now calls South Carolina home, where she lives with her wonderfully supportive husband, awesome son, and a canine critique group (if tails aren't wagging then the story isn't working!). When not writing, she can usually be found in the kitchen trying out any recipe that calls for rhubarb, working on her latest tapestry project or playing catch-up with her reading list. Please visit her at www.CarlaSmithauthor.com.

Go back to where it all started with Carla Susan Smith's *A Vampire's Promise,* available wherever digital books are sold!

TRUST YOUR INSTINCTS

Rowan Harper is nothing but a smart-mouthed bookstore clerk with a crappy love life on the night she walks into Rosie's Bar. Most of the drama in her life is borrowed from her best friend's adventures. But when she meets Gabriel—tall and movie star gorgeous—everything changes. Never mind that she turns down the drink he offers, or that he brims with secrets she can't begin to guess at. He ignites a desire in her she never suspected—and shows a fascination with her she can't explain.

He has no family, no job, no bank account; he knows where she lives and her favorite flower. An aura of mystery cloaks him, even as Rowan grasps for facts, even as she fears an answer that could destroy her happiness. Gabriel can guide her through a wonderland of new sensations. But only if Rowan trusts him enough to follow . . .

Winner of the OKRWA "Finally a Bride" contest.

CARLA SUSAN SMITH

A VAMPIRE'S PROMISE

A Vampire's Promise Novel